SHIPWRECKED

First published in the UK in 2024 by Usborne Publishing Limited,
Usborne House, 83-85 Saffron Hill, London EC1N 8RT, England, usborne.com

Usborne Verlag, Usborne Publishing Limited, Prüfeninger Str. 20, 93049
Regensburg, Deutschland, VK Nr. 17560

A CIP catalogue record for this book is available from the British Library.

Trade paperback ISBN 9781474999908

Waterstones exclusive paperback ISBN 9781836041566

7495/1 JFMAM JASOND/24

Printed and bound using 100% renewable energy at CPI Group (UK) Ltd,
Croydon, CR0 4YY.

SHIPWRECKED

JENNY PEARSON

Illustrated by NICK EAST

USBORNE

BEFORE WE GO

You never know what a person is truly made of, or who they truly are, until they are tested – at least that's what my dad thinks.

Usually, I tend to think the exact opposite of my dad – but that's more out of habit than accuracy. And having had quite a bit of time apart, what with him being at home in Singapore and me being marooned on an island somewhere in the Pacific, I can probably admit that I *might* have had a bit of an attitude problem.

I wish I could tell him that I didn't really disagree with him about *everything*, and while he was always *very* wrong about his aftershave being *subtle*, he was always bang on the mark about me.

I wasn't the best I could be.

You see, now I know what I'm made of because I *have* been tested – if you don't believe me, *you* try being stung by **Julian Jehoshaphat**. Julian, by the way, is a jellyfish with a personal vendetta against me and, despite our history, I think I'll miss him when we leave here.

But being serious for a moment, because I can do that now, I've been tested in ways that are bigger even than Julian.

Ways that have forced me to look inside myself.

I've seen and done – and also eaten – things that I never thought I would. And I think, after everything I've been through, I might be a better person.

I'm sad that my dad might never know that.

I think he might even be proud.

I guess I'm proud.

Lina has forced me to say I am so often that I think I've actually started to believe it.

Last night for example.

We – that's me, Lina, and my other best friend and castaway, Étienne – sat round the campfire and did one of Lina's enforced bonding exercises.

When we first started these I found them uber-awkward, but now...how can I describe them? They make you catch the good and sometimes it can be the tiniest thing that keeps you going. Last night we looked out at

the black horizon and we spoke about how we were proud of each other.

Proud for still surviving.

Proud that we saved Tarquin's teeny turtle babies. All one hundred odd of them.

Proud of our friendship.

And, as far as Lina is concerned, we are proud that no one has let the fire die out.

This isn't strictly true. Étienne and I have had a few minor issues, but we've kept them quiet because Lina *really* has a thing about the fire. That **Lord of the Flies** book is to blame. It's a story about a load of kids who were stuck on a desert island like us. Things did not go well for them AT ALL, which Lina blames on them for letting the fire go out. As a result, she's been fixated on keeping ours burning at all times. Étienne and I decided it's best if she doesn't know that we have, on occasion, forgotten about it.

In the spirit of catching the good, I want to tell you that things here haven't been as bleak as William Golding – the guy who wrote **Lord of the Flies** – made out. We've done much better than the kids in his story. We

didn't turn into total savages, and nobody has made any truly heartfelt attempts at killing anybody else. I think that should be noted down if we don't make it.

Because today we face another test. We are going to leave this island and hope we find our way home.

But, in case we *don't* find our way home, I've documented how we ended up as castaways and what we've done since we arrived on the island. It's also a guide of sorts. There are tips based on what I've learned about survival. And there's also a lot about what I've learned about myself and the person I want to be.

So here is the story of **the Spectacular Survival of Sebastian Sunrise** (and Lina and Étienne too).

Don't tell them I put them in brackets. It's not that they aren't equally important, they're the most **spectacular** bit really, but I was going for the whole alliterative title thing.

SURVIVAL TIP #1

MAKE A TEAM WITH THE BEST KIND OF PEOPLE

I suppose I should start with the events that led up to our **Spectacular Shipwrecking**. The reason I was anywhere near a deserted island in the Pacific Ocean can be traced back to Lina Lim's aggressive sales techniques. There's this competition our school runs at the end of the year to raise the most money for **Climate Avengers**. The top fundraising team is awarded a place on the **Climate Avengers** Summer Camp on Tonga, an island in the Pacific. **Climate Avengers** is an environmental project where you learn how to protect the planet. You learn about the ecosystems on the island and get to see all sorts of cool animals, like dolphins and turtles, and help them by collecting rubbish from the ocean. While I was keen to see a turtle, the rubbish collection part didn't fill me with joy to be honest.

Granted it's not your regular school trip, but I don't go to a regular school. I go to Beaufort International School, in Singapore. Like a lot of things, I didn't really appreciate it before I became a castaway.

Beaufort International is different from most schools – kids come from all over the world and learn to become Global Citizens – I'm still not completely sure what one of those is, although having lived on a remote and deserted island for months might make me one of the best Global Citizens Beaufort's ever had. Go figure.

Alone, I didn't stand a chance of winning the fundraising competition, but I teamed up selling cookies with Lina Lim and Étienne Stark, and Lina Lim, as I said, has some pretty fierce sales techniques. Étienne also sold a ton of boxes because his mum works at the university, and it turns out students love cookies. We are the only Year Sevens to ever win.

Étienne has been in Singapore since he was five, but Lina and I only moved there at the start of secondary school. My first run-in with Lina was when she ploughed right over the top of me in swimming training. Outraged, I whipped up my goggles and shouted at her, but she didn't apologize.

Instead she smiled and said, "You swim like a donkey!"

and splashed off. We then spent the rest of the session trying to kick each other or drag each other back by the foot to get in front. I honestly don't know how we went from that to being best friends.

Lina's mum comes from America and her dad comes from Singapore. She'd lived in America her whole life but moved for her parents' work. They started a company out here – don't ask me what they do because Lina explained it once and I didn't understand a word.

Lina is probably a better swimmer than me – not that I'd ever admit that to her face – she loves reading and has so many fluffy key rings attached to her school bag I'm surprised she can lift it.

She has a very strong sense of right and wrong – when it comes to what other people are doing. This can be a little tedious because she is always saying stuff like, "Sebastian, have you considered the consequences before you do that?" If I was busy considering consequences all the time would those ducks from the outdoor market ever have been saved from ending their lives in a pancake?

Exactly.

Étienne Stark has a French mother and a Scottish father and an accent all of his own. He is the smallest kid in our year, has terrible eyesight and feet that are WAY too big for his body. He reckons he's going to grow into them any day now and we'll all be sorry when he suddenly shoots up to seven feet tall. Meanwhile, he spends a lot of time tripping over and asking me to get stuff off high shelves. He reminds me a bit of one of those tarsier monkeys with the big goggly eyes that are cute but a little alarming looking.

Étienne has faith. He told me that the first time I met him, right after he'd kissed me on both cheeks then laughed at my confused expression. To be honest, I didn't imagine I'd be spending much time with Étienne, but we kept getting paired up with each other because our surnames both begin with S and, without even noticing, we just ended up merging together.

Étienne says we became friends because he feels compelled to help me. I think it's really because of my **spectacularly** magnetic personality.

As you'll have figured out, my name is Sebastian Sunrise. My dad is British and a Vice Admiral in the Royal Navy, which he tells me is pretty important, and I don't like to talk about my mum. I think my dad's job has made him have very exacting standards. Or maybe he's always been like that and that's why he's so good at his job. Either way, I'd say his parenting style leans heavily on his naval background. He says things like, "Get that room shipshape, Sebastian!" or "You don't have to like it, you just have to do it!" and when I'm running late, which is often, "Time and tide waits for no man, Sebastian."

The thing about my dad's exacting standards is that I figured out pretty early on that I was never going to meet them, so I guess I stopped trying.

I am average-sized and unremarkable to look at, apart from the fact that I have a condition called heterochromia, which means absolutely nothing unless you're a Pacific Ocean smuggler pirate – which I will come to later. But basically, I have one blue eye, which I must get from Mum, and one green eye, which must come from Dad.

Oh, and I guess you wouldn't describe me as a model student. See, after bagging myself a place through the biscuit-based endeavours of my friends, it looked like it was touch and go as to whether I was even going to be allowed to go to Tonga. Let's just say that I've had an eventful year at school and my report wasn't what you might call *glowing*.

Alongside a lot of pretty poor grades, my teacher, Mr Gravina wrote, "The problem with Sebastian is that he just doesn't think and, as a result, disaster and trouble have become his closest and most constant companions."

"That's not a very nice thing to say about Lina and Étienne," I said to Dad, trying to laugh it off, but to be honest the report had got to me. I stomped up to my room and immediately took to my computer to search for lawyers to sue Mr G for slander. Turns out good lawyers don't come cheap and the ones that work on a no-win-no-fee basis were neither forthcoming nor professional when I spoke to them about my case.

As it happened, Dad wasn't really on board with my idea of suing the school either. He told me I had to take responsibility for my mistakes. There'd been a few – an accidental fire in the school conservation area; the time I'd unintentionally locked the PE teacher in the store cupboard; the time I'd poured plaster of Paris down the sink in the art room. It had hardened and ruined the whole of the Art and DT block's plumbing. I suppose if I had secured the services of a lawyer, they'd have had a job on their hands.

Anyway, the night of the *bad school report*, Dad had called me away from my internet lawyer search and said, "Sit down, Sebastian," in a voice that was bordering on a shout. And I did sit, because when my dad says to do something, you do it. I think he sometimes forgets that I'm his kid and not a member of his crew.

He cleared his throat and straightened his collar. Dad looks like he's wearing a uniform even when he isn't. You know those guys you see in films where they have a wardrobe full of the exact same shirts, trousers and shoes?

Yeah, he's one of those – white shirt, navy jumper, chinos – it's all he wears when he's "off duty".

He placed the report on the table. "You just seem all at sea – wild, even. I'm worried that the course you're steering is the wrong one."

I said, "I'm fine," but made no effort to hide my irritation at yet another water-based saying.

"I'm here to help you, Sebastian, but it is up to you to find your own way. To navigate your own waters."

I groaned inwardly. Or maybe it was outwardly because he said, "Stop groaning and listen. I don't recognize you any more. I don't know, you seem...*lost*. I know your mother leaving—"

"It's nothing to do with her," I snapped, but now I realize I was probably wrong about that.

My mum and dad have been separated for just over a year. They'd always had problems, but I think the move to Singapore was what finally did it for them. I overheard them arguing about it. Mum didn't want to go. Dad said we didn't have to move. She said he should, but without her – that a separation was what she wanted.

When it all happened, they'd given me a choice of who to live with. Mum's the kind of woman who will give you a Twix and a Fanta for breakfast and wake you up in the middle of the night to drive fifty miles to try out a new restaurant. Dad is the kind of person who will shout at someone about dental health and for being irresponsible for keeping a kid up on a school night.

I'd chosen Mum. I guess because I thought she was the fun one. But it turned out she didn't choose me. She wanted to go off and try to make it as an actress in America. Apparently she'd been close to success, before she'd had me.

She held my face in her hands, kissed my cheeks and said, "Your father can give you what I can't, Sebastian." I told her that wasn't true, what I wanted was the latest VR gaming console, but neither of them had been forthcoming with that. Then she'd said, "Your father needs you." Which puzzles me to this day. I have literally zero clue what my dad needs me for. He's a grown man. He can pretty much do everything for himself. Except for squeezing through the garage window when we accidentally lock ourselves out, but I can't believe she'd leave me behind just for that.

But that's what she said. And then she left, and I ended up with Dad anyway.

Dad and I stood on the doorstep, our whole house packed up in boxes ready to be shipped off to Singapore. He had his arms crossed behind his back, showing absolutely no emotion as Mum, in floods of tears and making promises to visit every holiday, got in a taxi and drove away. He just nodded at her as she closed the car door. Once she had rounded the corner I was feeling very upset and very confused and very angry, but then I turned to Dad and I thought he looked like someone who was trying to hold all those emotions in too. Which you'd think might have made me feel a degree of empathy for him. But it annoyed me. He shouldn't have let her go.

He said, "This isn't your fault, Sebastian. Your mother does love you."

Had I thought it was my fault? I think I'd blamed him – his exacting standards. Maybe he made Mum feel like a failure too. But I guess part of me believed there must be something about me she didn't like for her to leave me behind.

"Things are complicated...she is complicated...she had a very difficult childhood and..." He stopped, his face suddenly etched with pain. "I don't know if I'm saying too much. I wish I could help you make sense of this."

To me, it sounded like he was scrabbling around for excuses.

So it became just us, and we are very different people, and I had no idea how that was going to work.

Dad said, "We'll be okay. Two lads together, hey?"

I didn't answer.

"I know you wanted to be with your mother," he continued, "but this will be fine. Good, even."

I realized then he must have felt like the consolation prize. So, I said, "Dad, I might have chosen Mum, but you came an incredibly close second. Maybe if you worked on being a little less strict and a bit more fun—"

He cut me off before I could finish, saying, "It doesn't matter who you chose, Sebastian. Because I choose you."

I think I should have said something back. But I didn't.

So, we were both sitting in the kitchen, the report on the

table and my chances of becoming a **Climate Avenger** looking pretty slim.

"Please can I go?" I said.

Dad rubbed the bridge of his nose and suddenly looked very tired. "With comments like this I just don't think I can let you. This year has not been smooth sailing."

"I'm sorry!" I said. "Things just happen to me. I don't do them on purpose. I really want to go. I really want to have the opportunity to do something good."

To be honest, my reasons for going on the trip were not completely altruistic, unlike Étienne and Lina, who were very motivated to save the planet. I just didn't fancy staying at home over the summer holidays without them – and with only my dad and the housekeeper for company.

Dad told me to go upstairs to my room so he could think. I reckoned there was no way the trip was happening, so I started to plot ways to get myself there without him knowing.

Luckily, I didn't have to hide in the drum of a washing machine, which is, according to the internet, one of Singapore's top exports to Tonga. When he called me back down to deliver his verdict he said, "Maybe a bit of hard graft and being part of a team that's working for a good cause is just the thing you need." Then he added, "Besides, you earned your place selling those cookies."

I'd only sold six boxes, but I still punched the air and said, "Get in!" which by the look on Dad's face was too much, considering the situation.

He sighed and said, "Promise me you'll stay out of trouble and not do anything stupid. Make me proud of you, son. Make yourself proud."

I said, "I promise." But only because that's what you do to get what you want.

On the way to get our flight, I told Lina and Étienne how close I'd come to not being allowed on the trip and I complained about the injustice of Mr Gravina's harsh words. Lina wasn't having any of it. She held up her hand to stop me from talking and told me that she thought that maybe Mr Gravina did have a point and that I should take on board what both my dad and my teacher were saying – that maybe I did need to think more.

But I didn't want to take any of that on board. So, I didn't.

Which is possibly why, less than thirty-six hours later, I had already broken the promise I'd made to my dad about not doing anything stupid. And it's probably also why Lina, Étienne and I were bobbing about very lost and very wet and very cold, somewhere in the Pacific Ocean, wondering what had happened to the others.

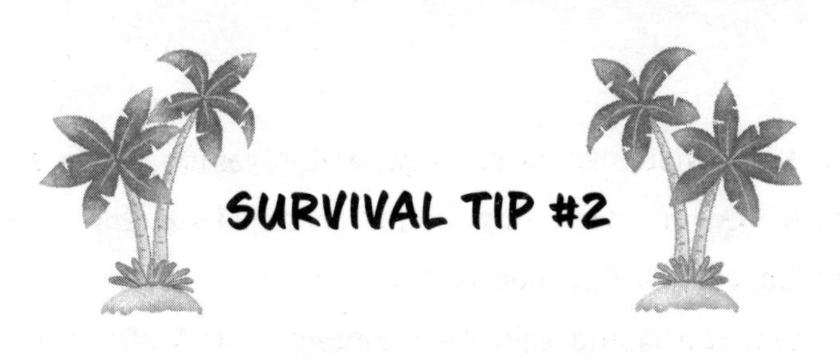

SURVIVAL TIP #2

IT'S BEST NOT TO CHALLENGE PEOPLE YOU HAVE ZERO HOPE OF BEATING

That first morning at **Climate Avenger Camp**, we had an orientation meeting given by the camp leader, an Australian guy called Beecham. His bleach-blond hair, which looked like fishing rope, was bundled up on his head and held back with a blue bandana. He had deeply tanned and weathered skin that looked like biltong and a massive tattoo of a turtle on his back, which made me think he must be a really big fan of turtles.

We'd arrived in Tonga late the night before and, as it had been dark, we hadn't been able to see much of our surroundings. We'd unpacked our backpacks, gone straight to bed and fallen asleep to the sound of the lapping ocean. It had taken me a little while to drift off. I was *very* happy to be away from home. To have the freedom that came with being away from Dad. He was probably in bed in his ironed pyjamas reading some military book. I'd wondered what Mum would be up to – but I really had no idea. She'd called before I left and told me she'd sent me a Lakers baseball cap for my trip. It hadn't arrived on time. Maybe she hadn't actually sent it.

The next day, Étienne woke up first, seeming to want to start avenging the climate immediately. I think he pretty much cartwheeled out of bed and shouted, "IT'S MORNING!"

Moments later, he burst out of the hut door in his green **Climate Avengers** T-shirt, multi-pocketed khaki shorts and baseball cap. I buried my head under my pillow in the hope that I might get a few more minutes of shut-eye, but then he burst back in and said, "IT'S SO BEAUTIFUL! The sky is so blue, the sea is so blue, the sun is so yellowy-white, the sand is also so yellowy-white."

"That is a very moving description," I said.

He beamed. "*Merci!* Now get up, lazy skeleton, let's meet the others. I can't wait to start protecting our environment!"

By the time Lina, Étienne and I arrived at the meeting hut, all sporting our standard-issue **Climate Avenger** uniforms over the top of our swimmers, Beecham was just chiming his little cymbals to get everyone to quieten down.

We sat cross-legged on the hessian mat with the other Avengers and went round introducing ourselves. Looking at the kids there, I grew increasingly worried for the climate if it was up to us to avenge it.

There was a boy called Orlando, who reminded me of a stick insect because his limbs were so long and twiggy, a girl called Rashida, who spent the whole time picking at a scab on her knee, another kid called Fabio who, for some reason – possibly extreme glare-concerns – was wearing three pairs of sunglasses (one on his face, one on his head and one on a chain around his neck), and there was also a girl called Camilla or Celia, who was basically a human smear of suntan lotion. She even had it on her eyelids. There were quite a few other Avengers, but I can't remember much about them, and it doesn't really matter, because none of these kids feature in what happened to us.

But the next set of kids you do need to pay attention to.

I was just about to say, "My name is Sebastian Sunrise," when Benedict Phan, Lukas Zukas and Francesca del Core strolled into the room and stole my thunder.

People gasped when they saw them.

I'm not kidding you. They walked into the hut and the

other fifteen or so kids gasped. Fabio swapped the glasses that were on his face to the ones hanging round his neck – I suspect to check he wasn't seeing things. Even Rashida looked up from her gammy knee.

No one has ever gasped when *I've* walked into a room before. Except the time I went trick or treating at the old people's retirement home, but I think that was because the severed head I was carrying was a bit too realistic for people of such advanced years.

Anyway, the reason for all this gasping is that Benedict, Lukas and Francesca are genuine **mutants**.

Alright, they're not really **mutants**.

They just look like **mutants**.

Okay, they don't look like actual **mutants**.

But they are the tallest kids I have ever seen, all of them coming in at over six foot. They're unarguably a remarkable sight to behold.

Benedict, Lukas and Francesca attend the Beaufort International school in Hong Kong. I remembered them from the Rising Stars section of the Beaufort International newsletter. Benedict and Lukas, despite being in Year Nine, played basketball for the Sixth-Form team and were pegged to be future legends. Francesca was only one year above us but she'd already played in the Italian under-17 volleyball team.

These were the types of kids my dad wished he'd had. I know this because when he saw the newsletter, he shook his head and quietly muttered, "Their parents must be so proud."

After overhearing that, I'd gone out into the yard to try and shoot hoops, but I was *not* the most accurate. I accidentally hit Mr Chua from the apartment next to ours and knocked him and his walking frame into the ornamental fish pond. Dad ended up shouting at me for causing trouble and inadvertently wounding a koi carp.

Sorry, I digress. So, on seeing Benedict in real life, in all his towering tallness, with his extra-shiny teeth and extra-shiny hair, and Lukas with his broad shoulders and extra-shiny teeth and extra-shiny hair, and Francesca with her infectious smile and extra-shiny teeth and extra-shiny hair, I had three main thoughts:

1. Maybe the climate does stand a chance if these guys are involved.
2. I have taken against them all for reasons I cannot quite articulate but that seem completely justified.
3. I must find out what toothpaste and hair products they are using.

Étienne leaned in and whispered to me, "They are all just so sparkly." Which, for some reason, he seemed pleased about. It only made me like them even less. I'm the sparkly one.

"Yes," I said, through gritted teeth. "They are very sparkly, but so is an electric fence when you touch it."

Étienne slapped his hand on my shoulder. "Sebastian, why do you pretend not to be nice? I know you don't mean to be unkind."

But it was too easy for me to dislike them, because I didn't like how they made me feel about myself. Which is probably why I ended up challenging Benedict later that evening. Even as I was doing it, I knew it would most likely turn out badly.

I just didn't realize quite *how* badly.

After our introduction meeting, we were given a site tour. Then it was lunch. We had a plant-based burger, and something called breadfruit, which I think was supposed to be a bit like sweet potato fries, but had the texture of bread – which is where I guess the name came from. To me, it tasted like a sigh.

Following lunch, we had a *talk* about the environment. It was as interesting as it was horrifying. Beecham told us a lot of miserable facts. For example, did you know that by 2050, scientists reckon there will be more plastic in the ocean than fish? He showed us photos of these massive floating garbage islands. We learned that fish, birds and sea turtles mistake the plastic in our oceans for food and eat it and die. It was a bit of a mood killer, and everyone was a bit quiet by the end of the day. The whole scale of the plastic problem seemed overwhelming. But then Beecham clapped his hands together and said, "There's a saying that the greatest threat to our planet is the belief that someone else will save it. But here at **Climate Avengers** we try to make a difference. Do you want to make a difference?"

Étienne was the first to jump to his feet. He clutched his hand to his chest and shouted, "I do!"

I saw Benedict smile and I wasn't quite sure if it was in a good way. I decided it probably wasn't, so not wanting to leave Étienne standing up on his own, I stood up and said, "Yeah, I do, I guess."

Lina popped up between us and said, "You can count me in!"

Benedict Phan then said, "Let's get drastic over plastic!" Which I didn't think made sense, but it got the other kids on their feet vowing to get drastic over plastic too.

Beecham whooped. "You guys are awesome! Tonight, we meet for pre-mission bonding! Be at the campfire at seven. But tomorrow work starts: we're going on a 'clean-up the Pacific Ocean' boat trip!"

I didn't say anything but cleaning up the *whole* Pacific Ocean seemed a little overambitious in my opinion – I can tell you from experience that's a *lot* of water, no matter how *drastic* you are.

At seven we went down to the beach and sat round the campfire. Beecham introduced us to a man called Lakepi and a woman called Panisi, who were from Tonga and part of the climate-avenging crew. He then went over the itinerary for the next day, reminding us to wear our full avenging uniform, including baseball caps, and to bring suntan lotion, water and a whole lot of enthusiasm.

Étienne shouted, "My middle name is enthusiasm!"

All the other avengers smirked but Beecham said, "The ocean thanks you for your passion, little dude."

Beecham then went through a few safety things and, to be honest, I was probably not paying my most maximum attention until Benedict mentioned the **pirates**.

"Is it true, Beecham, that pirates have been spotted around here?" he asked, a flash of excitement in his eyes.

Lakepi made a tutting noise and shook his head sorrowfully, which made me think the answer was yes.

Beecham pressed his palms together. "Not pirates as such, but it is true there are smugglers in the area. Some of these people are just trying to make a living in the wrong way, but others are bad people, dangerous people," he eyed us all over the crackling flames, "but they won't be anywhere near the waters we sail, so, my little climate dudes, you can all relax."

My dad had told me stories of modern-day smugglers. He'd been involved in capturing a few and, stupidly, I thought then that it might liven things up if we bumped into a band of smugglers illegally smuggling smuggled things during our trip.

"What sort of thing are they smuggling?" Lina asked.

"All sorts, but we have a big problem with turtles being trafficked for their meat or to make medicines. It's a lucrative business. Traffickers make a lot of money from stealing and selling turtles on," Beecham shook his head. "Sad times."

Étienne said, "Very sad times. I'm going to pray for all the turtles tonight."

Which made the other avengers snigger again.

Beecham cast a look of disappointment around the group, then said to Étienne, "You're a bit like a turtle."

I thought, no he isn't, he's a bit like a tarsier monkey.

Before anyone started sniggering again, Beecham continued, "Yeah, little avenger dude. It seems to me that, much like a turtle, you are comfortable in your own shell, and by that I mean you are secure in who you are."

Which I supposed was true. Étienne was very happy being Étienne.

Then Beecham said, "Some of us might want to contemplate being more like a turtle." He looked around the group, his eyes settling on me.

I felt a bit uncomfortable and shifted on the mat. "Yeah, I'm changing my goal of becoming an astronaut to transforming into a turtle."

There were a few giggles but, even then, something about what Beecham was saying got to me.

Beecham then told us how he'd spent a wonderful summer tagging turtles so they could be tracked and that they were one of the most majestic animals in the ocean. He then chimed his little cymbal, and we had one minute's silence for all the trafficked turtles, which he called our remarkable reptilian relations. Yup, Beecham really loves turtles.

I have since tried to blame what happened later that evening on Beecham. After our briefing, it was *him* who'd made us participate in some friendly beach games for bonding purposes. But when I mentioned I might look for a lawyer to sue **Climate Avengers** for the role they played in our shipwrecking if we ever make it home, Lina said that it was poor form to sue a charity and that I wouldn't have a leg to stand on, what with it being completely and undeniably my fault.

Anyway, that evening when Lina, Étienne and I were drawn to play volleyball against the **mutants**, we obviously suffered a crushing and humiliating defeat. I did not react very well to being crushed and humiliated. I guess I get that from my dad.

We all shook hands and Benedict said, "Nice try, guys." And that, I think, was what set me off.

I angry-whispered to Lina, "Did you hear that? How rude!"

Lina pulled a face. "He said *nice try*, Sebastian. How is that rude?"

"Yeah, but in a nice try, *loser*, kind of tone, don't you think?"

"No, I *don't* think," Lina said, which did not feel very supportive.

"Neither do I," Étienne said. "I think he was being nice."

But I couldn't let it go and later, after the last embers of the fire had died and before I could think things through, I challenged Benedict, Lukas and Francesca to a boat race, out to the furthest rocky islet from the beach.

And Benedict, not one to turn down a challenge, had said yes.

I don't know why I decided on a boat race. I suppose it was seeing the line of little wooden fishing boats down by the shore that gave me the idea. Maybe I thought being an admiral's son might somehow make me good at rowing. If I'd challenged him to a game of football or to see who could clean up the most plastic, things would have turned out differently. If I hadn't been *me*, things would have turned out differently.

After lights out, when Beecham was safely in his hammock, and Lakepi and Panisi were asleep in their huts, we snuck out to meet the **mutants** down on the water's edge. Lina said she absolutely wasn't taking part, it was a stupid idea to go for a row in the dark, we couldn't possibly win and she was going to read her book by torchlight while I made an idiot of myself and poor Étienne.

Étienne also said he would possibly prefer to spectate rather than participate because he wasn't much of an oarsman and suffered terribly from seasickness.

I said, "Fine then. I'll do it by myself. *I'm* not one to walk away from a bet." I said the *I'm* with extra emphasis to imply that *they* were ones who would walk away from a bet, which made them, unquestionably, a bit rubbish.

Lina said, "It's not our stupid bet, though, is it? It's yours. There's no way we're going to beat them."

"You can't know that for sure!"

"Just look at Étienne!" Lina gestured towards him. "No offence, Étienne, but you're half their height."

"I am not offended by what is true," Étienne said.

"What are you trying to prove, Sebastian?" Lina continued. "Why do you always do stuff like this?"

I didn't answer the *what was I trying to prove* question because I didn't know the answer at the time. Of course, now I realize I had major inferiority issues, issues with my dad and issues liking myself – probably because I thought my mum didn't want me. But that sort of self-awareness only came to me after having spent a fair stretch of time on an island with a goat named **Giuseppe Garibaldi** and a turtle called **Tarquin Tarantino**.

So, at the time, I said, "Please, just do this for me and I promise I won't ask for anything else. There will be no more *stuff*. Go on, Lina, Etsy, purrrrleeease?" I may have dropped to my knees and clasped my hands together for effect.

"My name is *not* Etsy."

"Sorry, Étienne. So, how about it, buddy?"

He did a little sigh. "Oh, I don't know. Is this such a good idea? I don't like the look of those clouds."

"Those clouds are just clouds. There's nothing to worry about," I said, slinging my arm round his shoulders, oblivious to how **SPECTACULARLY** wrong I had just been. I was too distracted by the **mutants** heading towards us, looking rather magnificently athletic in the moonlight, to think about clouds.

"Please guys, you're my best friends. I really need you to do this. Backing out would look worse than losing."

Lina did a big huff and snapped her book shut. "Okay, but this really is it. No more getting in trouble or persuading us to do things we shouldn't be doing for the rest of the trip. After this we are only saving the climate and nothing else."

I saluted. "Understood!"

"And you're not to sulk when we lose."

"When do I ever sulk?"

Lina raised an eyebrow.

"Fine. No sulking! You guys are the best!"

"We know," Lina replied drily.

"You won't regret it!" I said, **SPECTACULARLY** wrongly again.

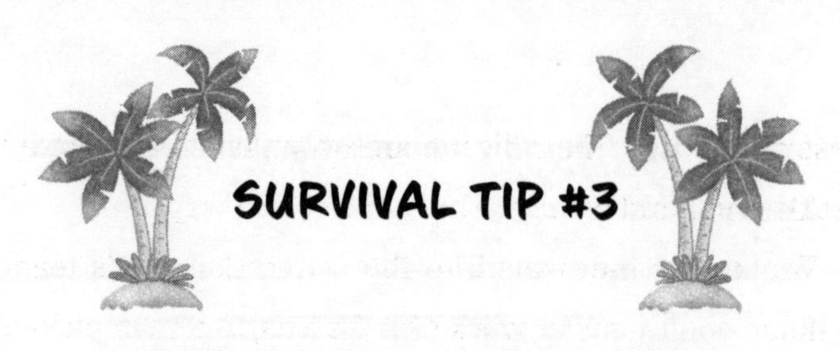

SURVIVAL TIP #3

NEVER UNDERESTIMATE OMINOUS-LOOKING CLOUDS

The little islet that I had chosen for us to row to was much further out than anyone had realized, which was the first of our problems. The second problem was the sudden and dramatic change in the weather. And our third problem was the current – which made all our attempts to paddle back to land, completely and utterly futile.

You know those sayings you hear about respecting the sea? My dad is always bleating on about them but, yeah, listen to those, they're right on the money. That evening, Benedict and I did not think for one moment about the sea being dangerous.

As self-appointed team captains, we both selected a small fishing boat to borrow from the line of boats that had been pulled up onto the beach by people who did not deserve to lose their livelihoods thanks to a stupidly reckless kid and his ego. That's me by the way.

We pushed the boats into the water, Benedict's team making slightly easier work of it than us, and then picked up the oars.

"To that rocky islet over there," I said, pointing at the rocky islet, which no one had worked out was much too far away.

Benedict, Lukas and Francesca raised their oars, bashed them together and shouted, "Go, Team!"

Lina, Étienne and I tried to do the same, but oars are quite heavy and, lacking the upper body strength to get them above our heads, we ended up waving them around in quite a pathetic manner. We followed this oar-waggling with our own call of, "Go, Team!" Which was not quite as rousing due to the fact that Étienne was quite half-hearted about it and Lina didn't even bother to join in.

We'd been rowing for about twenty minutes and were reasonably far from the beach and unreasonably far from the **mutants'** boat, when the rain started. I tried to motivate Étienne and Lina to catch up by periodically shouting, "Tortoise and hare, guys, tortoise and hare," but even that didn't spur them on.

At the first drop of rain, Lina said, "That's it. I'm done. Let's turn round."

"It's nothing, just a passing shower," I said.

Étienne put down his oar and wiped his glasses. "I told you I didn't like the look of those clouds, but you never listen."

"Give me ten more minutes of effort, guys," I pleaded. "Look, I think they're getting slower."

"Do you think maybe the lashing rain might have something to do with that?" Lina said, a little snappily.

"I would hardly call it *lashing*." Although I have to admit, it had got heavier quickly – much heavier.

Étienne shivered. "I'm getting a bit cold." His hair was plastered to his face and his **Climate Avengers** T-shirt was stuck to his body.

"That's because you've stopped rowing. You'll soon warm up if you start again. Get that blood pumping! Come on, five more minutes. I think they might have stopped for a break!"

They had stopped for a break. Not because they were tired, but because they could see what was heading our way.

I might have seen it too, but I was busy trying to prove something I was never going to prove. I pushed the oar towards Étienne. "One last effort. We'll overtake them, declare the win and then turn back."

He mumbled something about patience being a virtue and picked up his oar.

"Atta boy!" I said, trying to ignore the fact that the rain was absolutely hammering.

Étienne then muttered something about me either being sent from God or a test from God. It was probably the second, but I wasn't too bothered – at least he was rowing again.

Lina said, "For goodness' sake, let's get this over with so we can get back to land," and joined in too.

It was only five minutes later when the first wave hit.

We pitched to one side, then the other, and a huge amount of water rushed aboard.

I think we knew then that we were in trouble.

Suddenly, all the stories my dad had told me about small boats getting battered at sea came flooding back and a lump of cold fear formed in my stomach.

Looking very green and very scared, Étienne grabbed hold of the side of the boat and said, "I don't like this."

I looked out to the horizon and saw what the **mutants** must have seen.

"Woah," Lina said, which was as good a response as any to the line after line of waves – giant ones – heading right for us.

"Those waves look big," she said. "Really big."

Panic rippled through me. "They are a little on the large side."

Étienne gulped and tugged my sleeve. "Look! The other boat!"

Francesca was standing up, waving her arms to attract our attention and shouting. We couldn't make out what she was shouting, but I got the strong impression that she was suggesting that it might be a good idea to turn back. This was confirmed when Benedict and Lukas turned their boat round and began paddling frantically against the current towards us.

Étienne dropped his oar and said in a voice I shan't ever forget, "Good Lord, have mercy."

A wave, dark and monstrous, rose up. It was easily three times as high as their boat, and it was barrelling right for them.

Francesca was still standing when it struck.

I remember seeing her go under.

One minute she was there – the next she was gone. They were all gone.

I don't remember much after that. Just noise and water and the feeling of my body slamming into wood. Desperately trying to hold onto the oars. Not knowing which way was up and which way was down.

The panic. The fear – for myself and for my friends.

The screams.

Then just the dark and the cold. Then nothing.

I came round to the sun beating down on my face. It took me a moment to realize where I was, but when I felt the rocking motion of the boat, reality hit. I was curled up in a space at the bow of the boat. My legs were wrapped round an oar. Slowly, I pushed myself to sitting. Everything hurt – my mouth especially. My fingers found their way to a deep cut on my lip, and I winced. I looked for Étienne and Lina and relief spread through me when I saw they were both there.

"Is everyone okay?" I asked.

Étienne was sitting at the back of the boat, rocking back and forth, his glasses on the wonk. He had a few scratches on his arms and legs but seemed to be in one piece, physically at least. He looked very pale and very scared, which was understandable. I probably looked the same. I felt the same.

I would not describe Lina's expression as one of fear. She looked relieved when I first sat up, but her mood quickly changed to one of unrestrained anger. She dropped her book – which looked damp and tattered and, rather than checking whether I was okay, she pulled me towards her by my T-shirt and shouted in my face, "SEBASTIAN, THIS IS UNBELIEVABLE! EVEN FOR

CLIMATE AVENGERS

YOU!" Then she let go, sank back onto the floor of the boat and hung her head and sobbed.

It would be fair to say that I've seen her looking chirpier.

I looked around me. It *was* unbelievable. Water stretched out endlessly to the horizon. Sea and sky, that's all there was. We were in the middle of nowhere.

"You're okay though?" The guilt at what I had caused to happen through my stupid boat race hit me, and it was so strong it caused my voice to wobble.

"OKAY?" Lina shouted.

"They're gone, they are all gone," Étienne said.

"We're lost somewhere in the middle of the Pacific Ocean," Lina continued. "I think it's fair to say we are the furthest we could be from okay, Sebastian! We've been out here all night and we're stuffed, that's what we are!"

"Are you hurt?" I asked.

She shook her head. "Battered and bruised but other than that no, I'm not hurt. No thanks to you."

"We're all going to die out here!" Étienne wailed. "This boat is tiny, and the ocean is so massive." He looked at me. "What have you done, Sebastian?"

The guilt hit me again – bigger than any wave. Étienne was right, our boat was small. We'd managed to keep hold of all three of the oars, but when I looked out at the huge expanse of water around us, it seemed ridiculous to think they'd be any use. We were miles from anywhere. There was no sign of the other boat – of Benedict or Lukas or Francesca. I was desperate to say something that would make us all feel better, but I couldn't think with fear flooding my brain. "Things might not be as bad as they seem," I began. "Let's not panic."

"Not as bad as they seem? Are you kidding me?" Étienne said, paying little attention to my advice about not panicking.

"No, I'm not kidding you. I think we should take stock and assess things – see if we can figure a way out of this less-than-ideal situation."

It was Lina's turn to start panicking. "Less than *ideal*? Are you *kidding* me?"

I swallowed the sob that was threatening to come out. "I'm not kidding you either. If you haven't noticed, now really isn't an appropriate time for kidding."

"*That* is something we can agree on!" Lina turned her head away like she couldn't bear to look at me. "Thanks to you, Sebastian, we are in the middle of the Pacific Ocean and no one knows we're here! We're going to drift out here for ever, never to be seen again, until we die of thirst or are eaten by sharks or pecked to death by pelicans." She turned back to face me, her eyes flashing with anger. "You *had* to make that stupid bet, didn't you?! And now

Benedict and the others are missing and—"

"—in my defence—"

"—there is no defence!" She shouted so loudly I jumped.

Lina closed her eyes and did a deep sigh. When she opened them, she seemed a little calmer. "Look, giving you a heads up, I am feeling a lot of emotions. I'm very cross with you, but I know you didn't mean for this to happen, so that makes me cross with myself for being cross with you. Really, I'm just cross with the whole situation. I'm scared and I don't know what to do and it all feels hopeless. I will probably take it out on you, for a while at least, and you will just have to deal with it."

"I think that's probably fair enough," I said. "I also think it is a bit premature to give up. I'm sure someone is coming to rescue us. I bet the others got right back on their boat and made it to shore. They're athletes, you know, they're strong. They've probably already raised the alarm and help will be on the way. Someone will come, you'll see. They'll come. They have to."

We all wanted to believe it was true. I'm not sure if anyone did though.

No one said anything for some time and, wanting to fill the heavy silence, I heard myself say, "Have you actually paid attention to a pelican's bill? Because I have and I'm not convinced they are all that sharp or stabby. No way could one of those peck us all to death."

I had hoped to sound encouraging, but I obviously annoyed Étienne, because he stopped rocking and let out an almighty roar.

"Are you alright, Etsy?" I asked, politely.

Étienne shouted, "No I am not alright! Maybe you should pay less attention to pelicans' bills and more attention to when Lina and I are telling you something is a bad idea! You never learn! And for the billionth time... Don't. Call. Me. Etsy!"

Étienne isn't what you'd call *the fighty type*. He is usually very kind and caring. Anyway, that day he forgot all about being kind and caring and he sort of **supermanned** towards me, fist first.

The boat rocked, Lina screamed – or it may have been me – but luckily I jumped up and caught his fist before he landed one on my nose. "Étienne, calm down! This is not helping anyone!"

"What *is* going to help, Sebastian? WHAT!?" he demanded, then he burst into tears and collapsed into a heap in the small space next to Lina. She put her arm round him and glared up at me. I stood over them, watching Étienne struggling to slow his breathing, while I struggled to control the panic building inside me.

"D...don't worry," I said, "when my dad finds out we're lost at sea, he'll search for us and find us."

"What if he doesn't?" Lina said quietly, bitterly.

"I'll think of something," I said, with no clue of what that something would be. "For now, let's try and think clearly. Look around. There might be something on board that could help."

"Oh yes, there's an on-board motor hidden under my seat," Lina said, very sarcastically.

"There might be something."

Étienne and Lina didn't move but I began searching anyway. Not that there was much to search. I was beginning to think that it was a lost cause when my fingers found a latch under one of the seats.

"It's a lid!" I said.

"Brilliant, a lid is *exactly* what we need," Lina said.

"To a hatch, and these things might be useful."

Inside the storage locker I found:

1. A coil of rope
2. A small rusty bucket
3. A fishing line and some rusty hooks
4. A fairly blunt hatchet
5. Two distress parachute flares
6. Three bottles of water

"Any food?" Lina asked.

I shook my head. "But do not worry. We can survive a few days without food as long as we have water, and I realize we are in a spot of bother—"

"A **spot** of bother?" Lina laughed a little manically.

"But we have some very useful items here."

"We should use the flares, quick!" Étienne said, grabbing one from the pile. "Someone might see us!"

I snatched it back off him and read the instructions. "My dad's told me about these. The best time to send a distress signal into the sky is when there's someone there to see it. When there is land, another vessel or a helicopter in sight. Do you see any of those things, Étienne?"

I don't think Étienne was listening. He yanked it out of my hand and before I could do anything about it, he'd whipped off the bottom and shot the parachute flare – which advertised itself as being capable of firing 300 metres up into the sky – downwards into the boat.

Flames crackled and smoke immediately started spewing from it as it bounced around by our feet, threatening to set us and the boat on fire. It was difficult to see – Lina was coughing and shouting about being stuck with a couple of idiots, I was wafting my arms around trying my best not to panic, but panicking anyway, and Étienne was tumbling about screaming. Thinking quickly, I grabbed the bucket and managed to scoop up the flare and chuck it overboard.

Eventually the smoke dispersed, and Lina emerged from the cloud it left behind looking thunderous. She was sitting with her arms crossed and her brow-crumples deeper than the waters below us.

Étienne had the decency to look a little shamefaced about almost setting fire to our boat. "I...I'm sorry...I..." He looked down at his hands. "I don't know why I..."

"Never mind," I said, trying to remain upbeat and keen to adopt a *no-blame* atmosphere. "I'm sure we'll do much better when it comes to deploying the second flare. When there's *someone* around to see it."

"How do you know that's going to happen? Do you see anyone, Sebastian? Do you? Because I don't!" Lina let out a frustrated shriek and stomped her foot. "I cannot believe this is happening!"

I looked around – there was nothing other than ocean and sky. And my best friends' terrified faces.

"Someone will sail by and spot us and, if not, the others will have made it back and got help and they'll come looking for us. Or I bet my dad will send the whole Navy to find us." I took a deep breath to stop my own terror overcoming me and grabbed hold of an oar.

"Someone will find us, I'm sure. But, until then, we paddle."

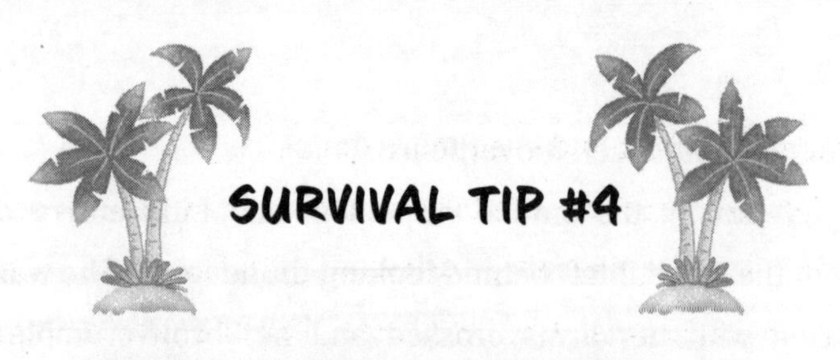

SURVIVAL TIP #4

NEVER OFFER YOURSELF UP TO BE EATEN, YOUR SO-CALLED FRIENDS MAY TAKE YOU UP ON IT

It wasn't too long before the question as to where we were paddling came up. I had suspected it would, mainly because it was what I had been wondering since I'd first taken hold of the oar and with a stirring call of, "Onwards!" had started to row.

"It feels better than sitting here and waiting for the pelicans," I said. "You never know, we might find land."

My whole body hurt, and I could tell that Lina and Étienne's did too by the pained looks on their faces, but we kept at the oars. Desperate situations somehow seem less desperate if you are doing something rather than nothing. If only to give you a sense of purpose and control, and even if that something turns out to be paddling in circles as the sun sets and the waters around you grow worryingly dark and even more ominous.

We took it in turns to take a break. Lina would sit and read her book, which had dried out in the sun, and shoot me an occasional hostile glance. Étienne would stare hopefully at the horizon. And to stop myself from going through a never-ending list of *what ifs* and to lift the mood, I would sing.

As the hours passed, we grew more and more tired and more and more hungry. I could sense the atmosphere aboard **HMS Saviour** (as I had christened the boat for reasons of motivation and positivity) had taken a turn for the worse when Lina shouted at me to, "Stop with the singing, Sebastian! We are not rowing our boat down a stream and we're not going merrily or gently and life is currently a nightmare and not at all a dream and I'm so close to throwing you overboard!"

That outburst was unhelpful for two reasons. Number one, she had already vetoed me from singing **What Shall We Do with the Drunken Sailor** and I was all out of nautical-based songs and, number two, it caused Étienne to start crying again.

He looked out to sea, where the sun was lowering below the horizon, and sniffed. "I'm going to die out here, aren't I?" He wiped a long string of sobbing-snot down his now rather sunburned arm. "I'm never going to see my parents again."

"You can't think like that. I know things are bad—"

"Do you?" Lina shouted. "Because the incessant jubilant singing sort of suggests otherwise!"

"I was trying to rally the troops."

Lina turned away and muttered. "For someone who isn't a massive fan of their dad, you sound an awful lot like him. *Very* admiraly."

Her shot hit its mark, but I didn't show it. This was not the time to descend into petty squabbles.

"As I was saying, things are undoubtedly bad. Really bad. I know that is all down to me, but I don't believe this is how we're going to die, Étienne. We need to concentrate on what we are going to do right now," I said. "It's going to get dark soon and there's no land in sight. I think we may have to accept that we are going to be sleeping out here tonight."

Étienne closed his eyes and whispered, "Lord help us."

"I'm sure he will," I said, though I had some niggling doubts about that, "but just in case, I will do everything I can to get us out of this mess, I promise. I'm going to fix this."

Étienne started sobbing again, although quietly this time. He took off his glasses and dabbed the tears from his eyes and said, "I want my parents."

Lina swallowed hard. "I want mine too."

"Me too," I said, but I realized that it was my dad I wanted the most. He'd always been there when things were hard. Like the time I broke my arm when I fell out of a tree and when Mum crashed the car because she ran into a stop sign. He was always calm in an emergency. He made me feel safe. I'd forgotten that at some point.

Lina did a big sniff, then glared at me. "I'm never going to forgive you for this, Sebastian."

I said nothing, because if I were them, I wouldn't forgive me either.

I felt completely and utterly miserable. Lina was right – I'd gone too far this time. What was wrong with me? Why did I always end up getting in so much trouble? I looked out at the waves and wondered what it would be like to not be me. To be someone that my dad could be proud of. Someone I could be proud of.

I was unable to sit in quiet reflection and feel sorry for myself for very long because it turned out Lina was not done telling me off. She glared at me so hard I wondered if her eyeballs might drop out. "What, no clever comeback from the massive mouth of Sebastian Sunrise? I said I was *never* going to forgive you – did you hear that?"

"I did and I understand. I am really, really, *really* sorry. The most sorry anyone could ever be in the history of the world ever."

"Really? You're always sorry after a catastrophe, Sebastian."

"I promise you I am the sorriest of sorry. And if the worst comes to the worst and we run out of food and one of us needs to get eaten for the others to survive, I think it should be me."

"*That*", Lina said, "isn't even up for debate."

EXPECT THE UNEXPECTED, ESPECIALLY WHEN IT COMES TO FISH

That second night on the boat was almost as dreadful as the first. None of us got much sleep. The sea, which hadn't been too rough during the day, became far more furious in the darkness.

And so did Lina.

I tried to point out that the weather wasn't my fault, but I couldn't really argue when she said, "The reason we are out in it is, though, Sebastian."

The rain lashed down like a barrage of bullets. The waves grew bigger and bigger. As the front of the boat climbed each new crest, we would find ourselves almost perpendicular to the sea. At that angle it was impossible to cling onto the sides and we would all slide to the back of the boat. Then the back would rise upwards and we'd get thrown forward, towards the bow. It was the see-saw from some watery version of hell.

Above the sound of the hammering rain and the crashing waves, I could hear Étienne vomiting and praying and Lina vomiting and screaming. I tried to shout back to them that everything was going to be okay but, to be honest, I didn't know if we had it in us to survive another night as ferocious as the one before. Fortunately, while the waves were big, they weren't nearly as destructive and, at some point, the storm passed. I could have cried with relief – I think I probably did.

We all curled up – Étienne at the back, Lina in the middle and me at the bow – and tried to sleep. I rolled over and that's when I remembered that I'd put something in the zip pocket of my shorts.

"Look!" I said quite proudly, "my emergency Bounty bar!"

"Oh, that's *just* what we need, emergency chocolate. Not a radio or a rescue boat. A coconutty taste of paradise is what's going to save us," Lina snapped, but she ate her portion anyway.

Then, with the water calm and the sky clear, we were finally able to get some much-needed sleep.

That second morning there was a moment, just after I woke up, when I forgot where I was. A few blissful seconds when the horror hadn't found me. But when my eyelids flickered open, the first thing I saw was Lina's angry face looming over me and I remembered.

"Good morning, sleeping beauty," she said. "Did you sleep well?"

By the tone of her voice, I could tell it wasn't a genuine question, but I answered anyway. "I have had more restful nights." I sat up and stretched. I must have woken late because the sun was already high in the sky. My body ached and my clothes were a crispy salty layer stuck to my skin.

"You don't say." She sat down next to me, and I propped myself up on my elbow.

"I'm worried about Étienne," she whispered. "I'm worried about all of us, but I'm especially worried about Étienne. He hasn't said a word since he woke up. I think he might be in shock or something."

I looked over to where Étienne was sitting at the other end of the boat. A sad little figure, hunched over with his head hidden between his knees. His face was red and peeling and his hair was sticking up in all directions. I felt terrible seeing him that way. I had to do something, so I scrambled over to him and gently put my hand on his shoulder.

"Étienne?"

No response.

"You okay, buddy?"

He shrugged my hand off.

"Étienne, can you say something please, so we know you're okay?"

"Of course he's not okay!" Lina said. "Look at him. Look at us! We're stranded in the middle of the Pacific Ocean! The largest and deepest ocean on the whole planet! Do you know it covers over a hundred and sixty million square kilometres? How is anyone going to find us in that much water?"

"I don't know if sharing facts like those is *that* helpful," I said.

"You don't like facts? Then you better buckle up because I've got a load more for you. I'm hungry, I'm thirsty, I'm tired, I'm battered and I'm bruised. Nothing about this is okay, Sebastian. The sooner you realize that the better."

I felt sick. Sick from hunger. Sick from the seawater I'd swallowed the night before. Sick from the rolling of the boat. But most of all sick at the thought of what I'd done to my friends. They looked so miserable – so defeated.

I got to my feet. "I'll tell you what we're going to do," I said with as much confidence as I could muster. "We're going to survive. We are going to stick together. We are going to be brave—"

"I don't think one of your motivational talks is going to help now," Lina interrupted.

I knew she was right, but I carried on valiantly trying to be motivational and inspiring by saying empty things like, **"Once you choose hope, anything is possible,"** and **"You never know what the next moment might bring."** Then the next moment did bring something quite astonishing.

It brought a fish.

From the actual sky.

Not that I realized that it was a fish, what with it being in the air and not the water. Where fish are supposed to be.

It showed up from out of nowhere, walloped me on the side of the face and knocked me to the deck, where it started attacking me. It flipper-flappered around on top of me all slimy and slippery. I screamed and tried to wrestle it off, desperately calling out for mercy. Which I know isn't something a fish can give, but it was a traumatic event on top of an already traumatic event, and I was not thinking that clearly.

"Get off me!" I shouted and when that didn't work, I called for the assistance of my so-called friends.

My screams of, "Save me!" were met by a noise I

couldn't quite place. I caught sight of Lina and Étienne's faces and I saw that they were laughing.

"Stop laughing!" I yelled. "I'm under attack!"

"Yes! By a fish!" Étienne squealed and clutched his stomach and started rolling about like it was the funniest thing he had ever seen. I think perhaps, due to the extreme stress of our situation, hysteria had set in.

"Help me!" I yelled as my face was slapped repeatedly by fins.

After what felt like an age, Lina and Étienne finally composed themselves sufficiently to free me from my aquatic attacker.

Together they managed to get hold of it and chuck it back into the water and it swam off without so much as a backward glance. I'd thought it was about the size of a tiger shark when it was wrestling me, but it looked embarrassingly smaller – mackerel type proportions – in the water.

"That was unbelievable!" Lina said.

"You can stop smiling about it!" I snapped. "I could have been mortally injured by that bird-fish thing!"

Étienne started sniggering again.

"Look, I understand that a fish isn't the most terrifying of things to be attacked by, but you don't expect fish to leap out of the ocean and wallop you in the face."

"At least it lightened the mood," Étienne said, the shadow of a smile still on his lips.

"Well, yes," I agreed, "at least it did that."

"Do you think we should have kept hold of it? You know, for food?" Lina asked.

We hadn't eaten anything since the rather squished Bounty bar, but that had been hours ago and the queasiness I felt at being at sea was also laced with a fierce hunger. A hunger that was only going to get worse.

"You have a point," I said. "If another fish momentarily thinks it is a bird and flies aboard **HMS Saviour**, I say we keep it."

"What are the chances of another fish leaping aboard the boat?" Lina said. Her tone suggested that she didn't think it was very likely.

But she shouldn't have been so negative. Because what we witnessed next was truly **spectacular**.

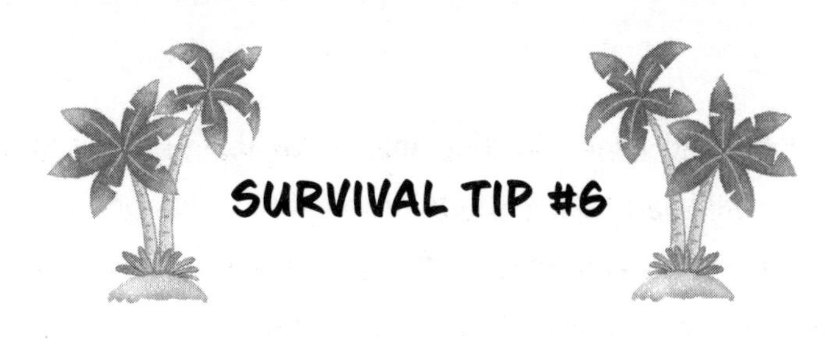

IF YOU CAN, PACK CONDIMENTS

If one fish hurling itself onto **HMS Saviour** was unexpected, a whole bucketload was even more surprising. About twenty fish must have fallen from the heavens into our little vessel that day.

"What the heck!" I shouted, shuddering and jumping about trying get the slippery little devils off me. "Where are they all coming from? Is it actually raining fish? Or am I hallucinating? I can't be hallucinating. I'm the only practical one among us. I can't lose my head or we'll be doomed. Doomed I say! Get it together, Sebastian!" I said, and then, for some reason, I slapped my own face with the fish I'd pulled out from inside my T-shirt.

"Look," Lina said, calmly removing a fish from her lap and pointing out to sea. "It's incredible!"

I hopped about, kicking my leg so the fish that had made its way into my shorts dropped to the floor. I did a full body shudder, made a few retchy noises and then I looked.

What I saw *was* incredible.

I've never seen anything like it before or since. Stretching out in a shimmering silver blanket above the waters around us, was a shoal of flying fish. Or maybe you call them a flock once they're airborne. I'm not sure, I'll have to look it up – if we make it home.

There were hundreds of them. They broke the surface of the water, their tails waggling furiously until their wing-like fins, which were stretched wide, caught the wind and they soared like gliders above the twinkling waters of the Pacific Ocean. I reckon they travelled about a hundred metres before they dropped back below the waves.

"Woah," said Étienne, which I think just about summed it up.

"Isn't that something," I said. "I never knew fish could fly."

"Oh, double woah!" Étienne said pointing at the water. "Do you see those?"

Around the boat were some larger shapes. Bigger fish,

greenish in colour, with extra-long foreheads and fierce eyes that reminded me of Mr Anderson-Tubbs, our very mean and very bald science teacher.

"Mahi mahi," Étienne said.

"Whatty-whatty?" I asked.

"Also called dorado or dolphin fish," Étienne replied, very knowledgeably.

I must have looked surprised that he knew what they were because he explained apologetically, "My dad ate one on holiday once."

Lina leaned over the side of **HMS Saviour** to get a better look. "They're trying to hunt the bird-fish."

"They're going to have a job getting at them from the water," I said, watching the flying fish soar through the sky. "They must be three or four metres above the water level?"

Lina shielded her eyes. "Maybe even higher."

Then a flock of actual birds showed up, circling the sky above the fish-birds. "Blimey, what are those?" I asked.

"They look like pterodactyls," Étienne said.

"Your dad eat one of those on holiday too?" Lina asked.

"No he didn't, and I didn't say they actually are pterodactyls," Étienne said. "Just that they look like them."

“The way our luck’s been going, I wouldn’t be surprised if pterodactyls did show up,” Lina said. “But I think those are frigate birds. I watched a documentary about them once.”

“What are they holding in their beaks?” I squinted. “Red balloons?”

“I don’t think they’re carrying anything. That red puffy bit looks like it’s part of their body. I wonder why they’ve suddenly shown up?” Étienne said.

He didn’t have to wonder for too long, as one of the birds swooped down and plucked a flying fish right out of the air in quite an aggressive manner.

“Poor flying fish! They’re being attacked from above and below!” Lina said.

“But look at them,” I said. “They don’t give up! They’re in the water, then flying out of the water, then diving back in. They’re fighters! Survivors! Like us! It’s a sign!”

Lina turned to me. “Are you seeing the same thing I’m seeing? Because I’m seeing a flying fish massacre out there.”

“That’s nature, that is,” I said. “Powerful and dreadful and wonderful all at the same time.” And then I did a little nod because I was kind of pleased with how that sounded.

“Thank you, David Attenborough,” Lina said.

“You’re welcome,” I said, because when would being

compared to David Attenborough be anything but a huge compliment?

When the frigate birds and the flying fish and the mahi mahi had moved so far away from us it was difficult to still make out their shapes, our attention was forced back to our situation. There were quite a few flying fish in the bottom of **HMS Saviour**.

"If God can give us food, maybe he will rescue us too," Étienne said.

Lina did not do very well at hiding her feelings about that comment because she plastered them all over her face.

Étienne looked at her, a little hurt. "I'm entitled to my opinion, Lina."

"I'd hardly call this food! Look at it!" she said, gesturing to the fish.

I have to admit, they didn't look that appetizing, what with them only being very recently deceased.

"And God certainly didn't bring them! The mahi mahi scared them onto the boat."

"Who do you think told the mahi mahi to do that?" Étienne said.

"Er, themselves! It's not like God is sitting down there on the bottom of the Pacific Ocean issuing instructions!"

"He is everywhere," Étienne said so ominously it made me almost want to start checking around.

"Everywhere, *really*?" Lina pushed.

"Yes. Everywhere. He is all powerful."

"If he is *all powerful*, how about he sends me a double cheeseburger with a side of fries and a chocolate milkshake, rather than a load of horrible-looking fish! I mean," she said picking one up and pulling a face, "you don't really think we're going to eat these, do you? There's no way, this is going anywhere near my mouth!"

I was kind of with Lina on that, but it turns out you'll eat anything when you're hungry enough. And that evening, as another day of aimless bobbing about in the Pacific drew to a close, our need for sustenance grew stronger than our objection to eating raw fish.

"Think of it as eating sushi," I said, not very convincingly, as I handed a flying fish corpse to Étienne. "It isn't about taste – it's about getting the calories and nutrients we need to keep our bodies working."

"I can't stand sushi." Lina held hers up in front of her face. "There really isn't any way to cook this? You're sure there's no matches?"

I shook my head. "You checked too."

She did a massive huff. "I'm never going to forgive you for this, Sebastian," as if she hadn't already made that abundantly clear. After a few aborted attempts, she finally took a bite out of the side.

"How is it?" Étienne asked, grimacing.

"You know, not bad," Lina said and a line of flying fish juice dribbled down her chin.

My stomach spasmed at the sight. "Really?"

"No! Not really! It tastes awful, truly, truly horrible and I want to pull my tongue from my mouth and throw it into the sea so I never have to taste that again, but what choice do we have? Now you eat some, Sebastian!"

"You know what? I'm not that hungry and I've probably got enough nutrients stored in me already—"

"**EAT IT!**" Lina roared, jabbing a fish right under my nose. "I want to see you eat some!"

"I can't. I'm a vegetarian," I lied.

"You know I know that isn't true! And a cauliflower falling out of the sky is even less likely than a fish, so just **EAT IT!**" She then rammed the fish onto my lips and tried to force it in, but I kept my mouth firmly clamped shut.

"Are you kissing that fish?" Étienne said.

I opened my mouth to say, "No, I am not snogging a fish," and Lina saw her chance and rammed it into my mouth.

I immediately pulled the slippery morsel of digustingness back out and retched again.

"Just eat it," Lina said, with a sigh. "You know you're

going to have to eventually."

I knew she was right. I did a sigh big enough to match hers, took hold of it by its weird wing-fins, took a breath, took a bite and swallowed. At least, I tried to swallow, but the lump sat in my mouth for a bit while my stomach worked very hard against me by contracting ferociously to try and make me spit it out. Eventually, and very heroically, I managed to get it down.

"*And?*" Lina said. "How did it taste?"

It took me a moment before I could speak. "Probably would taste better with a bit of soy sauce and wasabi."

MAKE SURE YOU WISH FOR THE RIGHT THING

We spent the rest of that day rowing and hoping beyond hope that we were heading *somewhere.* Despite the seriousness of our situation, our spirits – Étienne's especially – were lifted by the wildlife we saw on the way.

A pod of dolphins followed us for a while, which, when we were finally sure they weren't sharks, was completely **spectacular** and something I won't ever forget. They moved so gracefully, so effortlessly, their silver-grey bodies diving down and then resurfacing almost like they were dancing.

We also saw a huge turtle paddling deep below us. It was a dark shadow at first, but when it moved closer to the surface of the water its shell glistened a dappled orangey-yellow in the sunlight. It cut through the water in this deliberate and unhurried way and had the feel of something majestic and ancient.

And then there were the shoals of fish. So many fish, in so many colours – electric blues, fiery reds, emerald greens and brilliant silvers. Each shoal moved like it was one being. The fish would all head one way, then abruptly they'd all change direction. It was so mesmerizing to watch, it almost made us forget where we were. What we were facing.

That evening we finished our first bottle of water. We'd been good – rationing it out carefully and only taking sips when the thirst became too much. But, even if we kept drinking as slowly as we were, we knew that we wouldn't have long left until we ran out.

It was something that played on our minds.

And there was still no sign of a boat or a search plane.

"How can there be so much water and yet so little to drink?" Étienne said, looking out across the miles of blue that stretched out around us.

"It messes with your mind, doesn't?" Lina said. "But no matter how bad it gets – we can't drink the seawater. It's toxic, our bodies won't be able to get rid of the salt and we'll end up more dehydrated than when we started."

"Drinking seawater can scramble your brain too, can't it?" I asked. "At least, I think that's what my dad said."

Lina shifted in her seat and stretched out her legs. "If you drink enough of it and you get mega dehydrated, eventually delirium will set in."

Étienne turned back to look at us. "But if we run out of water, we're going to get dehydrated and delirious too, aren't we?"

"Yup," Lina said, very matter-of-factly, but I could tell she was anxious.

"That's something to look forward to," I said.

"We've got another night to survive first; we might not even reach the point of delirium if we drown," Étienne said miserably.

"Another cheery thought, Etsy," I said. "But don't worry, I think we have it in us to survive to the point of delirium."

"You certainly won't get through another night if you call me Etsy again."

"Point taken. I must say, being lost at sea is definitely bringing out another side of you."

Étienne narrowed his eyes. "Is that so?"

"Yes! A very excellent and assertive side of you! Not at all like a tarsier monkey!"

"What are you talking about? Are you already delirious?" Lina asked.

I realized that my comparison of Étienne to a tarsier monkey was something that I hadn't actually shared with the world.

"No. Nothing," I said and swiftly changed the subject. "Come on, let's start strapping things down to the boat in case we have to endure another storm like last night's."

Mercifully, the **HMS Saviour** was cradled by a far gentler beast that third night – the sea was calm, almost still.

Despite this, and our bone-tired bodies, we still struggled to sleep.

I suppose it is difficult to quiet your mind when you're facing possible death by drowning or delirium or starvation or pelican attack.

The guilt continued to gnaw at me too. My mind whirred angrily within my skull. I questioned again why I was so stupid. Why I did these things. Whether I was the reason Mum had left. I thought about the damage I'd caused in the past through all my actions. So many stupid, mindless, thoughtless actions. And the pain I was causing in the present.

Why couldn't I just be better?

Lina gave a low whistle, which snapped me out of my self-indulgent despair-spiral.

"Would you look at all those stars!" She sort of breathed

the words rather than spoke them. “The sky…it’s…it’s **spectacular**.”

It really was breathtakingly beautiful.

“That’s one positive about being out at sea,” Lina said. “No light pollution.”

“There aren’t this many stars usually, are there?” Étienne asked.

“There are, we just haven’t been able to see them clearly like this before,” Lina said.

“I’ve never seen anything like it,” Étienne said, his eyes wide and glinting behind his glasses in the moonlight.

Lina sighed. “You’d never believe something this beautiful existed – would you – if you hadn’t seen it with your own eyes.”

“A bit like flying fish. I’d never believe those things were real if I hadn’t been smacked round the face with one.”

“Way to ruin the moment, Sebastian,” Lina said.

“Sorry, I don’t know why I did that. You’re right. It is incredible.”

“Almost makes you believe there could be a god,” Lina said.

“That’s because there is,” Étienne said.

“It is scientifically imp—”

I tuned out of their discussion about whether God

exists. They'd had it a million times before and always ended up agreeing to disagree.

Instead of listening, I looked up at the star-studded sky. My eyes scanned the silver-speckled darkness, hoping to spot a shooting star so I could make a wish to be a different person once we were rescued. A better person. A person who was a bit more like Lina – so fiercely loyal and hard-working. Or to be somebody like Étienne, who was so kind and caring and intelligent. Although I might ask to leave out resembling a tarsier monkey.

But a person who wouldn't do all the stupid things I did. A person who wasn't me.

A light, brilliant and vivid, suddenly streaked across the sky and it felt like the universe was offering me a chance.

"There!" I shouted and jumped to my feet, "Did you see it? A shooting star!"

I wish to be better.

"I did! Amazing! Oh look! There's another!" Lina shouted.

"And another!" Étienne said, getting to his feet.

"There's loads of them!" Lina said, spinning round, trying to take it all in. "Look at them all!"

"A shower of shooting stars!" I said. "The sky is surely putting on a show for us tonight!"

"Are you wishing?!" Lina asked. "You'd better be wishing!"

"Yes, I'm wishing," Étienne said.

"Me too!" I said.

"What are you wishing?" Lina asked.

"I can't tell you that or it won't come true," Étienne said, quite correctly. Everyone knows there are hard and fast rules associated with wishes.

"Okay, but we are all wishing for the same thing, right?" She looked from me to Étienne like she didn't trust us.

Which I suppose was fair enough, I had used up my first wish on myself, which in retrospect, was not brilliant of me. I used my wishes after that for the good of the group though.

"We can't tell you!" Étienne said.

"I know, but you *are* both wishing that we'll be resc—"

"Shhh!" Étienne said and rammed his finger over her lips. "Don't say it, or it won't happen! Understand?"

Lina nodded and Étienne slowly took his hand away, eyeballing her until he was certain she wasn't going to speak.

"I think we all know what we've got to wish for, Lina," I said.

"Fine—"

"World peace," I said.

"What? No!" she shouted. "Don't wish for that! Oh, that sounds bad. But you know what I mean. Leave it for people who aren't stranded in the middle of the Pacific to wish for peace."

After the shooting stars had stopped their shooting, and we had made our last wishes for whatever it was we had to wish for but couldn't say, we lay back down in the boat and hoped for sleep to find us.

"It's really quite something," Étienne said dreamily, his eyes fighting to stay open. "The strength of the brightness against the dark."

"Some things shine their brightest in the darkest of times. A bit like us," I said. "Hold onto that thought."

This moment of silent reflection was quickly ruined by Lina and Étienne splutter-laughing.

"Sebastian, that really was quite possibly the *corniest* thing you have ever said," Lina howled. "You read that on a tea towel or something?"

"It's like being stuck out at sea with the world's worst motivational speaker," Étienne said, I think rather unkindly. I thought I had been very motivational. Then I realized that was probably how my dad felt every time he told me one of his naval mottos. I promised myself that if I ever made it home, I'd never roll my eyes or groan at him again.

Once they'd stopped giggling and teasing me, silence eventually fell over the boat again.

"You're right though, Sebastian," Lina said quietly. "Let's try to be the best versions of ourselves. I've been reading this book ready for IGCSE—" She took it out from where she had rammed it under one of the seats.

"Lina," I interrupted, "we're going into Year Eight, why are you reading IGCSE texts?"

"To get a head start."

"That's so you," I said.

"Nothing wrong with working hard, but shh, Sebastian, and listen. The story is about this group of kids whose plane went down and they ended up stuck on this island and they completely lost the plot—"

"Did they drink the seawater?" Étienne said sleepily.

"No, but they turned on each other and they got into big fights, and they went a bit savage, and they started seeing things that weren't there and some of them died and they put a pig's head on a stake and it was all awful. Really dreadful stuff. Promise me we won't do that."

"We can definitely promise you that we won't impale a pig on a stake," I said. "Where would we get one from for starters?"

"What were they even doing putting a pig's head on a stake?" Étienne asked. "Seems like a very odd thing to do."

"I think it was a peace offering to a beast," Lina said.

"Crikey!" I said. "When I broke Madame Aurelie's window in that French lesson, I just gave her a pot plant."

"I remember, but I'm not talking about pigs! I just want you to promise that we'll stay friends. Whatever happens."

I propped myself up on my elbow and said, very earnestly because I was being very earnest and I knew how lucky I was to have them, "Of course we'll stay friends. Whatever happens. I promise."

SURVIVAL TIP #8

STAY HYDRATED

The following morning, I was woken, quite forcefully, to an unbelievable sight.

The words "**WAKE UP!**" were being bellowed into my eardrums and I opened my eyes to find Lina's face looming over me yet again. Her slightly deranged expression wasn't the unbelievable sight. It was something much more exciting.

Lina gave me a shake. "Look!"

"What is it?"

"Just **LOOK!**" she yelled.

Étienne and I sat upright and looked to where Lina was pointing.

"Oh! Wow!" Étienne scrambled to his feet, his chin already starting to wobble. "Is it really—"

"Land!" I cried. "I see **LAND**!"

My heart leaped, and I clambered over to the side of the boat, tripping and stumbling in my excitement – desperate to get a better view of the small, green island that had appeared out of nowhere.

"LAND! Man the oars!" I shouted, blinking back the tears I hadn't realized I was crying. "We are saved!"

Our excitement did not make for a unified effort when it came to rowing. We clattered the oars about everywhere, with no timing or rhythm. Our arms ached and our bodies were weak from the days at sea, which meant we got nowhere fast.

Eventually I stopped and took a moment to catch my breath. "Guys, I think we need to approach this in a more united manner. Let's not panic, the island's not going anywhere."

"Fine. On three," Lina said.

After that, we made a much better job of it, and we moved slowly but steadily. I was even allowed to sing **Row Row Row Your Boat**, which I think lifted our spirits even higher. Even Lina joined in by the fourth round.

We decided to approach the island from what we determined to be the south-west side, although we had no clue which side it actually was because we had no idea of our bearings. It just sounded good when I said, “Let’s approach from the south-west side.” It sounded like something my dad would say.

The other side of the island – the north-east, we supposed – was far more rugged. Angry-looking rocks jutted out from the sea like giants’ teeth, making it impossible to steer the boat through them and the white surf flinked off the imposing jagged cliffs. There would be no place to moor there and none of us fancied scrabbling up rocks.

So, we rowed what we decided was due south, and from the dark, bottomless waters of the open sea, we navigated ourselves round the twisting arc of a coral reef into waters that were almost as still as a mountain lake.

“We’re in a lagoon.” Étienne’s oar became still as he took a moment to appreciate the beauty of the place. “It’s –” his eyes shone – “wonderful.”

It really was. The waters around us seemed to change from dark inky blue, to purple, then bright blue and turquoisey green.

“How can the ocean be so many colours?” Lina said, not really to anybody.

A lightness lifted up in my heart again. It was as if the atmosphere changed the moment we’d crossed to the other side of the reef. I felt almost giddy with thanks that we hadn’t perished at sea. “You’d almost think we’d stumbled across paradise."

Lina said, "I don't want paradise, I want home."

I didn't know what to say to that. She was right, of course.

Étienne took up his oar again. "This will do for now though. Come on, let's get ashore, my bum's had enough of this bench."

We paddled across the lagoon, occasionally stopping to point out the shoals of glittering fish that darted about around us, and into the mouth of a sandy cove that was lined with palm trees and backed onto a dense green forest.

"It doesn't look inhabited," Lina said. "I see no signs of life – no housing or smoke or anything really."

"I think you're right," Étienne said, pushing his glasses up his nose.

"No one to help us," Lina said, and for a moment silence fell over the boat. We knew that our troubles weren't yet over.

When the waters grew lighter, to the point where we could see the rocks on the bottom of the sea floor, we carefully climbed over the side and, with burning muscles, pulled the boat up, high onto the island sands so the tide wouldn't steal it from us.

Walking on solid ground was the strangest sensation. Heavy, wet shoes did not help. My legs didn't feel like my own and the ground didn't feel that solid. It felt like it was moving from side to side, like the waves. The whole world was swirling. When I looked at Étienne, I could tell that he was experiencing the same thing because he was staggering about all over the place.

"My legs feel like rubber," he said in a rather wibbly-wobbly voice. "Do your legs feel like they're made of rubber? They won't do as I want them to. What's wrong with my legs? Are they even there? Are these your legs or my legs, Sebastian?"

And then he fell over.

Then I fell over too, because my legs *really* didn't feel like mine and in my slightly heightened state of euphoria, I wasn't sure whether I did have someone else's legs attached to me.

"What's wrong with you two?" Lina asked, looking remarkably stable on her feet – almost like she'd been planted. Clearly she had far superior sea legs to me or Étienne.

Étienne, lying flat on his back, staring up through the feathery leaves of a palm tree at the brilliant blue sky, started opening and closing his arms and legs. "Look! Sand angels!" he beamed. "I love the ground. Have I ever told you how much I love the ground? It is just so...**grounding**. I've never thought about that word before...*grounding*. It really is a perfect word. Grounding, grounding, grounding!" He sang those last three groundings very operatically.

Lina eyed him suspiciously. "Do you think we need to give him some water?"

But I was on Étienne's side. "You know what? I think I love the ground too. I think I love it more than the sky, definitely more than the sea – yup, I think the ground is my favourite!"

"Hmm. I'm getting you *both* some water. You two are clearly delirious," Lina said, and stomped back to the boat.

I might have been a *teeny* bit delirious, but I wasn't just delirious from dehydration. I was also delirious from the fact that we were no longer at sea. We were on dry land, and if we were on land, we had a chance of survival. A chance of someone finding us. A chance of getting home. Through the fear that had wound itself round my insides, I felt a glimmer of hope.

After Lina had shared out the water, each of us only daring to take a couple of sips, I lay back on the sand. A tiredness so deep and consuming, a tiredness that I have never felt before or since, took its hold on my body.

The sun was just peeking out from the horizon when I came round, so I must have slept right through the whole day and night. I sat up and saw that Étienne and Lina had fallen asleep either side of me, their faces red from the sun.

For a while I watched them sleep, saying silent apologies and making promises that everything would be okay. They looked so peaceful – despite everything they had just been through.

Étienne suddenly bolted upright, screaming, his hair sticking up in all different directions, and started bicycling his arms and legs – flinging sand all about the place, which woke Lina.

Startled, she jumped to her feet and shouted, "Sebastian!" as if I was to blame.

"He's having a nightmare," I said and grabbed hold of Étienne. "It's okay, you're okay!"

Lina said, "Well, stop him!"

I gave Étienne a good shake. "Wake up. You're having a nightmare!"

His eyes finally focused, and he looked around, confused.

"You okay now?" I asked.

Étienne placed his hand on his chest and breathed in deeply. "I had the worst dream. I was still at sea, and I was being attacked by flying mahi mahi the size of pterodactyls."

"That sounds awful," I said. "So, I imagine you must be very relieved to wake up and discover that you are not under attack from giant-bird-fish-dinosaurs and, instead, you are stranded on a desert island."

Étienne rubbed the sand out of his eyes, his hands were still shaking. "Yes, I suppose this is the better of those two options. Just."

Lina slumped down on the floor next to us. "This really is a nightmare, isn't it?"

Étienne nodded and looked at the ground and whispered, "Please, God, help us."

The heaviness of our situation bowled into me again but before I could let it paralyse me, Lina said, "I'd be delighted if your God does help us, Étienne, but in case he's busy, we're going to have to help ourselves. We should go and explore the island. Find out what's here and familiarize ourselves with our surroundings."

"Now?" I asked.

"You have something else planned in your diary? You never know, it might be inhabited. We could walk through and find a town on the other side of the undergrowth."

We looked towards the thick, green jungle that hugged the beach. It seemed very unlikely that anyone could be living in there.

Lina stood up and cupped her hands round her mouth.

"HELLO! IS ANYONE THERE? WE NEED HELP! WE HAVE BEEN **SHIPWRECKED!**"

Étienne and I struggled to our feet – my legs still feeling quite peculiar – and joined in.

"HELLO! HELLO! ANYBODY?"

We carried on shouting for quite some time, but there was no answer. We sat down on the sand, more than a little dejected.

"Maybe we're too far away for anyone to hear us. Let's get going – we'll have to scour the whole island," Lina said. "There could be someone here. Maybe."

"Not *all* of the island, though, surely?" Étienne said. "I'm not up for some big excursion. We've been at sea for the past few days. I really think we deserve a little R&R."

"R&R?" Lina said.

"Rest and relaxation," I clarified.

"Yes, I know what R&R means, but in case you've forgotten, we're not on some all-inclusive holiday."

"How about we compromise and have a little scout round the beach and that bit of forest over there today. We can go on a bigger mission tomorrow," I suggested.

Lina screwed up her face, while she considered this suggestion. "Okay, small scout about today, big exploration tomorrow. But we need to locate a water source and start making the camp before nightfall."

"The camp?" Étienne said. "Can't we just sleep in the boat tonight?"

"Absolutely not. If someone does arrive here to rescue us, I want to have built the best castaway camp ever in history. I want the newspaper reports of our discovery to talk about how ingenious we've been. How we've whittled our own kitchen utensils from palm trees and built a fully functioning kitchen out of coconut husks. I'm not having people judging us and thinking we were rubbish castaways."

"That sounds like a lot of unnecessary hard work," I said.

"That's what you sign up for when you make friends with an overachiever. But first things first, we need to start a fire to alert passing ships or planes to our location. A fire is our best chance of rescue. We still have one flare left but we should save that for the right moment – when someone is near to see it."

"That seems reasonable," Étienne said.

"But listen to me and listen good. In that book I'm reading, there was a lot of bother over the fire and, I'm just saying, if one of you lets it go out, things aren't going to go well for anybody. But mainly you. Understand?"

"The pig-head book?" Étienne asked.

"That's the one. It's an examination of whether, deep down, evil lurks in all of us. It just takes certain circumstances, like the one we're in, for it to come out."

"Thank you, Lina, for that cheery thought of the day," I said. "Personally, I think challenging situations bring out the good in people. That's what my dad tells me anyway."

"Are you going to start waffling on about how we are like stars?" Étienne said.

"I just don't think there's any evil in either of you," I said.

"Let's hope that's true," Lina said, clapping the sand off her hands. "Now, come on, we need to collect wood and, later, I'm going to show you how we're going to use Étienne's glasses to start a flame – I saw it done in a movie once."

Lina strode off purposefully towards the boat and I could tell she was going to make us work hard.

I turned my head to look at Étienne. "My legs still feel a bit like marshmallows." I stared down at my trainers, which had dried and hardened in the sun. A salty crust had formed over them, making them feel tight on my feet.

Étienne flapped his legs about like a dying fish. "Where even are my legs? I need to put them back on if she's making us walk somewhere."

"Do you think we need a bit more to drink?" I said.

"Yeah, probably."

SURVIVAL TIP #9

CHOOSE A LEADER CAREFULLY

By the time Étienne and I had ziggle-zaggled our way across the little patch of white sand back to the boat, Lina had already retrieved the hatchet.

"I think we're going to need a leader," she said.

"Okay, I'll do it," I said. I wanted to – I wanted the chance to do something good, to prove that I wasn't a complete catastrophe of a person.

"No, I meant I should do it."

"Guess it will be up to Étienne to decide between us then," I said.

"What makes you think I don't want to be the leader?" Étienne said.

"Do you?"

"No, but I don't like the assumption that I wouldn't. Or

the thought that you wouldn't even consider me to have leadership potential."

"Of course you don't like that assumption. It was a bad one and I apologize. I think you'd make a fine leader, Étienne." That was quite a massive lie. Étienne would be a useless leader – Lina would walk all over him – but I needed him on side.

"Sucking up isn't going to make me pick you, Sebastian."

"A boy with scruples! I admire that. So who is it going to be, Étienne, my old pal?"

"I choose Lina."

"What?! Why?!"

"She's the one holding the hatchet. Never vote against someone with a weapon, I say."

"But I have military experience – my whole body is practically a weapon!"

Étienne pulled a face. "Military experience?"

"It's true! Well sort of…okay, my dad has told me some stories."

"Too late now anyway, Sebastian," Lina said, giving me the smuggest of smug grins. "Étienne has very sensibly picked me and, as leader, I am going to instruct you on what you're going to do first."

I gave Étienne a very strong look and muttered, "You'll

only have yourself to blame when she's got us weaving hammocks from palm leaves."

"That's actually not a bad idea," Lina said. "But in the meantime, we have three main objectives. **Number one** is to build a shelter. **Number two** is to search the island – to see if anyone is here and to find food and a safe source of water – and **number three** is to make a fire. Everybody in agreement?"

I did not want to agree because I was still a bit annoyed about not being voted in as leader and I did not appreciate her bossy tone. However, it did seem like a reasonable plan.

"Can I add a number four?" I asked.

"Depends what it is." Lina eyed me suspiciously.

"My number four is to have fun. If we can. I think we should try, at least. Things are going to be hard, and I don't want us to feel too desperate or bleak, you know? So, yes. **Number four** is to have fun."

Lina tilted her head. "I'll think about it. Now, come on." She nodded decisively towards the forest. "Let's chop down some wood. We'll need quite a lot if we want to build a fire and some sort of camp."

"Okay," Étienne said, running behind her and looking more than ever like a lost little tarsier monkey.

"We'll need to make the fire somewhere that's in plain

sight, so our rescuers can easily see it. It will need to be a decent size too."

"About the size of the fire Sebastian accidentally started in the school conservation area?" Étienne asked.

"Goodness, no! We don't want the whole island to end up ablaze. Think the size of the school bonfire."

"Understood!" Étienne said.

"After that we should try and catch a fish or something," I suggested. "Actually, why don't I have a go at that now?"

"No!" Lina snapped. "We work together as a team – I don't want you going off on your own and turning into some savage hunter and losing your mind."

"Are you thinking about your pig book again?" I asked.

"It's called **Lord of the Flies** and I think it should serve as a warning to us all about what could go wrong if we're not careful. I shall read you both some this evening to help you understand."

"It just seems like it could be quicker if I went—"

"Nope, leader has spoken," Lina said and marched purposefully towards the forest. "Keep your eyes out for any signs of human life and your wits about you."

"She's going to be unbearable – you do realize?" I whispered to Étienne as we kicked our way through the sand and up a bank smattered with coarse grass.

"I think she'll be fine. Give her a chance."

"Ooh look! A coconut!" Lina suddenly stopped and pointed at a tiny brown ball *very* high up in a tree. "Up you go, Étienne, go and get it."

Étienne shielded his eyes against the brilliant sunlight. "How on earth do you expect me to get up there?"

"By climbing!" Lina said.

Étienne looked at me for support that he wasn't going to get. Instead, I gave him a big grin and said, "Up you go, Étienne! Our leader has spoken."

SURVIVAL TIP #10

CONSIDER PROTECTIVE CLOTHING

I was expecting Étienne to refuse, but I think the bone-gnawing hunger spurred him on to have a go and he handed me his glasses. "Look after these."

I looked through them and the world warped and blurred. "Blimey, don't you struggle with them?"

"Very funny. Just don't break them."

"Listen to him," Lina said, "those glasses could be what get us rescued. I need them to start the fire."

"Hero glasses. They're cool," I said, "but seriously, Étienne, can you see without them?"

"Not brilliantly, so I can't afford to have them falling off and smashing."

"Got it. Good luck!"

Climb true, my little monkey friend, you've got this.

He didn't have it.

Lina and I watched as he wrapped his legs round the trunk and attempted to pull himself upwards. It became clear within mere moments that there was no way he was going to make it all the way to the coconut. He might look a bit like a tarsier monkey, but he certainly couldn't climb like one.

"Am I close?" he asked, desperately trying to pull himself further up the tree.

"Er...closer than you were," Lina said, diplomatically.

"It is...very hard work," he panted as he grappled to pull himself higher, "and I...am...already very tired... but...must get...food."

"Keep going," I said, "almost there!"

Lina frowned at me. I shrugged. He was nowhere near *there*, but I didn't want to knock his confidence.

After a period of persistent struggle, where he made it no further up than shoulder height, he eventually dropped down and admitted defeat.

"No matter. It was a valiant effort," I said, handing him back his specs. "Now step back, let a professional have a go." I imagined I'd be rather good at shimmying up a coconut tree and quite liked the idea of being the food provider for the group again. After all, it was me who'd had the Bounty bar and me who'd captured that

flying fish in the boat.

Lina scrumpled up her face. "A professional what? Coconut collector?"

I ignored her, walked through the decaying coconut shells that were scattered around and got a handhold on the tree. "Today we shall feast on coconut!" I declared and then I commenced my climb with real resolve.

A resolve which ran out within minutes, when I discovered how hard climbing is and how tired I still was and how much energy I didn't have. I sort of ran out of steam and ended up stuck halfway up.

The real problem, though, was that I also didn't have the courage to climb back down. I suddenly became acutely aware that even though I was nowhere near the coconut, I was also nowhere near the ground.

"What are you doing?" Lina shouted up, a little impatiently. "Where's this coconut feast you promised us?"

"I think he's having a rest," Étienne said. "Are you having a rest, Sebastian?"

"Yes, Étienne, I'm taking a little zizz halfway up a coconut tree!"

"You know what I mean. Are you okay?"

"I'm fine. I'm just taking a moment, that's all."

I carried on clinging to the trunk, desperately

wondering what to do, while they carried on looking up at me, wondering what I was doing.

"You're stuck, aren't you?" Lina asked. "Admit it."

"No!"

"You sure look like you're stuck," she continued.

"I'm just taking a moment to enjoy the view."

"And how is that for you?" she asked.

"It's slightly ruined by somebody squawking at me," I told her, my arms starting to ache.

"What can you see from up there? Any sign of human life?" Lina asked hopefully.

"I can see trees, lots of trees. That's about it." I wasn't high enough up to get a proper view.

"Sebastian," Étienne said kindly. "Are you sure you're not stuck?"

"Absolutely. I'm not stuck, I'm just unable to progress any further up the tree and also unable to work out a way to get back down." My arms were really hurting now. I glanced up at the coconut, a furry egg in a feathery green nest. It seemed impossibly out of reach.

"So stuck then," Lina said, with very little sympathy in her voice.

"No, not stuck, as I said, just unable—"

I was going to say *unable to get down,* but I suddenly did get down. Very quickly. Much quicker than I would

have liked, in fact, because my arms gave way, and I shot down the tree with my legs still wrapped round it. I went so fast and there was so much friction that I think I saw smoke.

I'll tell you something for nothing, coconut tree trunks are not smooth. They are very barky and ridgy and at the gazillion miles an hour I was plummeting, bark and ridges are not good things.

My poor backside bore the brunt of it.

I'm glad I didn't know this would become a recurring theme during my stay on the island, because I may have lain down in the sand and given up right there and then.

My shrieking – yes, there was shrieking – caused a whole load of colourful birds to burst out of the jungle in a chaos of flapping and screeching. This startled Étienne so much he threw himself to the ground and covered his head with his hands, like he was sheltering from gunfire.

I landed heavily on the sand. Then jumped up clutching my sore bum and began hopping about.

"Eee ooo ahh ahh! Hurts! Bad! Bad bum…oh the pain… like…real…bad, bad bum!" Rather than check if I, the person with an actual problem, was okay, Lina ran over to Étienne and said, "Étienne, are you alright? Don't worry, it was just some birds."

"Why are you asking *him* if he's alright?" I shouted, dancing by them. "I'm the one who has skinned my bum!"

This did not illicit the reaction of sympathy that I was expecting.

Instead they both looked like they might be about to giggle, until I stopped dancing and glared at them with my most deadly glare and they thought better of it.

Lina looked up at the coconut. "Do you want to give it another go?"

I did not answer because I gave her a look that said all I needed to say.

"Maybe we'll leave the coconut for today," Étienne suggested.

"Agreed, let's see if we can find something else to eat," Lina said. "We'll figure out a way to get it down another time. Maybe we could throw rocks at it or something?"

Étienne glared up at the coconut. "I'm going to get it, somehow. That coconut will be mine. I swear to you."

"That's very determined of you," I said, although having watched his attempt, I thought it was wholly unlikely. "We'll have to call you Étienne the coconut hunter."

"No!" Lina shouted. "No one here is being referred to as a hunter, okay? I am not having either of you turning into savages on my watch." Then she stomped off towards the trees, swinging her hatchet and ordering us to follow, in quite a savage way herself.

I looked at Étienne. "Is coconut hunting that savagey?"

Étienne shrugged. “I think it’s that book of hers talking again.”

“She threatened to read it to us later,” I said. “Maybe we’ll see what all the fuss is about then. In the meantime, we’d better do as she says, because *somebody* here voted her in as leader.”

“Right, you two,” Lina said when we caught up with her. “We need water and wood for a fire and for shelter and keep an eye out for food.”

“What sort of food?” Étienne asked.

Then, right on cue, **Giuseppe Garibaldi** made his first entrance.

SURVIVAL TIP #11

SEARCH FOR A SOURCE OF WATER

Giuseppe Garibaldi was not called **Giuseppe Garibaldi** when we first met him. In fact, he did not have a name.

He did not have a name because he was a goat.

Étienne was responsible for christening him and many other animals on the island, for reasons I shall discuss later.

Giuseppe emerged from the undergrowth on bandy, knobbly legs, lazily chomping on some shrubbery.

Lina, in answer to Étienne's question as to what sort of food, pointed her rusty hatchet at Giuseppe and whispered, "That sort of food."

Étienne gasped.

I gawped.

And Giuseppe gulped.

I thought at the time that it was a coincidental swallow. I now realize, of course, that Giuseppe understood *exactly* what we were saying right from the start.

Étienne looked frantically from Giuseppe to Lina. "What do you mean? You can't mean...no!"

Lina nodded and, eyes glinting in a slightly menacing way, she raised the hatchet aloft. She took a silent step towards Giuseppe, who was happily attending to the lower leaves of a tree.

Another step.

Then another.

Étienne shot me a worried look. Considering Lina had been so concerned about us turning into hunting savages only moments before, she was doing a pretty good impression of one herself. It was *most* perplexing.

Sure, I was hungry – famished even. We would need sustenance and soon, but I felt there should be just a little more discussion before we slaughtered a goat.

Étienne must have thought that too because he shouted, "NO! LINA! NO!" before she got anywhere near Giuseppe.

Étienne's impassioned outburst spooked Giuseppe, who immediately stopped his lazy chomping and started his frantic bolting instead.

Have you ever been hit in the stomach by a frantically bolting goat?

Didn't think so.

I have.

Wouldn't recommend it.

I flew upwards and backwards and landed on my already very sore backside and **Giuseppe Garibaldi** trampled over the top of me and disappeared off into the trees, completely unconcerned as to whether I was okay.

"There goes dinner," Lina said, looking at me crossly, as though she thought I was somehow responsible.

"It was Étienne who spooked the thing!" I shouted, scrambling to my feet and blinking pain-tears out of my eyes. "And you were the one who was against us becoming savages!"

"Savages are out-of-control killers. I am the opposite of that. I am a very considered killer."

That was, frankly, unnerving.

"I couldn't stand by and watch you murder an innocent animal!" Étienne said.

"You didn't complain about the flying fish," Lina muttered, which seemed like a fair point.

"We didn't kill those, they sacrificed themselves!" Étienne said, which also seemed like a fair point.

Lina folded her arms. "Oh, yes – the gift from God. I don't think a shower of fish is going to save us now, and besides, how do you know that goat wasn't sent to us by God for our dinner?"

Étienne spread his arms wide. "It's not here now, is it?"

"That's because you scared it away!" Lina said, then she did a big sigh, which she always does whenever she is about to speak to us like we're a couple of idiots. "Étienne, Sebastian, listen, I don't like the idea of eating goat any more than you do. I'm quite a fussy eater normally."

"That's true," I said. "She takes *ages* choosing in the school canteen."

"Yes, alright, but if we're going to survive, we need to eat."

"We don't have to eat *goat* though," Étienne squealed.

"I don't understand why I'm being blamed for this," I said.

"We *could* have had coconut –" Lina said in quite an accusatory tone – "but that didn't happen. You should have let me kill the goat."

"Lina, no!" Étienne gasped again. "I can't imagine you would be capable."

"She wasn't really going to kill it," I looked at her, "were you?"

"I was."

"Oh."

"I think we need to be realistic about what it's going to take to survive out here," she continued. "It isn't going to be easy."

Étienne said, "Can't we just look for some fruits and vegetables? I don't think we need to massacre poor **Giuseppe Garibaldi** on day one, do we?"

"Who?" Lina and I said at the time.

"**Giuseppe Garibaldi** – the goat," Étienne replied, like it was obvious.

"Don't give it a name!" Lina said. "That will make it harder to kill."

"Oh, I had not thought of that." Étienne smiled innocently, which made me think that he had thought *exactly* of that.

I don't think Lina realized because she said, "It doesn't matter now, but in future, if we see a chicken or a pig or anything we could catch for food, don't name it."

"Okay, I won't," Étienne lied.

Lina tipped her head back and exhaled. "Cripes, I'm thirsty."

I ran my tongue over my parched lips. "Me too."

"Come on, let's keep looking," she said. "There's got to be a source of fresh water somewhere."

We ventured deeper into the undergrowth, the ground changing from sand to rock and vegetation. It smelled rich and green and wild. It was clear no person had passed through before. It was really beginning to feel like we were the only ones on the island.

"Hey," I said. "Do you think that goat might have belonged to someone?"

"Giuseppe looked like a free spirit to me," Étienne said.

"HELLO?" I shouted. "Anyone missing a goat?" There was no answer other than a few hoots and caws from some birds.

As we trekked further into the jungle, the creepers became dense and tightly entangled. Insects – some alarmingly big, some small – buzzed about us. Étienne performed what looked like a very elaborate dance when one landed in his hair.

Lina used the hatchet to cut a way through the interwoven green creepers, as she called out a seemingly never-ending list of **keeps** and **don'ts**.

"**Keep** your eyes out for water; **keep** your eyes out for berries; **keep** your wits about you – there may be snakes; **keep** up..."

"**Don't** eat anything without checking with me; **don't**

get lost; **don't** step on anything dangerous; **don't** sing that annoying song about going down to the woods today, Sebastian..."

It was quite tiresome. My eyes were ping-ponging about all over the place looking out for stuff, and I was beginning to get the impression Lina had a problem with my singing. That couldn't be true because our music teacher told me I have a very interesting voice.

Eventually we came to a halt outside what looked like an entrance to a small cave.

Lina placed a finger on my lips and cut me off right in the middle of my song. "Sebastian, will you hush for one moment, please! Listen."

She edged closer to the cave, her hand cupping her ear. "Do you hear that?"

I frowned and looked at Étienne, who shrugged – clearly as clueless as me.

"I hear dripping," Lina said, and then, because we must have still look confused, "Water, guys, I hear **water**."

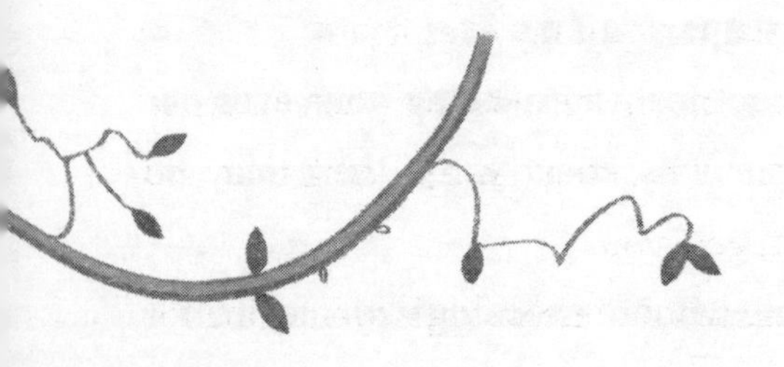

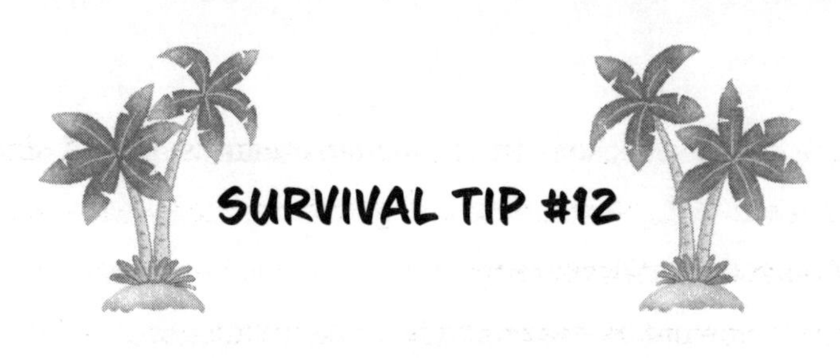

SURVIVAL TIP #12

A BIGGUS LEAFUS CAN MAKE A VERY HANDY CONTAINER

We clambered over the rocks and further into the cave. Lina led the way, adding to her seemingly endless list of keeps and don'ts. "Don't slip; don't rush; keep together; keep a hand on the rock..." Followed by, "Don't roll your eyes, Sebastian."

What? How...? I thought.

Before I could lie and say I wasn't rolling my eyes, she said, "Don't pretend you're not."

I looked at Étienne and rolled my eyes again.

Then she said, like some mystical being who can sense what's happening without looking, "Keep doing that and we shall see how far it gets you."

I stopped then because I'd done enough eye-rolling for

one day, not because I was worried about where it would get me.

It was dark and pleasingly cool inside the cave and nice to be out of the humidity of the jungle, even if it did smell a bit dank and musty. It wasn't a very big cave, more a gap in some rocks, but all three of us could fit inside, with room to swing our arms about if we wanted to.

"See if you can find where the dripping is coming from," Lina instructed.

"Why don't *you* see if you can find where the dripping is coming from," I mumbled so she wouldn't hear.

Obviously, she did hear. "I am, Sebastian. Look, I think you need to drop the attitude before we fall out and you end up tumbling down a rocky cliff."

"Did you just threaten to hurl me from a clifftop?"

"No. But it happened to one of the kids—"

"In that book? Oh! It's bound to happen if the book says so."

"I just don't think you should take any chances. Now get looking."

Étienne placed his hand on my shoulder. "Come on, Sebastian. We are a team."

He was right, and so was Lina – I needed to drop the attitude. It's just I've always had a problem following instructions – which infuriates my dad. Even if I know it's the right thing to do, there is something inside me that wants to do the exact opposite. I can't explain it.

"Sorry, let's get looking for this drip," I said. But before I could start searching, a low growl echoed round us. I froze and immediately shushed the other two.

"Did you hear that growl?" I looked from Lina to Étienne, trying not to panic them unnecessarily.

They shook their heads.

"You don't think there might be a bear in here?" I whispered.

"In here?" Lina splutter-laughed. "A bear?"

"Why is that funny? A cave is literally where bears live!"

The growler growled again and I grabbed hold of Étienne's arm.

"You must have heard that!" I hissed. "Tell me that wasn't a bear!"

"That wasn't a bear," Lina said.

"It sounded like a bear! We need to get out of here before we're mauled to death!"

"It's not a bear," Étienne said. "It's my stomach rumbling."

Lina snorted. Then said, "Keep it together, Sebastian."

I felt my cheeks flush and I let go of Étienne's arm. "Of course it's not a bear. Only winding you up. How would a bear even fit in here? Obviously, it was Étienne's stomach rumbling...in a very loud bear-like manner."

Before Lina was able to jump on my mistake too brutally, a **splat** landed on my head. Normally a splat landing on your head is not a good thing, but this time it was.

"Hey! I found it! I found the drip!"

I tipped my head back, opened my mouth and let the refreshingly cool elixir of life in. It was only one drop, but it was glorious!

I appreciate that elixir of life might sound a bit OTT, but you'd have felt the same way if you were as thirsty as we were. It was a wonderful moment and I wanted to get that across to you by using the best words I know.

I climbed up the side of the cave to get my mouth closer to the source, but the drips were frustratingly slow. I stuck my tongue out as far as I could, but it still wasn't as satisfying as I hoped. I tried to get closer still but then Lina told me to stop licking the wall. I moved out of the way and let Étienne and Lina have their turn with their tongues out.

"We should put something under it to collect the water. That way we might get more than a drip at a time," I suggested.

"Pass me one of the water bottles," Lina said.

"I would, but they're back at the camp," I said.

"Seriously?" Lina said.

"Terrible oversight on your part as leader," I said.

"Any oversight was assuming you would have thought to bring them."

"Shall we try finding something else?" Étienne said.

We all looked around the cave for inspiration.

"Maybe we could use a big leaf? Isn't that what monkeys do?" Lina said.

"I am afraid I am unaware of the drinking habits of monkeys," Étienne said, which for some reason surprised me, what with him looking so much like one.

"Just go and get some big leaves," Lina said. "I'll wait here with the drip."

"Don't call Sebastian that!" Étienne said and then, before I could show my indignation, he apologized immediately. "I'm sorry, Sebastian. I didn't mean that, it is just the joke was right there, and I couldn't let it pass but I don't think you are a drip."

Bless Étienne, he really doesn't have a bad bone in his body. "Don't worry, it was a good joke," I said, and off we went in search of big leaves while our supposed leader stood waiting with her tongue out, lapping away like a giant gecko.

We took the hatchet and clambered back down the rocks. Étienne spotted some big leaves not too far from the entrance of the cave. I led the way, having quite a nice time swinging the hatchet about like some real-life jungle explorer.

"What type of leaves do you think these are?" Étienne asked as I began to cut one from the tree.

"Er, I think the Latin name for them is **biggus leafus**."

"You have no idea, do you?"

"I do not."

Étienne laughed but stopped when there was a rustle in the undergrowth behind us. We both swivelled round and crouched down, hearts pounding. I don't know why we crouched. Instinct, I guess. Those first few days on the island were quite stressful and anxiety-inducing. We didn't know what to expect, what we might find or what might find us. I think it is understandable that we were jumpy.

"What's that?" Étienne whispered, his voice trembling slightly.

"If it's a bear returning to its cave, you and Lina owe me a big apology."

It wasn't a bear though. It was Giuseppe.

When we heard him bleat, Étienne and I popped back up.

"It's that goat again!" I said.

"**Giuseppe Garibaldi!**" Étienne said, like he was meeting up with an old friend. "It's you! You scared us for a moment."

Giuseppe looked us up and down, pulled what can only be described as a very disinterested look and then turned back to the bush he was chomping from.

Étienne clapped his hands excitedly. "Oh, Giuseppe, you clever thing! You are our saviour!"

"Our *what*?" I said because my brain had not processed what we were seeing as quickly as Étienne's brain had.

"Our saviour! **Giuseppe Garibaldi** has shown us the way!"

SURVIVAL TIP #13

THERE IS A LOT TO BE LEARNED FROM NURSERY RHYMES

Giuseppe Garibaldi carried on munching away at the bush, and I tried to work out why Étienne had become overexcited at the sight of a mangy-looking goat eating its dinner.

"Praise the lord for Giuseppe!" Étienne said. He actually had tears of joy in his eyes.

"Étienne," I said slowly. "Are you having a breakdown?" Because I couldn't think of any other reason for such a jubilant reaction.

"Look what Giuseppe has brought us, Sebastian."

Oh dear. "Do you want to have a little sit down for a moment?"

"The berries, don't you see, Sebastian, Giuseppe has brought us to food!"

That's when I finally realized why Étienne was so overjoyed. Giuseppe *had* led us to food. Well, sort of. He hadn't really led us there – more we'd stumbled across him. Also, the *food* part of that statement turned out to be a little sketchy. I'll explain about that later.

At the time we were ecstatic, and I heard myself say, "Well done, Giuseppe! Good boy!"

"Praise be to Giuseppe! Lord of the Goats!" Étienne cried and we linked arms and danced in circles for a bit, chanting, "All hail, Giuseppe! Lord of the Goats!"

He glanced over his shoulder at us, unmoved by our display of thanks and turned back to his tucker.

"Hang on," I said. "That little blighter's going to eat the lot if we don't stop him!"

Étienne gasped. "It is true! Enough, Giuseppe, Lord of the Goats. Please, leave some for us!"

Unsurprisingly, Giuseppe did not react to Étienne's heartfelt pleas to stop eating.

I started clapping and shouting. "Make some noise, scare him off!"

Étienne joined in with some highly ineffective **whoops** and **cooeees** and **shoos**.

"Get out of it, bad Giuseppe! Clear off!" I hollered and waved my hatchet about feeling a little bit terrifying and powerful and a bit excellent at the same time.

Not that Giuseppe noticed – he still didn't move.

Until Lina showed up.

She didn't even have to say anything. Giuseppe took one look at her and fled. Then she threw her arms in the air, all exasperated. "You let it escape again!"

My mouth dropped open and I was going to throw a whole lot of words in her direction regarding her goat-terrifying presence, but Étienne said, "We did find some berries," and gestured to the bush.

Lina raised an interested eyebrow – at least I think it looked interested, it's not always easy to tell with eyebrows – and marched towards the bush. She said, "I'll take that, thank you," and snatched the hatchet out of my hands as she walked by me.

"What are they?" she asked, holding the branch up.

"They are berries," I said, trying carefully not to use a tone that sounded like I thought she had said something stupid, even though she had. We had literally just told her they were berries.

"I know that, but what *kind* of berries? You can't just eat any berries you know – they could be poisonous." Lina was not as generous as I had been when she was selecting the tone she used.

"Giuseppe seemed to enjoy them," Étienne said.

"Giuseppe is a goat." Lina plucked a berry from the

branch and held it up to examine it.

"I think they look fine – a bit like longer blackberries," I said. "Maybe they're called **blongberries**?"

"There's no such thing as a **blongberry**," Lina said.

"There should be, it's a great name," I said.

Étienne examined one closely. "I think they're mulberries – I've eaten them before."

"See, they'll be fine," I said. "There's a nursery rhyme about going round a mulberry bush – they can't be deadly."

"There's also a nursery rhyme about the plague and **Rock-a-bye Baby** is about a baby falling out of a tree, so I'm not sure that logic works," Lina said.

"There's never a nursery rhyme about the plague!" I said.

"There is – **Ring-a-Ring o' Roses**. When you sing a-tissue and fall down, you're falling down dead."

"Actually, I think the pretty maids all in a row in **Mary, Mary Quite Contrary** are dead too. Isn't it about a cemetery?" I said, and then realized I wasn't helping my argument.

"**Three Blind Mice** is about Mary Tudor chopping up some noblemen who crossed her as well," Lina said.

"Seriously?! What is wrong with people? Imagine singing about that sort of stuff to kids!" Étienne said.

"Bearing all this in mind, what do you want to do about

these maybe-mulberries?" Lina said holding the probably-a-mulberry in my face.

"I don't think **Here We Go Round the Mulberry Bush** has anything about death in it, does it?" I quickly ran through it. "...'on a cold and frosty morning...this is the way we wash our hands...wash our face'...okay so far...'comb our hair...this is the way we tie our shoes'... No, I think we're good!"

Étienne shook his head. "Such a weird song."

"So looking at the scientific facts that: one, **Giuseppe Garibaldi** the goat has not dropped down dead after consuming the mulberries; two, the nursery rhyme 'Here We Go Round the Mulberry Bush' does not involve death via poisoning, and three, we are all really, really definitely hungry – shall we agree that the probably-mulberries, aka **blongberries** as it just sounds better, are safe to eat?" I said.

"I'm really not sure," Lina said. "I think I heard that you should rub a berry on your lips first to see if you have a reaction to it."

"Rub it on our lips?" Étienne said.

"Yup and wait and see. If your lips don't blow up like a pufferfish, they're probably safe to eat."

"So we could rub the blongberries on our lips now and see how it goes. But let's also take some back to the camp

– the camp we are yet to build by the way – then we won't have to schlep out here again," I said.

"That is a good idea, Sebastian," Lina said, which was big of her to admit because everyone must have realized that I was sounding much more like a leader than her.

"Okay," she continued, "you can be the guinea pig, Sebastian. You rub your blongberry if you're so certain it's safe."

"Fine," I said and smushed the blongberry onto my lips and gave it a good rub.

"How does it feel?" Étienne asked, his voice full of concern.

"Perfect, not even a tingle," I said, "and rather tasty. Let's collect some more, and some water, then go back to the yet-to-be-constructed camp."

We were much slower on the journey back to camp. Each step across the creeper-matted floor was placed carefully, so we didn't spill our massive leaves of blongberries or the **cave-juice**, as I was calling the water. The concentration, the humidity and the constant battering of insects flying into our faces made it a difficult trek. Sweat trickled down my back and hunger coiled like a snake in my belly.

Étienne caught up with me and fell into step. "You are

very brave trying the blongberry out first."

"Thank you, I know."

"Are you sure it's okay? I'm ever so hungry."

"I really am, Étienne," I said, very confidently because I really was.

I was right to be confident about the blongberries because ripe ones are absolutely fine.

It's the unripe ones that can cause you some hassle.

As we later learned.

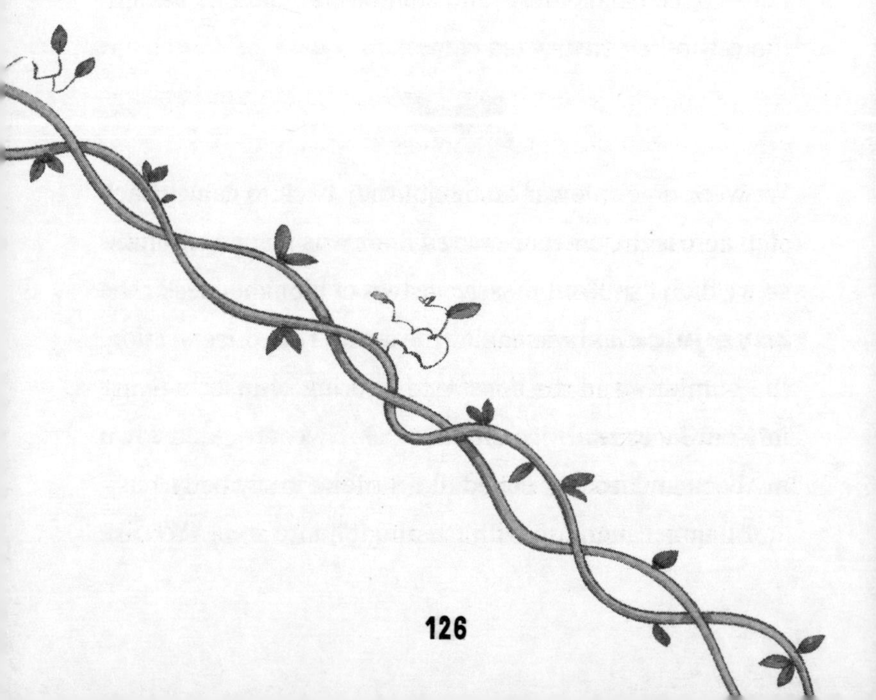

EXERCISE CAUTION WHEN TRYING NEW FOODS

Surprisingly, we didn't lose too much of the cave-juice-water on the way back to the boat and only dropped a few blongberries from our biggus-leafuses, so despite not managing to capture a goat to barbecue or get the coconut down, we chalked up our first hunting and gathering expedition as a success.

We topped up the plastic bottles, filled the rusty bucket and then drank the remaining water from our giant leaves. I don't think water has ever tasted as good as it did that first full day on our island.

"We should name this place," I said, leaning against **HMS Saviour**.

We'd decided we deserved a little rest after our busy morning of hunting and gathering. We had yet to build some form of shelter and make a fire, but fatigue stretched through our bones and none of us could find the energy to move once we'd sat down.

"I think we should name the island after Giuseppe," Étienne said.

Lina took off her battered shoes and dug her toes into the sand. "What is it with you and that goat?"

"He was here first – it only seems right we name it after him. Maybe **Garibaldi's Island**?"

"It doesn't have the right vibe," Lina said.

"What did they call the island in that **Lord of the Pig's Head** book of yours, Lina?" I asked.

"They never named it."

"Bit lazy," I said.

"I think they were too busy losing their minds to worry about naming their island," Lina said.

"In that case, I think we should definitely name ours," Étienne said firmly. "If you name something it makes you care for it more."

"I think we should name it after us," I said. "Isn't that what happens if you discover a place? Like when Captain America discovered the US?"

"Captain America did not discover America," Lina said. "It was Christopher Columbus and there were already people living there when he arrived."

"Er, no. He discovered Columbia, *obviously,*" I told her. "So, who's name should we give to our island? Hmm. No offence, Étienne, but **Stark Island** sounds a bit...stark."

"None taken. I would prefer something more uplifting."

"It should be **Sunrise Island**," Lina said, before I had to give my arm-and-leg-based reasons as to why **Lim Island** didn't sound that positive either.

"You think?" I was surprised Lina had suggested my name. I felt sure she would have wanted her name in there somewhere. I suppose there was no arguing that I had the best surname when it came to island naming.

"**Sunrise Island** sounds great," Étienne said. "Very fitting. And the sun is a big feature out here."

It certainly was. The sun was almost white now and high in the sky, making our shadows nearly disappear under us.

"It needs to be an uplifting name," Lina said, "and also it will serve as a reminder as to whose fault it is that we're here in the first place."

"**Sunrise Island** it is then," Étienne said, with a decisive nod, and the name was set.

I grinned. It was kind of cool to have an island named after me, even if Lina had managed to twist it into some kind of punishment.

"Right, on that note, I think I'm ready to try a **blongberry**," I said.

"You could eat a couple then we can go get some firewood while we wait to see if it has any adverse effects – it might make you swell up like that Violet Beauregarde in *Charlie and the Chocolate Factory*," Lina said. "And if it all goes wrong, at least you'll have an island named after you."

"Now that I'd like to see," Étienne said, then immediately added, "I wouldn't really, Sebastian. I don't want you to swell up like that at all, I don't know why I said that."

"I'm sure I'll be fine." I chomped down a couple of blongberries before I could think too much about inflating like a giant blue beach ball.

The blongberries tasted good. I could have gorged on the lot right there and then, but I knew it was best to be cautious.

"And?" Lina said, her eyes studying me intently.

"Actually, very tasty!" I stood up and brushed the sand off my shorts. "Right, let's go and get this firewood. I'd rather do something than sit around and wait."

Lina eyed me suspiciously. "Are you sure you feel okay?"

"I feel fine, apart from the massive graze on my

backside from that coconut tree. I'll let you know if I don't."

"That was very brave of you, Sebastian," Étienne said earnestly.

"I only ate a couple of blongberries," I said, but secretly I did feel pretty brave. Although I did keep picturing myself as a massive swollen blongberry.

Lina made us collect a huge amount of wood. When she was finally satisfied that we had enough, she pointed us to the spot she decided would be perfect for the fire. Not too close to the shoreline and not too far from where we would construct our shelter. We marked the edge of the fire with some rocks.

Lina cleared her throat ready to give her next barrage of instructions.

"I'm going to need your glasses, Étienne," Lina said as she rearranged my already perfectly placed firewood. "I'm going to show you how to start a fire. Go and get me dry coconut husks for kindling and a bottle of water."

"What do you need water to start a fire for?" I asked.

"You'll see. They did it in **Lord of the Flies**, but I've seen it done in a movie too. It could take a while though."

"In that case I think we should eat first," I said.

"I am absolutely famished," Lina said. "Do you think the blongberries are safe to eat?"

I was still my regular size, my regular colour and very much alive so I said, "I do indeed!"

"Then let's eat!" She took up a handful of blongberries, handed some to Étienne and then popped one into her mouth.

I clutched my throat and dropped to one side, "Wait! I was wrong about the blongberries. In fact, they should be renamed blong-a-wrongberries. They actually are deadly! I'm sorry, dear friends!"

Étienne and Lina looked unimpressed.

"That's just not very funny," Étienne said.

"Stop messing about, the blongberries are fine," Lina said.

Étienne and Lina began eating the blongberries tentatively at first. But soon they were guzzling them down with relish.

"So good!" Étienne said. "Better than goat any day of the week."

"I'd only eat the riper ones, though, if I was you," Lina cautioned, and she carefully selected only the deepest-purpliest fruits before cramming them into her mouth.

I grabbed another handful and gobbled it down. "I quite like the greenish ones – they are a tangy taste sensation!"

Lina shrugged, "Suit yourself. If you get a runny tummy, you have only got yourself to blame."

"I won't get a runny tummy. I have a stomach of steel."

I did get a runny tummy, but that wasn't the worst of it.

After we'd finished eating, and before what happened to me had happened, Étienne and I collected up some coconut husks as instructed. There were many empty shells scattered about the beach. We checked them for remnants of coconut flesh, but the birds and insects must have got to them first, which was disappointing. We vowed that the next coconut to fall would be ours.

Arms loaded, we carried the coconut husks back and fetched the water bottle and presented them to Lina. She told Étienne to drip a single drop of water onto the lens of his glasses. "It is to help bend the light, so it creates a more focused beam."

Étienne dripped the water onto the lens of his glasses and then we sat back and waited while Lina angled the lens at the wood.

After what felt like an eternity, but on reflection was probably no more than a few minutes, I said, "How long is this going to take?"

"A little patience, please, Sebastian," she said tartly and moved Étienne's glasses about again, trying to focus the circle of light on the dry tinder.

"Maybe it only works in books and movies," I said.

Just as those words passed my lips, smoke rose from the brown fibres, and we all whooped in both surprise and delight.

Étienne clapped his hands together excitedly. "It's working!"

Lina handed him back his glasses, then crouched down low and started blowing on the glowing embers. Within several healthy puffs, the small flame that had flickered into life grew bigger and stronger and we all moved back as the heat became too intense to bear.

"Go and fetch some green leaves," Lina instructed. "That will create more smoke, which will hopefully be seen by any passing ships or planes."

Instinctively, we all looked out to sea, hoping to see the silhouette of a passing vessel on the horizon, and when one was not there, we looked up into the sky, only to have our hopes dashed again.

"Someone will come soon, I'm sure," I said.

And Lina nodded and Étienne said, "Me too."

It was about this time that the hallucinogenic effects of unripe blongberries hit me right in the face like an unexpected flying bird-fish.

SURVIVAL TIP #15

BEWARE THE BLONGBERRY

I actually remember quite a lot of what I imagined under the influence of those under-ripe blongberries. Any gaps in my remembrances were later filled in gleefully by Lina and Étienne. One minute, I was sighing wistfully at the horizon, hoping against hope that a cruise liner would appear. The next, I was crawling about in the sand trying to get away from a **coconut monster**.

Just to be clear, there was no coconut monster, but at the time I could have sworn that there was a coconut running about the beach in a hula skirt and sunglasses, trying to whip me with a stick.

"Sebastian!" Étienne cried, as I attempted to pounce on top of my imaginary coconut-attacker. "What are you doing?"

"What am *I* doing? What are you *not* doing, you mean?" is what I think I said.

"We're watching you dive about on the sand for reasons that, presently, are quite unclear," Lina said.

"Help me catch the little blighter, would you?" is what I apparently said next.

"Catch what?" Étienne asked, quite reasonably, as they could not see the little coconut fella I was convinced was repeatedly trying to jab me in the butt with a stick.

"The coconut-guy, *obviously*!" I shouted quite angrily, feeling incredibly frustrated that they were leaving me to fend him off alone.

I launched myself to the ground and wrestled about a bit, kicking sand everywhere. Then, believing that I had caught the non-existent coconut baddie, I shouted, "Ah-ha! Now I've got you! Prepare to be desiccated."

Lina said, "Sebastian! Stop messing about! What *are* you doing?"

I was about to say, "What am *I* doing? What are you *not* doing, you mean?" again, but then I noticed something weird about her face and shouted, "**ARGH!!! WHAT IS WRONG WITH YOUR FACE?!**"

Her hands whipped to her cheeks. "What do you mean what's wrong with my face?"

"Why is your nose all big and your eyes all swirly

and your ears so flappity?" I yelled.

Apparently, this freaked Lina out big time, until Étienne set the record straight.

He said, "There's nothing wrong with your face. Don't listen to him! Sebastian is currently spinning in circles," Étienne said.

"But why is Sebastian spinning in circles?" Lina asked.

To which I replied, "Because the coconut's got me!" Then I spun around a few more times, before I threw myself to the ground and rolled about trying to escape from the clutches of an imaginary coconut.

"I think he's hallucinating," Étienne said. "Sebastian, try to stay calm, I think you're hallucinating."

I stopped still, my eyes darting everywhere. "Who said that?"

"I did!" Étienne said trying to stay calm. "Sebastian, are you okay?"

"No. Who said **yabadabadoo**?"

"Nobody said **yabadabadoo**," Lina said.

"Would you shut up!" I snapped.

"I was answering your question!" Lina protested.

"Not you! The coconut! It keeps shouting **yabadabadoo** and it is very annoying! Can't you hear it?"

"A coconut shouting? No, I can't." Lina turned to

Étienne. "I think you're right – he's hallucinating."

Then I said, "I'll **yabadabadoo** you in a minute, coconut monster! Have the courage to show yourself!"

At this point, Étienne put his hands firmly on my shoulders and said, "Sebastian, I want you to sit down and drink some water."

I responded to his concern by stroking his face and saying, "Does the cute little monkey want a nut?"

Étienne informed me that he did not want a nut and that it would be best for everybody if I sat down, calmed down and drank some water.

My head swivelled about, then I cupped my hand to Étienne's ear and whispered. "I think the coconut monster has gone."

Étienne tried to say something, but I squished my finger to his lips. "Shhhhhhhussh, he might be hiding. Be very, very quiet. As quiet as a quiet thing or he'll hear us."

Lina scowled. "I knew he'd be the first to lose his mind!" she said, putting her hands on my shoulders and assertively guiding me to the floor. "Sit down and drink some water."

She handed me a water bottle and I began chugging away on it. Then she turned to Étienne. "I'm not sure why Sebastian is acting so strangely, but in my opinion, it could be one of three things. One – the stress of our situation has caused Sebastian's brain to short-circuit, which is highly possible. Two – he's suffering delirium through dehydration, also highly possible. Three – those green mulberries have caused hallucinations and weirder-than-usual behaviour, which I think is both highly possible and the most probable."

"What shall we do? Will he be okay?" Étienne asked.

"Sebastian will be absolutely fine, I'm certain. At least, I hope I'm certain. I'm sure it will wear off. I think..." Lina said.

To which I said, "**Yabadabadoo!**" Then fell back in the sand and passed out.

Étienne told me later he was genuinely worried that I was either going to die or be stuck in a hallucination for ever. Luckily, neither of those things happened. I did learn though, that eating green blongberries is **NOT** a good idea. Maybe I should write a nursery rhyme about that.

When I came round from my blongberry-induced coma, I felt really very normal, but did remember feeling very *not* normal before I'd zonked out.

I propped myself up on my elbow. The fire was still burning, Étienne was poking it tentatively with a stick and Lina was standing over him instructing him on how to poke properly.

There was a big pile of sticks next to them – they'd obviously been busy collecting supplies while I was sleeping.

"Sebastian! You're okay!" Étienne's lips spread into a huge smile.

Lina was beaming too. "Thank goodness, the coconut warrior awakes!"

Étienne put his stick down and came and kneeled down next to me. "We were so worried about you, Sebastian. How do you feel now?"

I thought about it, and realized very quickly that I had one strong and overriding feeling.

"I feel like I need to go to the toilet, right NOW!"

My stomach cramped like it meant something big and dramatic and horrifying was going to happen very soon. "Oh, no!" I groaned. "NO!" I jumped up and ran round in circles desperately trying to work out a place I could go that would afford me some privacy.

I spotted a pile of sticks leaning together haphazardly and rushed inside just before I did something horribly **spectacular**.

When I came back to the fire, I was met by two very stony faces.

"Unbelievable!" Lina shouted, pointing the glowing end of her pokey stick at me. "Do you have any idea how long that shelter took to build?"

"*That* was our shelter?" I looked over at the lopsided thing. It was basically a few long sticks propped up against each other with some leaves stuck on top. It can't have taken *very* long, surely?

"It took AGES!" Lina snapped before I said anything to the contrary, which was probably a good thing because, looking at the throbbing vein in her neck, I don't think my guess of fifteen minutes would have gone down brilliantly.

"We were going to sleep there for the night, Sebastian!" Étienne said, quite angrily for Étienne.

"I...I...had to go. I'm sorry, I couldn't help it. It was a desperate and sudden and frankly, terribly stressful situation."

"Sebastian!" Lina shouted. "I just...I...I...I mean in our shelter, *really*?!"

"Where else was I supposed to go?"

Lina held her arms and gestured about madly. "Literally anywhere BUT the shelter! Sheesh, Sebastian!"

Étienne shook his head and looked at me from behind his specs with humongous and disappointed eyes. "Oh, Sebastian."

"Can you go in and clean it up?" Lina asked.

"Errr, probably not easily. It was all quite dramatic—"

"Stop!" Lina held her hand up. "Spare us the details."

"I'll help you build a new shelter. A better shelter."

"We're certainly not sleeping in there tonight," Lina said scowling.

"I think that is a very wise decision," I said.

Étienne threw another load of sticks onto the fire and placed some green leaves on top to make more white smoke.

"So, we build again?" I said.

"*We'll* build again, *you* will be building for the first time," Lina said.

When Lina was finally satisfied there was enough wood on the fire for it to keep burning for a while, we traipsed across the white sand, Lina swinging her hatchet purposefully, on the search for more building supplies.

The sun was lower in the sky now, and not quite so intense. The jungle throbbed with the sound of insects. Colourful butterflies flittered about, and a heady perfume rose up from the dense greenery. Carefully, we placed one foot after the other, making sure not to trip on the tangled foliage that carpeted the forest floor. We climbed over fallen trees, twisted vines and palm saplings while Lina searched for the "perfect" branches to chop down for the new shelter. Just as I was about to launch into a second round of **The Bare Necessities**, which I think had served to lighten the mood after my accidental bottom-based destruction of our sleeping shelter, Étienne let out a little squeal. It sounded like a good squeal.

CLIMATE AVENGERS
CLIMATE AVENGERS
CLIMATE AVENGERS

"Hey! Are those breadfruit?" he said, grabbing my arm with one hand and pointing at a tree that had large leaves and was festooned with knobbly green balls, with his other.

Lina gasped then shouted, "YES! Those *are* breadfruit!"

When we'd had them back at the **Climate Avengers** camp, I'd thought breadfruit was a very poor and unnecessary substitute for regular fries, but that day my stomach flippety-flipped in delight.

Étienne plucked the largest breadfruit down from the tree, then took the hatchet from Lina and hacked it into pieces.

"Ripe," he said, before sinking his teeth into a chunk. Cheeks bulging, he passed the remainder to Lina, who took a bite and then passed it on to me. Which I'd like to think was a peace offering after the shelter incident.

If you've ever tried raw breadfruit, you might not think it tastes of much. I guess it tastes a bit like a starchy, slightly sweet custard. But that day in the jungle it tasted like ambrosia – the food of the gods. Of course, after we'd been on **Sunrise Island** for quite some time, breadfruit – and fruit in general – began to lose its appeal, but right at that moment it was wondrous.

We ate hungrily. Pulling down green globes and prising them apart before sinking our whole faces into the flesh.

We must have looked animal-like, gnawing so feverishly.

Once we were bordering on the painful side of full, Lina wiped her face on her arm and let out a truly leader-worthy belch. “We should come back, get some more of these later and then we can have breadfruit kebabs on the fire tonight.”

“Belly likes that idea.” I stuck out my stomach, which now had a pleasing curve to it, and patted it cheerfully.

Lina frowned at me, shook her head and muttered something about me being, “So weird,” which I ignored because I was just too happy about being so full.

Étienne and I were then tasked to act much like donkeys, carrying the branches Lina cut down back through the forest to camp. She’d chop, we’d carry. Every time we returned to pick up the next load, she’d ask if the fire was still burning and remind us to add more wood if it needed it.

“Don’t worry,” Étienne said, “you can count on us.”

“Totally,” I said. “They said the one I accidentally started in the school conservation area could have burned for days, if the fire brigade hadn’t arrived quickly, so really how hard can it be?”

Turns out quite hard.

Eventually, Lina was satisfied that we had enough sticks to start the rebuild of the shelter.

She stood over the pile and nodded. "Excellent, now let's get going before it gets dark."

"I've been thinking," I said.

"Wonderful," Lina said, not sounding very genuine.

"I wasn't sure about the last design."

Lina crossed her arms. "Oh really?"

"I'm thinking that we could build a multi-room complex. Maybe with a separate living room, dining area and sleeping quarters?"

"I shall look forward to watching you try to achieve that," she said.

"Sounds very...ambitious," Étienne said, diplomatically.

"I want it to be nice for you. I want you to have a comfortable home while we're stuck here."

Nobody said anything.

I'd said *home*.

In that moment, we all remembered just how far away from home we were.

SURVIVAL TIP #16

IN DIFFICULT TIMES, REMEMBER, MUSIC IS A VERY POWERFUL MOOD LIFTER

Étienne was correct that my suggestion for a multi-roomed shelter was a little overambitious. Especially because neither he nor Lina seemed to be fully on board with my vision. I mapped out the rooms with a border of stones and small rocks, so we were all aware what we were working towards. It quickly became apparent that the construction of the **"Ritz of Sticks"** as I had named the building was going to take many stages.

"Let's start with the bedrooms," I suggested. "Lina, I thought you could have the one at the front with a sea view."

"The one by the door, so I'm the first to be eaten if a bear comes calling?"

"There is no bear," I said.

"I'm making a point."

I had meant it to be a nice thing and I was annoyed she hadn't seen that, so I said, "You *are* the leader, and you *are* the one with the hatchet so, if there are any bears, you'll have to deal with them."

"I don't think a hatchet will help me fend off a surprise attack from a jungle bear."

"Hang on," Étienne yelped. "There aren't really bears, are there?"

"Probably not," Lina said.

"*Probably?*" Étienne glanced over his shoulder at the forest and gave an involuntary shiver. "But we can't be certain there isn't some sort of beast out there in that jungle."

I shivered too. "Who knows what's out there."

Lina threw down a stick. "NO! Absolutely not. It's only day one! I can't have you two losing your minds and thinking there's a beast on the island! That's what happened to the boys in my book and it did not end well for them. You need to get it together!" Then came a barrage of keeps and don'ts. "Keep your minds clear! Don't give into paranoia. Don't...blah blah blah."

To be honest, halfway through her rant I stopped listening and started planning a beautiful shell-decorated toilet for the outhouse.

Anyway, she *eventually* finished up by saying, "Do I make myself clear?"

"I don't think a bear would stand any chance against her," I muttered to Étienne.

He whispered back, "You're probably right."

"We're clear, Lina." I bent down and handed the stick back to her. "There's no beast in the jungle. Just butterflies and breadfruit and I am a fan of both."

She brushed a strand of hair out of her eyes and regained her composure. "Good. I was just checking that's what you thought."

We worked *tirelessly* on the first room of the **Ritz of Sticks** that evening. We had a few engineering difficulties. Once where we hadn't fixed the stick walls securely enough and the whole thing collapsed. And again, when the walls were secure, just not secure enough to withstand the force of me crashing into them. It wasn't my fault – I'd been attacked by a hermit crab. Little blighter fixed itself right onto the end of my foot. Even though I was wearing my salt-encrusted trainers, its pincer managed to pierce my big toe.

I hopped about and fell backwards into the east wing of the **Ritz of Sticks**, completely demolishing it, while shouting, "Get the **RUDE WORD** thing off me!"

Because I was on an island in the Pacific, I actually said

the rude word because no grown-up would hear me.

Neither Lina nor Étienne rushed to my aid. Instead, Lina took one look at the crab, licked her lips and said, "Mmmmm, crab!"

Étienne gasped, but I'll give it to him, he reacted quickly. He dived at my foot and wrenched the hermit crab off, which was eye-wateringly painful, but a relief all the same.

Lina held her hand out and said, "Mmmmm, crab," again.

Before she could do anything, Étienne launched my crustacean attacker back into the sea shouting, "Run home, **Herbie Herbertson**! Run home!" I had no idea that Étienne had such a good throwing arm.

Lina did not look happy. "**Herbie Herbertson**?"

Étienne shrugged. "He looked like a Herbie."

"What did you throw him for?" she blasted.

"I thought you wanted to eat him."

"I did! I still do! But you threw him into the ocean! We'll never find him now! Why did you do that?"

"I didn't want you to eat him! I wanted him to find his way home."

I thought this was quite sweet, even a bit moving, considering the parallels with our own situation, but I don't think Lina had the emotional mind space to think like that, because she shouted, "It's a HERMIT CRAB, Étienne! Its home is literally on its back."

I looked up from inspecting my poor toe. "He might return. Although I don't think I could eat him now that I know his name is **Herbie Herbertson**."

Lina stomped her legs like a toddler and let out a frustrated growl. When she finished having her little episode, Étienne said, I think quite bravely, "Everything okay?"

She pushed back her tangly hair from her face, picked up a stick and started to rebuild the east wing of the **Ritz**. "Everything is wonderful. Just wonderful," she said, as she started strapping sticks together in a very angrified manner.

Étienne and I looked at each other. Behind his glasses, his eyes were even bigger than usual. We both knew it would be best not to delve any deeper into Lina's thoughts when they were quite clearly very angry ones. Instead, we started helping her with the rebuild.

I didn't even get three words in to **Whistle While You Work** before she snapped, "No singing, Sebastian. No singing." Then she pointed a stick from me to Étienne. "You think I *want* to eat Herbie? I don't even like seafood, but this is an extreme situation. I want to survive, and I won't have you making me feel bad about it."

We worked in silence after that – apart from a few huffs and tuts and sighs from Lina when Étienne or I had apparently got in her way or placed a stick in a manner she didn't like.

It was Lina, though, who started humming the song about half an hour later, when her crossness had subsided. She's never been able to stay mad at anyone for *that* long. I joined in immediately and Étienne started up too. Étienne has a very good voice. He used to be a choirboy, but he doesn't like singing in public. I don't think he has the self-confidence. I've tried to encourage him to blast the words out with more ambition, like I do, but he says what I'm doing is something that goes way beyond what can be described as singing. I'm not completely sure what he is trying to say by that, but I've decided to look upon it as a compliment.

The singing got louder and louder – that's one thing about being stranded in the middle of nowhere, it feels quite liberating knowing there is no one watching what you do. When I mentioned that to Lina after a very excellent and rousing rendition of **Circle of Life**, she said very sarcastically, "Oh yes, what a relief that there is no one around to listen to you butcher songs from *The Lion King*."

Which made Étienne giggle and then say, "Do that

opening bit again, Sebastian. That was quite…something. Are those the actual words?"

"Probably not, but my delivery is sufficiently convincing, and I think they sound close enough."

"Indeed," Étienne said.

"Okay, here goes." I took a deep breath and bellowed out the first lines with all of my motivation and Lina and Étienne joined in.

We carried on like that, singing and talking and teasing each other while we built what would come to be our home for much longer than we could have ever imagined.

By the time we called a stop to building for the night, the sun had disappeared below the horizon and the humming sound of the insects in the jungle had grown loud. The whole forest seemed to vibrate and throb as *things* within it began to stir.

We stood back to admire our work by the light of our fire and a few bats flew overhead, just visible in the darkening sky.

I tilted my head from one side to the other to fully appreciate our shelter. "It looks…it looks…" I wasn't quite sure how to describe it.

"It looks **EXACTLY** like the first shelter we built!" Lina exclaimed.

And she was right.

Which was annoying.

"Oh, rats," I said.

"It does bear a strong resemblance to the first one," Étienne admitted. "I'm sure we can make it feel like home though."

I sighed and looked out across the vast ocean towards the blackening horizon. We were so very, very far from home.

I felt the unfamiliar jungle pulsating behind me, like a beast breathing down my back, reminding me it was my fault we were here. It suddenly felt too much to bear.

"I...I..." I tried to say something – to find some words to apologize. But what words would be enough? I tried again. "I am so sorry. Truly I am. I don't know what... how to..."

I felt a hand find each of mine.

I looked from Étienne to Lina.

"We know," Lina said.

"Friends whatever." Étienne gave my hand a gentle squeeze and I felt like my heart might burst.

I nodded, blinking and sniffing to stop myself from crying. "Friends whatever."

"It's an excellent shelter, Sebastian," Étienne said. "The real **Ritz** has nothing on ours."

Lina nodded towards the fire. "Come on. I'm shattered.

Let's eat something before bed."

"Give me a second," I said, and I watched as they headed off towards the fire, wondering what I'd done to deserve two such **spectacular** friends. I vowed then that I'd find a way to get them home or die trying.

SURVIVAL TIP #17

KEEP AN EYE ON YOUR LIVESTOCK, ESPECIALLY GOATS

That evening, sitting round the fire, eating lumps of slightly burned breadfruit, which looked and tasted a little bit like coal, Lina started up her tradition of making us all say something we had done that we were proud of. I struggled and when I suggested my jubilant singing of the **Circle of Life**, she scowled and told me to choose something proper. I told her that I had to think about it.

After we'd found out that Étienne was proud to be our friend – *aww* – and Lina was proud of how she had handled the role of leader – debatable – she insisted on reading us some of **Lord of the Flies**. Which, to be honest, was pretty harrowing, but she said it was necessary so that we could learn from their mistakes.

She snapped the book shut at the end of a chapter and

eyeballed us. "So, do you see how the fire is important? We don't want a ship to sail past and miss us because we've forgotten to keep it burning, do we?"

It was an easy question, so I said, "We do not, Lina."

"We also don't want to accidentally set fire to the island, like they did," Étienne said.

Lina nodded. "Yes, and that too, *Sebastian.*"

I don't know why she said my name like that. Well, maybe I do, but that fire at school could have happened to anybody. "I think we're all in agreement about the fire being important, *Lina.*" I stretched back and did a big noisy yawn. "Let's chuck a load more logs on and then check into the **Ritz** for the night. I'm bushed."

On the way to the shelter, Étienne picked up a rock and placed it a few metres away, under a tree.

"What are you doing?" I asked.

"Day one," he said. "I thought we should keep track of how long we're here by laying a stone down every night."

Lina nodded. "Let's hope that we end up with a grand total of one."

We scrambled into the East Wing and pulled some big leaves over us to act as a blanket, albeit a waxy uncomfortable one, but it was better than nothing. Even though we were completely tired, it took a little while to fall asleep. Every little noise sounded strange and unnerving in the dark.

"We did it," Étienne whispered. "We survived our first full day here. We just have to keep doing that, surviving a day at a time until someone finds us. That seems doable."

"Absolutely. I'm sure Benedict and Lukas and Francesca have raised the alarm," Lina said. "They would have made it back onto their boat, don't you think?"

"Definitely," I said, but what I really meant was hopefully.

Étienne said his prayers, which ended with him praying for the others and everyone at home who would be worried about us. It made me think of Dad, and of Mum, and I had to take a few deep breaths to stop myself from crying. He also prayed for us, especially me, because apparently I needed help finding a way to forgive myself for the fact that our situation was all my fault. Which I think was supposed to be a nice thing, but sounded a little accusatory. Lina said a very loud, "Amen," after that bit.

The next morning we all woke up at the same time. This was not a coincidence but because we were woken up by the same thing.

Giuseppe Garibaldi.

He'd found his way into the **Ritz** and, having finished what was left of our pile of breadfruit, had moved on to chewing Lina's shoe.

Lina did not take this well.

She leaped to her feet, her hair as wild as her eyes, and screeched, "Get out of here, you dumb animal!"

On seeing Lina, Giuseppe did what she asked and bolted – her shoe still in his mouth.

Lina gave chase, but by the time she'd tripped over Étienne and me, who were still coming round in our leafy nest, Giuseppe was long gone.

"I don't believe it!" she shouted. "It took my Converse! What am I going to do now?"

"Dunno, hop?" I suggested.

Lina scowled at me and stomped off towards the forest. "I'm going to see if he dropped it nearby. Put some wood on the fire."

While Lina disappeared into the undergrowth, threatening to put Giuseppe into a curry, Étienne and I decided a dip in the lagoon might be a brilliant way to start the day. The turquoise water looked so inviting, and even though the sun was young in the sky, we were already sticky with sweat. Étienne placed his glasses in a coconut shell for safety, then we stripped down to our swimming cozzies and raced to the shoreline.

The water was clear and the cool side of warm. We waded in up to our waists, little shoals of fishes darting away from us, a kaleidoscope of colours. Étienne duck-dived below the surface, his bum momentarily flashing a hello to the sky. I watched him as he moved below the surface, his body rippling in the sunlight. Then he popped up right in front of me, splurted water into my face, grinned, and ducked below again. I swam after him and this time when he burst to the surface, I was ready and blasted water from my mouth into his face.

We messed about like this for a while, then floated on our backs, the sun warming our faces. I could see little rainbows through the water droplets on my eyelashes and for a moment the world was peaceful. I watched a streak of cloud drift over my head and tried to decide what it might look like. It couldn't think of anything other than a cloud, or smoke.

That's when I remembered the fire.

Following some frantic arm and leg flapping, I looked to the shore to see that our smoke signal was worryingly lacking in smoke.

"Étienne!" I shouted. "The fire, quick! We forgot about it!"

This was the first of many occasions that the fire went out. Luckily, Lina doesn't know about any of them.

I checked the horizon but, fortunately, there was no rescue plane or ship in sight. I don't actually mean **fortunately** because rescue-transportation would have been very welcome, but we knew that if Lina came back to find the fire was out, we'd be in that curry alongside Giuseppe.

Étienne bolted upright. "Oh, *mon dieu!*"

And I said, "Exactly!"

We tried to run through the water, splashing and tripping and not getting anywhere fast.

Running through water isn't that easy, especially when a humongous jellyfish arrives to block your way.

"Argh, jellyfish!" I shouted.

Étienne immediately stopped right behind me and squinted. "Where?"

"Right there!" I pointed to the pinkish translucent blob wafting around in front of us.

"Oh lord, it's massive!"

Before I could say, "What do we do?" Étienne somehow managed to leap past me and dive over the thing and was thrashing his way back to shore.

"Étienne!" I shouted, both shocked and impressed by his speed. "You left me!"

"I'm sorry! My fight or flight instincts kicked in. Just make a break for it!"

Sounded easy enough, but I couldn't. I stood there as the jellyfish undulated closer and closer to me. It was quite mesmerizing. I would have said beautiful, if I hadn't been so worried that he might shoot out a tentacly thing and cause me excruciating pain and possible death.

"Swim round it!" Étienne hollered from the shore.

I took a couple of steps to the side, but Julian seemed to follow me. I sidestepped the other way, but he followed me again. "He's hunting me down!" I yelped.

"He probably isn't," Étienne said as he put his specs back on. "I don't think jellyfish think like that."

"This one does!" I leaped back as he billowed even closer. "He's after me, I can tell."

"Why would he be after you?"

"He wants to eat me!" I cried.

"Jellyfish don't eat humans!"

"How do you know? Have you been watching all the jellyfish in the world?"

"*What*?"

"Didn't think so."

"It's more scared of you than you are of it."

"It doesn't look scared!"

"Sebastian, you're panicking."

"It might be a Portuguese man-of-war and cause instant death!"

"I doubt we're anywhere near Portugal, Sebastian. Just swim round him. It'll be fine. I'm going to put some more wood on the fire before Lina gets back."

"Don't leave me!"

"I won't be long – swim round it!"

Just swim round it. "Okay, I can do that," I said out loud, in an attempt to convince myself I could.

I stuck my head down and swam out far to the left, but when I popped my head up, there it was again, looking all wibbly and threatening!

"I swear to you, Étienne, it wants me!"

Étienne didn't answer because he was already halfway back up the beach, leaving me all alone trying to out-swim a very tenacious jellyfish. Honestly, no matter which direction I swam, it seemed to find me again.

Eventually, after what seemed like HOURS, but Étienne seemed to think was only minutes, I managed to get past the floppity thing and made a dash up the sand to safety, just as Étienne got the fire going again and Lina returned with her rather battered-looking trainer.

"What's wrong with you?" She looked me up and down and screwed up her nose.

I bent over and tried to get my breath back. "Jelly... giant...attacking."

"Jelly giant?" Lina said. "What's he talking about, Étienne?"

"There's a jellyfish in the lagoon."

"Really big," I puffed.

"How big?" Lina asked.

"Massive! Hey, aren't jellyfish considered delicacies in some countries? Maybe we should catch it and eat it?" I said, then muttered, "That would put a stop to him chasing me."

Étienne said, "I wouldn't say **Julian Jehoshaphat** was *that* big—"

"Who?" Lina interrupted, and then she realized what Étienne had done. She waved her non-shoe-holding hand. "Oh no. No, no, no, no. You are not naming everything on the island to stop us eating it."

"I'm just saying that I don't think Julian looked particularly big. Probably not worth bothering with," Étienne said.

"He looked pretty big when he was chasing me," I said. "I reckon he'd make a decent meal. It's eat or be eaten when you're **shipwrecked**, Étienne."

"Julian wasn't chasing you and he certainly wouldn't *eat* you! I doubt he was even aware you were there," Étienne said. Although, he was wrong about that. That jellyfish was after me from the get-go.

"Oh, Étienne! This naming thing cannot continue!" Lina said, just as a white gull with a hooked beak and untrustworthy eyes landed on the sand between us.

Étienne said, "Oh, it's **Gloria Goldberg**!"

Which made Lina shout, "Étienne, what did I just say?"

Surprised, Gloria flapped off with an indignant squawk.

"You said no naming things, but listen, I think it makes the place feel more friendly if things have names. You know, we could say, 'Look at good old **Giuseppe** there munching at the blongberry bush,' and, '**Julian** looks like he's having a nice swim in the lagoon today,' and, 'Did I tell you that I bumped into **Herbie** down by the rock pools and **Gloria** dropped by earlier...' You know, we could say stuff like that."

"*We could say stuff like that?*" Lina repeated very slowly, as though she was trying to unpick what Étienne had said. "Stuff like, *Gloria dropped by earlier*...and by Gloria you mean a gull?"

Étienne grinned. "Exactly! I think it might make the place feel less scary and maybe we won't feel quite so alone if we become familiar with the wildlife around us, instead of eating it."

"I sort of see your thinking." I waved at Gloria, who was perching on a branch. "Nice to see you, **Ms Goldberg**. Yeah, it does feel good. But I shall never be pleased to see Julian having a dip in the lagoon. I'm telling you, that jellyfish wants me."

Lina shook her head. "I'm stranded on a desert island with a couple of idiots." Then she threw her arms in the air. "I don't believe it, **Giuseppe Garibaldi**'s back in the camp! He's got some nerve."

Étienne clapped his hands together. "Yes! Lina that's it, you're joining in! Doesn't it feel great?"

Lina didn't reply. She started shouting very loudly, "Oi! Giuseppe, put that down!"

At first, I thought he had her other shoe, but then I realized that what Giuseppe had in his mouth was far more concerning than Converse.

Giuseppe had his jaws locked round our parachute flare.

We all shouted, "No, Giuseppe! Bad goat!"

"Stupid animal is going to waste our last flare and blast itself to bits in the process!" Lina yelled, which made Étienne emit a very dramatic wail.

I said, "Drop it, Giuseppe!" in my most authoritative voice. I sounded quite like my dad.

Giuseppe Garibaldi, quite surprisingly, did as I asked. Although he didn't drop it immediately. He trotted across camp, looking at me the whole way, and then proceeded to drop the flare into the fire, which was a little less than ideal.

We dived to the ground as a high-pitched shrieking sound filled the air. It was followed by an almighty explosion, a fierce bright light and, finally, a wave of intense heat.

When the smoke cleared, I honestly expected to see bits of frazzled goat everywhere, but Giuseppe was standing unharmed – apart from his slightly singed snout – and lazily chomping on our coil of rope.

I said, "So, guys, Giuseppe popped round earlier."

SURVIVAL TIP #18

IF YOU DON'T HAVE A ROPE – IMPROVISE

With the loss of the parachute flare, Lina became even more obsessive about the fire. I could understand it – losing the flare was more than a bit of a blow. It felt like we'd lost a lifeline.

"We need to concentrate on ways to maximize our chances of rescue," Lina said. It was the evening of the second day, and we'd just finished eating our charred breadfruit supper. "The building of the other wings of the **Ritz** will have to be put on hold."

"What do you have in mind?" I asked.

"Tomorrow, we need to investigate the island properly. Can you imagine if there's some five-star luxury holiday resort on the other side of the forest and we didn't find it because we didn't bother to explore?"

I felt it was unlikely – surely we would have seen some boats or planes if that was the case – but Lina was right, we needed to find out more about where we were.

"We could mark a big **SOS** sign on the sand with stones," Étienne said.

"Excellent idea," Lina said, which made him beam. "Anything else that may aid our survival?"

"We have a boat," I said.

Lina frowned. "We do."

I rammed a stick in the fire and it spat and crackled. "If there's nobody here and nobody comes, maybe we should think about using it."

"You can't mean going back out on the ocean?" Étienne said, clearly horrified at the prospect.

"Not straight away. I'm saying that it's an option. We don't want to be waiting on this island until we're old and wrinkly."

"I think we should wait as long as it takes for someone to find us," Étienne said.

"What if it's years and years?" I said.

"Sebastian, it was *awful* out on the ocean. I couldn't go back on the water willingly. I just couldn't."

"But we would be more prepared. We could store up loads of breadfruit and coconuts to take with us. Choose a day when the weather is fine."

"No," Étienne said. "I won't do it. Someone will find us. We have to believe that. It's only our second day here! I think we should give it a bit longer before we consider death by boat!"

He was getting upset, so I didn't push it any further. "Okay, fine. Forget I mentioned it."

We sat in silence for a while, listening to the crackle and spit of the fire. Lina picked up a stone and handed it to Étienne. "Why don't you go and put it by the other one, so we keep track."

Étienne sniffed, then swallowed, and gave me an angry sideways glance. When he went off to lay the stone, Lina leaned in and whispered. "I'm not staying on this island for years and years with you two. I've got plans – big life plans – and none of them involve goats or coconuts. A month. If we're still here in a month, and I hope with my entire everything that we aren't, but if we are, we'll talk to Étienne about trying to row back."

The following morning Lina announced our itinerary for the day over a breakfast of more burned breadfruit. We were going exploring.

"We need to discover if we really are alone." She picked up a stick and drew an outline of the island in the sand.

"We're here," she said, marking the shelter and the campfire. "The cave is over there, near the blongberries."

"Looks about right," I agreed.

"I think we need to aim for high ground. Remember when we rowed in? The north-east side of the island was all cliffs and rocks."

"Yup," Étienne and I said.

"Those are over here." She scratched out a few jaggedy lines. "I reckon we head there. If we climb to the top we might be able to look down on the whole island and see what's what."

After a little disagreement as to which way was north-east, we settled on a direction and decided that it would be best to walk along the beach and enter the jungle from the far side.

Lina put a load of sticks on the fire – enough to keep it burning for hours. Étienne set about marking **SOS** in the sand with stones and I went to fill up the water bottles with cave-juice. When our jobs were done, we headed out on our quest to find any signs of civilization.

Lina swung her hatchet about with free abandon and no concern about those behind her. She cut a way through the thick creepers and palm fronds – more than once I had to duck when one sprang back towards my face.

"What happens –" Étienne said, as he climbed over a

gnarled tree trunk – "if we do find people and they aren't friendly?"

"I've been thinking about that," Lina said. "It's a possibility, but we have our age on our side. I think most people would feel compelled to help a group of children."

"What about if they're cannibals?" I said. "I imagine age would work against us then. We're probably more succulent than some withered old person."

"Sebastian!" Lina swung round and a flutter of black-brown birds flew off through the treetops. "You did not just say that! The chances of you being eaten by a human are next to none – unless we run out of breadfruit, then I'm sorry, but your days are numbered."

I slapped at a mosquito that had landed on my arm. "I think the mozzies may get me first."

The walk to the cliffs took about an hour. The island must have only been a kilometre or so the whole way across, but with no discernible path through the forest and with the oppressively sticky heat, it was hard going. When we finally made it to the foot of the rocks, we slumped against them and took some swigs from the water bottles.

"It looks climbable," I said, gazing up at the rock face.

Lina swallowed, screwed the top back on the bottle and chucked it back to me. "Still, watch your footing.

We don't want to deal with any broken legs."

By the time I'd put the bottle back in my shorts' pocket, she was off.

Étienne let out a groan. "We're doing it already?"

"The sooner we get up there, the sooner we'll know what we're dealing with. Fingers crossed for an all-inclusive beach resort in close proximity," Lina called down.

I pulled Étienne to his feet. "Orders have been given – better get climbing."

I followed Lina and Étienne took up the rear. I could hear him behind me, breathing heavily and muttering to himself things like, "You can do this, Stark."

Lina was good at picking a route and pointing out foot- and handholds. She made it to the summit without much trouble and I'd almost pulled myself over the top when Étienne let out a shriek and there was a sudden hard yank on my leg. My hand lashed out and I grabbed hold of a shrub to stop myself falling.

"**HOLY LORD OF GOATS!**" I screamed. I had the top half of my body over the edge, but my legs were dangling over the side, with Étienne holding onto one, wailing at the top of his lungs that he was going to die.

Lina leaped over, grabbed hold of me and shouted down to Étienne. "It's not that steep, Étienne, you're not going to die. Climb up Sebastian – use him like a rope!"

I thought, *No, don't climb up Sebastian, climb up the rocks like everybody else*. But he scrambled over my back, all knobbly knees and jabby fingers. With a final foot to the face, he made it over the edge. I pulled myself over to find him lying on his back puffing and panting and thanking God.

"I think there's somebody a little more earthbound you should be thanking for your survival, don't you?" I said as I dusted myself down and inspected the scrapes and cuts that the climb had given me.

"Yes, thank you," Étienne said, "and thank you too, Lina. Lina...?"

Lina wasn't paying us any attention. She was standing with her hands on her hips, looking out over the island. Her jaw was tense and her eyes wide.

"Lina?" I tried again.

She glanced over at us, then her shoulders dropped, and she shook her head. "There's no one here. It really is just us."

I looked out over the mass of green jungle that was our island. I could see our beach and the cave, and the reef that surrounded our lagoon. The vast Pacific Ocean. But no other signs of human life. We were utterly isolated, and the thought knocked the wind out of me.

REMEMBER, THERE ARE NO SUCH THING AS BEASTS...

That evening, Étienne laid the stone to mark our third day on the island. The mood was quite sombre in our shelter afterwards.

"I didn't really expect to find anyone," Lina said. "I don't understand why I feel so disappointed."

"We lost a little bit of hope, that's why," Étienne said. "But we haven't lost it all."

"Yup," I said. "I've still got a decent amount of hope in me. How about you, Lina?"

The light from the fire outside was just enough for me to see her smile. "Yeah, I've got some in me too. Okay, new plan. Tomorrow, we set our minds to surviving. We'll collect wood and forage for food and water and build a new wing to the **Ritz**. Maybe even try and have a little bit of that fun Sebastian mentioned."

"I'm good with that," Étienne said.

"Me too," I said, but my mind had turned to home and to my dad and how far away he was. And then I thought of our boat.

Over the following days and weeks, we fell into a kind of island routine. We foraged and we ate, and we swam, and we slept, and we talked, and we missed home. And sometimes Étienne and I would forget about the fire. At night, we would say what we were proud of, and sleep huddled up together hoping that we'd be able to one day share everything we'd been through with our loved ones back home. And our pile of stones grew.

One day, we ventured past the cave-juice cave and discovered a tiny little freshwater stream. After a lot of dancing around and celebrating the end of cave-juice, we spent two whole days collecting the water in coconut shells – piling them up in a shady corner of the shelter.

Another day, we went beyond the stream and we found more fruit trees. There were breadfruit, bananas, blongberries and rambutan – which are about golf ball-sized, with bright red, fuzzy skin and look like they might come from another planet. When you peel away the outside, you reveal a glistening white fruit which reminds me of, but tastes nothing like, sheep eyeballs. We also collected all the coconuts that had dropped to the ground. And Étienne tried – unsuccessfully – to climb up to the coconut we had spotted on our first day.

"I'm going to get it today! It's day fourteen and that feels like a lucky number to me," he announced.

Lina and I sat and watched – munching through a bunch of bananas – as he tried to pull himself up the trunk.

"Thighs…are…burning," he stammered.

"You're doing great," I said, flinging a banana skin over my head.

"Am I further than last time?"

"Not re—"

I nudged Lina before she could finish. "Absolutely," I said, glaring at her. "You are definitely a little bit further up than last time."

Étienne dropped down and shook his arms and legs. "Maybe today isn't the day, but I reckon if I keep at it, I'll reach the top very soon."

"You totally will, Étienne," I said, although I wasn't sure about the *soon* part.

After a particularly long visit to the toilet towards the end of our third week, Lina told us she was concerned about existing on a diet purely of fruit. She said that our bodies needed protein to function properly and if we weren't prepared to sacrifice Giuseppe for our own survival, then we should really start trying to catch some fish using the rusty hooks we'd found aboard **HMS Saviour**.

Étienne wasn't sure. As a life-long vegetarian for environmental and animal-hugging reasons, he said he was still troubled by having eaten the raw flying fish that day when we were at sea.

"We are all troubled by that," I told him. "But Lina is right, we must think of our health."

Étienne couldn't be persuaded, but he did promise not to name any fish – should we manage to catch them.

We chucked more wood and leaves onto the fire and when Lina was happy it was sufficiently smoky, we trundled down to the lagoon in search of some dietary protein. I eyed the water suspiciously, looking out for **Julian Jehoshaphat**. Every time I'd been for a swim, since our first encounter, he'd shown up and I'd had to make a spirited dash for shore before he had launched an attack. Étienne said I was being ridiculous and that there was plenty of room in the lagoon for me and Julian, but Étienne couldn't sense Julian's evil intent like I could.

It wasn't Julian who showed up that day though.

It was **Tarquin**.

We'd been dangling bits of breadfruit in the water for maybe an hour or so without much luck.

"It's not working," Lina said, pulling up her line to examine the bait. "All we're doing is feeding the little fish."

"It does seem like that," I said. "Maybe we need to catch some of these little fish to use as bait to get us a bigger fish."

Lina and I had just started to argue about ways we could catch some little fish, when Étienne interrupted our heated discussion. Lina was incorrectly telling me it was not possible to scare fish into a corner, when he shouted, "Shut up and look!"

This was not a very Étienne thing to do, and we were both a little taken aback by his outburst, but then we saw a huge turtle swimming about in the lagoon.

"Wow," Lina said.

"Isn't it majestic?" Étienne said. "Look at it glide."

"Didn't Beecham say you can eat turtle meat?" I said, without properly thinking it through.

I don't think I've seen Étienne look so appalled.

"Sebastian! Shame on you! We're NOT going to eat **Tarquin Tarantino**!"

Lina shook her head. "There he goes again with the whole naming thing."

"Tarquin is an endangered species," Étienne continued, "and we are **Climate Avengers**, sworn to protect the environment and all its inhabitants—"

"I don't remember swearing an oath," I said, although I might have done and not paid attention.

"You wore the uniform, which means, by extension, that you agreed to the terms," Étienne clarified.

"And those terms include?"

"Not eating endangered turtles for a start!" Étienne shouted.

"It's okay, Étienne." Lina gave me a scowl. "Sebastian's teasing you, I think. We're not going to eat Tarquin, or any other turtle for that matter."

"Yeah," I said. "Without a can opener, I doubt we'd get the shell off anyway."

Étienne shook his head. "You are the WORST sometimes, Sebastian!" And then he stomped off up the beach.

"What?" I shouted after him. "It was a joke!"

He turned round and shouted back, "Watch out, Julian's right behind you."

I leaped forward and was out of that water in a flash, but when I looked back at the lagoon, Julian was nowhere to be seen.

"Now *that's* a joke," Étienne said and continued stomping up to the camp.

"Not a joke," I called after him. "A *trick* and not a nice one!" But he didn't seem to care.

I turned back to see Lina grinning.

"You can wipe that smirk off your face."

With our fishing attempt abandoned, we had to make do with more breadfruit kebabs for our evening meal. Later, when Lina made us say what we were proud of, I said I was proud of how well I'd taken to fishing. Lina very rudely spluttered when she heard that, but I shot her a very dark stare and she apologized. Lina said she was proud of how patient she was becoming. I could have spluttered too, but I have far more self-control. Étienne said he was proud of his tree-climbing progress.

I said, "You are doing brilliantly, Étienne!" Because he was still in a bit of a grump with me about the turtle-meat joke.

I was passing him some breadfruit when we heard a rustle in the undergrowth. Up until that point, the fire had done its job – it had kept us warm when the temperature dropped, it had cooked our food and it had kept any jungle animals away...

Instinctively, Lina picked up the hatchet and Étienne and I grabbed hold of each other and let out the teeniest of whimpers.

The bushes rustled some more. Whatever it was sounded big.

"What if it's a **beast**?" Étienne whispered.

I let go of Étienne's arm and picked up a glowing stick from the fire – just in case.

"It's not a beast!" Lina hissed. "There is no beast!"

"Then why are you holding a hatchet?" Étienne hissed back.

"To make you both feel safe."

The bushes moved about some more.

Étienne and I drew back, not feeling particularly safe.

"Was that a growl? I'm sure I heard a growl," I whispered.

"Last time you said that it was Étienne's stomach," Lina said. "Now stop being melodramatic."

"I fail to see how I'm being melodramatic," I angry-whispered. "We are stranded on a desert island and there is obviously a huge jungle beast that wants to eat us."

Étienne whimpered again, more loudly.

"There isn't a beast and it's not going to eat us!" Lina stood up and pointed the hatchet at me rather than in the direction of the approaching jungle beast.

"I don't think it's shown up for the barbecued breadfruit," I said.

This statement turned out to be completely incorrect because the beast which burst out of the undergrowth was **Giuseppe Garibaldi**. Once we had stopped screaming at his surprise entrance, he settled down next to the fire like he'd done NOTHING wrong. Then he nibbled away at the rest of my breadfruit kebab while I waited for my heart rate to come down from a gazillion beats per minute.

My attempts to shoo him away fell on deaf, furry ears and when Étienne invited him to stay, Giuseppe seemed to understand and snuggled into Étienne's side.

"Would you look at that!" I said. "That goat thinks you're its mum or something."

"I prefer to think of us as friends," Étienne said.

Giuseppe stayed there, like it was perfectly normal for a goat and a boy to be buddies.

Lina stared at them for a while, then shrugged. "Considering recent events, I think now would be a good time to read some more of **Lord of the Flies**. It'll remind us that there is no beast, it is just our minds playing tricks." She then selected some important chapters and told us we should pay particular attention to the scene when the leader was overthrown and how it led them to ruin.

Étienne listened intently, cuddled up and sharing his breadfruit with **Giuseppe Garibaldi**. With no goat-pal of my own to stroke lovingly, I decided I may as well do something useful in preparation for the next building phase of the **Ritz** and began weaving sticks together with long leaves.

I had concluded that our shelter was really too small for the three of us. I'd had enough of sleeping with Étienne's feet in my face and Lina's elbow in my armpit, and I had big plans for extension. The first being a toilet cubicle set very far back, just into the jungle, to avoid terrible smells from offending our nostrils. I had spent the time after my turtle-spat with Étienne collecting a whole pile of shells for decorative design purposes.

When Lina finished the chapter, she eyeballed me. "I think that gives everyone here a lot to think about." Then she asked me about the shells.

"They're to decorate the toilet," I said.

To which she said a very unimpressed, "*What*?"

Giuseppe Garibaldi made a snorting noise, which I refuse to believe was a coincidence.

I glared at them both then explained, "My mum used to say that you could judge a place by the standard of its toilets. If someone has bothered to take time to create an attractive environment in the bathroom, you can rest assured that care will have been invested elsewhere too."

To which Lina said, "*What?*" again.

I shrugged. "I just want to make the toilet I'm building nice, that's all."

Absent-mindedly stoking Giuseppe's back, Étienne said, "I haven't heard you talk about your mum before, Sebastian."

Even though he said it very kindly, I suddenly felt very hot and awkward and uncomfortable. Luckily, I was able to change the subject quickly because I spotted a great big lump moving up the beach.

"What's that lump?" I said, jumping to my feet and pointing in the lump's direction. "Haven't we had enough uninvited guests showing up for one night?"

"It's **Tarquin Tarantino**!" Étienne clapped his hands in delight, startling Giuseppe.

I stood up to get a better look. He was right. Tarquin was dragging himself up the beach using his flippers like little shovels.

"What's he doing?" I asked.

"I think he's here to lay some eggs," Lina said.

"Huh? I did not know boy turtles laid eggs," I said.

Lina gave me a withering look. "Seriously, Sebastian? They don't. Obviously, Tarquin's not a boy."

"In that case, maybe *she* is here to have a word with Étienne about being named Tarquin."

TAKE TIME TO MARVEL AT THE MAGNIFICENCE OF NATURE

Watching Tarquin dig a deep hole around herself and then pop out approximately one hundred luminescent eggs as I sat next to a goat named **Giuseppe Garibaldi**, is one of the most memorable experiences of my life – and you'll know by now that I've had a few.

The moon was full and high in the sky, and it felt like magic was happening right in front of our very own eyeballs.

Étienne kept gasping and saying, "Praise the Lord," and to be honest, watching what was unfolding in front of us, it made me think that someone really ought to be praised for it.

After the first egg plopped out, we had no idea how many others would follow and so Étienne gave that one a name. "Let's call it **Eggbert**," he announced.

The second was **Ethel**, the third **Ernest**, the fourth **Edward**, the fifth **Ermentrude** – that was my suggestion. The sixth **Étienne** – that was Lina's. At around egg number eleven we ran out of names beginning with **E**, so we named the next ones **Benedict**, **Lukas** and **Francesca**. Then there was a little pause, almost like Tarquin knew something should be said. We had a moment where we reassured ourselves that the others were strong, that they were probably home and most likely fine. And Étienne said a prayer for them.

Tarquin then set about laying the next lot. We decided there should be a **Beecham** because we all agreed he'd like that. Then, as more came out, we realized that maybe they needed names beginning with **T** because they'd hatch into turtles after all. So, we had a **Terence** and a **Tanya** and a **Timothy** and a **Trevor**, and then, as the eggs kept coming and coming, we kind of ran out of steam and stopped counting and naming and just sat and watched the spectacle.

"They look like little glowing moons," Lina said, her voice full of wonder. Then she thumped me on the arm and said, "To think you suggested eating her!"

"For the millionth time, it was a joke! And I would like to take this opportunity to remind you that you were up for barbecuing **Giuseppe Garibaldi**."

"Shhh," Lina said, looking at Giuseppe guiltily.

Étienne clutched his hand to his chest. "I almost feel like they're our babies, you know?"

Even though I had laughed at the time, I did know. I knew exactly how he was feeling.

We'd named them – well, most of them. They'd brought joy to **Sunrise Island**, and now they were ours to look after. Later, when I questioned some of the decisions we made and wondered if we should have done things differently, I knew we never could. Because of this moment.

Once Tarquin had finished laying her eggs, she used her flippers to cover them up with sand and then made the long trudge back down to the water. "It's a bit sad, really. The baby turtles being left all alone on this island to fend for themselves."

"Just like us," Lina said.

I've never felt more camaraderie with a reptile in my life. "They're not alone, though. We're here!" I said. "And even though I do not know that much about bringing up turtle babies—"

"Do you know *anything* about bringing up turtle babies?" Lina interrupted.

"I do not. But we're here for them and I think that counts for something."

Étienne nodded and said, "I do too."

That night we went to bed with a full moon above our heads, our bellies full of breadfruit and our minds full of turtle babies.

And with a goat sleeping across our doorway.

In the days and weeks that followed, we kept a close eye on the turtle nest. Even Giuseppe, who had decided that he was part of our group, would go down and stand guard. None of us knew how long it took for a turtle to hatch, and my guess of twenty-four hours was nowhere near.

We placed a ring of stones round the eggs, so we didn't forget where they were, and we waited for the turtle-babies to hatch. It did us all good, I think, to have something to look forward to. Even though no one ever said it out loud, every day that passed, our hopes of rescue faded a little bit more. But just in case, we kept the fire burning at all times. Well, at all times apart from the times when Étienne and I forgot. It was usually when Lina was off collecting water or fruit or had gone fishing at the other end of the cove. Really, we were astonishingly bad at remembering, but we always managed to get it going before Lina noticed, thankfully.

I had spoken to Lina one night, when Étienne was sleeping. I turned to her and said, "We said a month. We were going to talk to Étienne about sailing home. I counted thirty-two stones today."

"I know," she said. "Let's go when the babies are born. Let's wait until after that."

"Okay," I said, because while my insides still burned for home – for my dad, and for my mum – I was beginning to feel like I'd made a new one on **Sunrise Island**. Perhaps it had been a mistake to name it after all.

During the time we were awaiting the arrival of Tarquin's babies, I made excellent progress on the camp toilet. Even Lina was very impressed with the final product. I'd dug a deep hole, like a long drop, and then built a mound of sand up around it, which I had decorated in shells and interesting stones. Then I'd found some wood to use for a seat, which I then covered with some leaves after Étienne's bum-splinter incident. It was a toilet that I am confident any member of the royal family would be happy to grace with their backside.

We didn't get on to building the other wings of the **Ritz** though, which I came to regret later for reasons mainly to do with my competitive pride. I don't know what was stopping us. Maybe we'd grown used to sleeping so close together. Maybe we were scared to be on our own. Maybe we only had enough goats to guard one doorway.

The sun would rise and set, and the days slid by. We swam in the sea, we played on the beach, we collected food and water, we sheltered from the occasional storm, we fished, we kept the fire burning – mostly. We fell out sometimes and got on often. We'd found a rhythm, a rhythm we grew so comfortable with, it was sometimes hard to remember what life was like back home.

But the thing about rhythms is that they don't last for ever, and about six weeks after our turtle eggs had been laid, one dramatic day changed everything.

NO ONE EVER WANTS AN OTTER

On day sixty-two, I woke up early, peeled myself out from under Lina's armpit, stepped over Giuseppe – who was snoring so loudly I wondered if he had caught some jungle cold thing – and slipped off to my magnificently decorated toilet cubicle. Unfortunately, I did not have a successful visit as a diet of mainly breadfruit does bung you up a bit.

I thought I might go for a swim to, you know, get things moving. I was having a perfectly pleasant time paddling about in the shadows, keeping half an eye out for Julian, when I got distracted by what Étienne was doing. He was trying to get his un-gettable coconut again. Giuseppe was standing below him, lazily chewing on Lina's battered Converse. She wouldn't be too worried though, we barely wore shoes any more and had developed impressive hard pads of skin on the undersides of our feet. We'd got skinnier since we'd been on **Sunrise Island**, but we'd got stronger too, and Étienne had managed to get almost halfway up the trunk.

"Étienne! You're doing it!" I shouted. He'd never looked more like a tarsier monkey, and I'd never felt more proud as I watched him battling his way up the trunk.

Étienne turned to wave at me, but when he did, he suddenly stiffened. His mouth fell open and he dropped to the ground like an overripe blongberry. He jumped up immediately and ran towards me, eyes wide, shouting, "**BOAT!**"

"Boat?" It took a moment for my brain to process the word. I turned to look and there, just beyond the coral reef, was a boat. An actual boat. I'd been so used to seeing nothing but the blues of the sea and the sky, I couldn't believe it was really there. It wasn't a big boat. It was a small fishing boat, very similar to ours.

Étienne splashed through the water towards me, grabbed hold of my shoulders and shouted in my face. "**BOAT! SEBASTIAN! BOAT!**"

"I know," I shouted back, half laughing, half crying. "**BOAT!**"

Lina came bursting out of the toilet hut, frantically

pulling up her shorts. "What's going on? Did somebody say **BOAT**?"

Étienne and I both pointed towards it and shouted, "**BOAT!**"

She charged across the beach and thrashed through the water. She stumbled and fell but quickly popped up again yelling, "Who is it? Is it a rescue party?"

I shielded my eyes from the sun, struggling to make out who was paddling towards us. I couldn't see at all to start with – they were too far away and the glare made it difficult to see anything but three silhouettes. As they crossed over the reef and rowed further into the bay, Lina cried, "Is that...oh my goodness, it is! It's Benedict Phan... and...yes, that's Lukas and Francesca too!"

Étienne threw his arms skyward. "They survived! Praise the Lord, they survived!"

I really couldn't believe it, so I said, "I don't believe it! I really don't believe it!"

Étienne grabbed hold of me and shook me quite vigorously. "Believe it because that's them! They're here and they've come to save us!"

That turned out not to be strictly true, but in the moment, it looked like a boat full of hope heading right towards us.

I waved furiously. An incredible lightness – that

probably came from knowing that I hadn't caused three people to perish in the Pacific Ocean – spread over me.

Lina, Étienne and I held hands as we watched them approach – their strokes were slow but powerful. While they looked determined, they also looked exhausted and a little bit terrifying. They'd adapted their **Climate Avenger** uniforms with leaves and coconut husks. They

had mud of various brown and red hues streaked down their faces, and their hair was wild. If I thought they'd looked like **mutants** before, they looked like **warriors** now.

Giuseppe stood watching as we ran out to meet them. We threw a million questions at them as we helped drag the boat up the beach.

"Where have you been?"

"How did you get here?"

"What happened?"

"Is help coming?"

"Did *you* make those spears in your boat?"

"What's with the grass skirts?"

Benedict, Lukas and Francesca didn't respond. Slowly, they climbed out of their boat and stumbled through the water, and when they reached the sand they toppled to the ground like falling trees.

We stood over them for a moment, just staring, trying to process the fact that they had turned up out of nowhere and so unexpectedly.

I heard myself say, "Welcome to **Sunrise Island**. I hope your stay with us is a pleasant one. Can I get you anything today?"

Lina and Étienne both frowned at me.

"What? I'm being hospitable."

Benedict raised his head and said, in a very croaky voice, "Otter."

I pulled a face. "Did he say *otter*?" Seemed like an unusual request.

Lina scowled at me. "He said *water*, obviously. You two go and fetch some. Quickly. And bring some fruit while you're at it."

We did as we were told and brought a whole selection of the fruit we had stored up in the **Ritz**. They drank thirstily and ate in rather a savagey way, and then with no word of thanks – no words at all actually – they walked up the beach.

Étienne, Lina and I looked at each other, wondering what was wrong with the **mutants**. I shrugged and then we chased after them, firing more questions.

"Where've you come from?"

"How long have you been at sea?"

"Is that a loincloth under your skirt?"

Benedict held up his hand and spoke in a commanding voice. "Later. Now we sleep."

They disappeared into our shelter and didn't come out for hours.

Étienne, Lina and I stood there looking at the shelter, then at each other, wondering what to do next.

"What do you think happened to them?" Étienne whispered.

"I don't know. They survived – that's the main thing," I said.

We hovered about the doorway watching them sleep, impatiently waiting for them to wake up and answer our many questions. Waiting got a bit boring and staring at them started to feel a bit weird, so we decided to give the camp a tidy and get ready for when they did emerge.

When they finally came out, it was almost evening.

We'd prepared a huge feast for them – bananas and coconuts and berries and breadfruit. Lina had also managed to hook a couple of fish, so we had them cooking away nicely on some sticks.

When they walked over to the fire, we all stood up, like we were greeting royalty.

"Good sleep?" Lina asked. "You must have been exhausted – you've been out for ages."

Lukas nodded at Giuseppe. "We eating that?"

"No! Giuseppe is kind of…our pet," Étienne said.

"Your pet?" Lukas looked from Benedict to Francesca. "You hear that! The goat is a pet!"

They laughed, and I don't know why, but I blushed. I felt like they were saying that we were doing the whole **shipwrecking** thing wrong by having a pet goat.

"He's more one of the family," Étienne added, which only made them laugh more.

They sat down round the fire cross-legged and helped themselves to the fish.

Benedict bit the head off first, which was pretty horrible to watch. Once he'd swallowed it down, he said, "So, what have you lot been up to other than taming wild goats?"

COMPARISON IS THE THIEF OF JOY

Lina gave a *very* detailed account of what we'd been up to since the storm hit, which included **me** being hit in the face with flying fish, **me** falling down a coconut tree, **me** thinking there was a bear, **me** being knocked to the floor by Giuseppe and **me** hallucinating after ingesting under-ripe blongberries. Hearing it listed like that made me wonder if it was karma for what I'd done.

"You've been busy, Sebastian!" Lukas said in a way that I couldn't be sure if he was impressed or amused.

"We weren't sure if you guys would be okay after that storm," Francesca said. "I mean, you didn't look like confident rowers when we set out that night."

"We survived just as well as you guys," I said. "We were worried about you too. When we saw you knocked over by that wave it was hard not to think the worst."

"It wasn't much fun, but we got back on the boat pretty quickly. We hunkered down and sat out the storm. We rowed for a full day and ended up on an island about three days away from here," Benedict said.

"You've been there this whole time?" Étienne asked, offering round some breadfruit kebabs.

"Yup. Ah, more breadfruit." Lukas took one and nodded his thanks. "You know, when we make it back, I swear I will never touch the stuff again."

"What I'd give for a pizza," Benedict said.

We collectively sighed at the thought of pizza.

"What was your island like?" Étienne asked.

Benedict glanced around. "Much like this one, but we didn't have a lagoon."

"No lagoon? Too bad." I tried not to appear too pleased that we had clearly found the superior island. "Did your island have a name? Ours does, it's called **Sunrise Island**."

"Ours was just the island," Benedict said and I felt like we'd won that one too.

He waved his breadfruit stick towards the **Ritz**. "You've had a go at building yourself a shelter then?"

"We did have plans to extend," I said, feeling the need to explain. "The sleeping area might need a bit of work, but you should see the toilet."

Francesca raised an eyebrow. "The toilet?"

"Yeah, it's your regular long-drop system but I decorated it with shells and tried to make it welcoming, and, well, I just think you judge a place by the standard of the restrooms..." I trailed off, feeling a little self-conscious.

"Absolutely," Benedict said. "Shell-decorated loos are right up on the list of key things for survival."

"It's actually very pleasant," Étienne said.

"I'm joking, I think what you've got set up here is great – with your fancy loo and your pet goat!"

I still couldn't tell if Benedict was being serious.

"What was your camp like?" Lina said, quite hotly. "Better than this?"

"I wouldn't say *better*," Francesca said. "Maybe a bit bigger and more functional. I think our buildings were a little more like buildings...sturdy, shall we say."

"So better then," Lina replied flatly.

Étienne's eyes grew even bigger than normal. "Did you say buildings plural?"

"We have buildings plural," I said. "The shelter and the loo."

Francesca rose up a little. "We had a shelter each, a kitchen for preparing food—"

"We know what a kitchen is," I interrupted. Étienne

shook his head at me like he thought I was being rude, but it was Francesca who had suggested I didn't know what a kitchen was!

"—and a communal area for us to hang out in and also a special meditation room for when we need space and time to clear our heads."

"Wow!" Étienne said. "That sounds amazing."

"Yeah, amazing," Lina said, but she didn't sound amazed, she sounded annoyed.

"But we didn't have any animals," Benedict said.

"We did," Lukas said. "We had some pigs, but we ate them."

Étienne put a protective hand over Giuseppe. "We've adopted a fish and fruit diet here."

"It's better for your cholesterol," I said, although I wasn't one hundred per cent sure what cholesterol was. I just knew my dad's had got a bit high recently and he'd stopped eating red meat and swapped butter for something that claimed to have a buttery taste but was in fact, horrible. Although I imagine I'd find it okay now.

The thought of my dad caused a long, sad sigh to seep from me, which must have seemed odd to the others after listening to me talk about cholesterol.

Francesca gave me a curious look. "We've had fish too. There was a fishing net in our boat."

"We've had to catch ours by hand," Lina said boastfully.

"That's impressive," Benedict said.

"Yup. Anyway, how come you're here now?" Lina asked. "What made you leave your island if it was so great there?"

Francesca picked up a stick and began jabbing it into the ground. "We'd been there over fifty days; we had to do something. We agreed we couldn't stay there any longer."

"Why not?" said Étienne. "Fifty days isn't *that* long."

"We didn't want to keep waiting for someone to not show up and rescue us," Lukas said. "Fifty days could turn into a hundred, could turn into a year, could turn into ten years, could turn into a hundred years. Not a hundred years, we'd be dead by then, but you get my point."

Benedict nodded. "I asked myself what Coach Baggins would say, and I reckon he'd say, *Take control of the situation, Benedict.* So that's what we did. We've decided to row back."

I wasn't sure if taking survival tips from a basketball coach was a great idea – but it was hard not to be impressed by their courage.

Étienne gasped. "Row back!?"

"That's very brave," Lina said.

"Do you think that's a good idea?" Étienne blinked furiously. "You might get lost again, or drown, or...or get pecked to death by pelicans."

"It's better than doing nothing and I think we'll be

alright fending off the pelicans," Benedict said as he peeled himself a banana in a very arrogant way – if you can peel a banana arrogantly. "Plan is, now we've found you, we'll rest a few days, build up our strength and supplies then head out again."

"What if you don't make it? Don't you think it's too risky? You could die out there!" Étienne said.

"Fortune favours the brave," Francesca replied. "That's what my volleyball coach says."

I was beginning to have serious concerns about them basing their efforts purely on motivational half-time sports talks.

Lina must have too, because she said, "Do you have any evidence to back that up?"

"We made it to you, didn't we?" Francesca shot back with quite a lot of attitude, which shut Lina up.

"You could come with us," Benedict said. "You must have thought about trying to row back. You must have made plans?"

Lina and I caught each other's eye over the fire. Benedict saw and tilted his head, interested.

"Our plans are to stay alive not die at sea!" Étienne said. "We wait here and get rescued." Then he added quite proudly, "We also have **Tarquin Tarantino**'s babies to protect."

"Back up a bit...Tarquin's babies?" Lukas said. "Who is **Tarquin Tarantino**?"

"A turtle," Étienne said.

"A turtle?" Benedict, Lukas and Francesca said at the same time.

"Yeah, aquatic reptile, webbed feet, hard shell," I said.

"We know what a turtle is," Lukas said.

Étienne pointed down the beach. "She laid her eggs over there – do you see that ring of stones? That's where they are, and we are going to make sure nothing happens to them."

"What do you think might happen to them?" Lukas said, sounding confused.

I wasn't exactly clear about what we were protecting the turtles from and, by the looks on Lina's and Étienne's faces, I don't think they were either. I felt a little foolish. The others were going to try and row home and our plan was to sit around and keep an eye on some eggs. We knew we had to though, just in case. I guess, like any parent who has seen their kid being born, we just couldn't walk away.

When I say *any*, I really mean, *most* parents. I gave myself a shake before an image of my mum getting into that taxi could fully form in my mind.

"Who knows what might happen," I said. "Maybe

nothing, maybe something. We just want to keep an eye on the little fellas. We're **Climate Avengers** after all – we swore an oath to protect, remember?"

"It was amazing when we watched Tarquin lay them," Étienne said. He then told the story of that night, how the moon was so high and bright in the sky, how it almost felt magical. The others listened, hanging on his every word.

"Sounds pretty cool," Benedict said.

"Totally cool," Francesca agreed.

Étienne smiled shyly. "We even named some after you guys."

"Bit weird, but I guess I'm also a bit honoured that we have our very own turtles," Benedict said.

The flames of the fire crackled and, for a moment, we sat quietly. Even if they were a bit up themselves, it was nice to have new people around. Maybe they weren't that bad.

Then Lukas said, "Probably a decent amount of protein in a turtle egg."

Which slightly ruined the atmosphere.

Étienne leaped to his feet, grabbed a stick out of the fire and waved it in Lukas's direction. "You'll have to go through me and Giuseppe before you get anywhere near those eggs."

Étienne looked so completely angry, his eyes

determined and unblinking behind his wonky glasses, that we all burst out laughing. That only made him get angrier, and when Giuseppe let out a deep snore, we laughed even harder.

Poor Étienne. It was only after Benedict made Lukas swear that he wouldn't scramble Tarquin's eggs that Étienne finally calmed down.

We offered to let the others take the shelter for the night, but they insisted that we should sleep where we normally slept and that they would be fine round the fire. I thought they were being nice, but I heard Francesca mutter to Lukas, "Don't want that thing collapsing on us."

Too tired to argue about the obvious structural integrity of the **Ritz**, yawning and feeling very sleepy, we all trundled off to bed, followed by an equally sleepy Giuseppe, who took his usual place across our doorway.

Étienne bent down and gave him a kiss on the head. "*Bonne nuit à la meilleure chèvre du monde*."

So Étienne was kissing goats now. Island life really does do funny things to a person. But I couldn't help but smile. I think you could drop Étienne into all sorts of desperate situations and he'd still be able to find someone new to love and I love that about him.

When the chatter from outside had died down and all we could hear were the now familiar sounds of the jungle, the suck and heave of waves lapping on the beach and the rhythmic snoring of the others, Lina sat up and said, "Are you awake?"

When Étienne and I took longer than half a millisecond to answer, she jabbed us with her pointy elbows and hissed, "Wake up!"

"Hey! I am awake," I hissed back.

"I am now," Étienne said.

"I've been thinking," Lina said. "It's nice that the others are alive and they're here with their plan to row back, blah blah blah, but I think we need to be mindful that them being here could actually be trouble for us."

"How so?" Étienne said.

"Think how in **Lord of the Flies**—"

Étienne and I both groaned. Giuseppe might have groaned too.

"Hear me out. There are two separate groups here now, and it's clear those guys out there are the **Hunters**. They are already wearing the outfits."

"I don't think we're two groups," Étienne said. "I'm sure we can work together."

"You might believe that now, but I bet when they start wanting us to do things their way, it's going to feel very different."

I could see Lina's point.

"I think we need to keep an eye on them," she continued. "Make sure they know they are *guests* here on **Sunrise Island**. That they can't take over the place."

"I really don't think they'll do that," Étienne said.

I said, "I agree, Lina. This is my...*our* island and we run it the way we want."

"I'm going to pray for you both tonight," Étienne said, then he turned over and started whispering to himself. I didn't catch it all, but it was along the lines that he hoped we'd learn not only to see the best in others but also the best in ourselves. Then he wished **Giuseppe** life-long happiness and the same for **Tarquin** and **Eggbert**, **Ethel**, **Ernest**, **Edward**, **Ermentrude**, **Étienne**, et cetera, et cetera.

And then he prayed for home.

Home. My heart sighed and my thoughts twisted like jungle creepers.

I wondered if my dad really was searching for me. If my mum was even upset. What I'd say to them both. How I'd tell Dad I was sorry. Sorry for being difficult. Sorry for not choosing him. I'd ask Mum why she hadn't wanted to take me. Whether she regretted it now I was lost. I felt a flicker of satisfaction at the thought that she might be hurting. It would serve her right if she was. Then a wave of shame barrelled through me. I didn't really want her to hurt. I wanted to see them again. I wanted to see them both.

I thought about what Lukas had said – fifty days becoming a hundred, a hundred becoming a year, becoming ten. I couldn't sit and wait for ever to be found. I'd talk to Lina – try and persuade Étienne too. Once the turtles were born, I'd put my faith in our boat and take my chance with the sea.

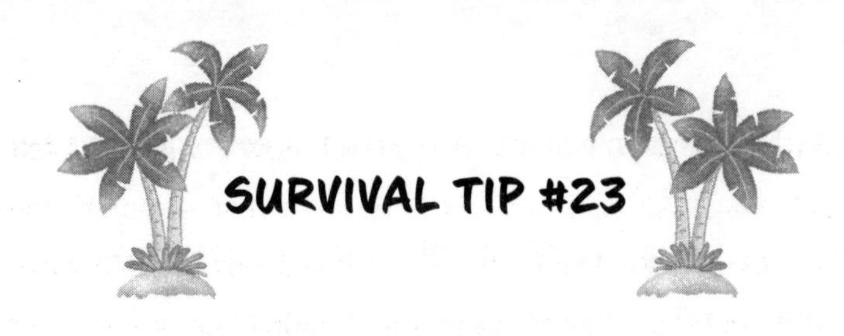

SURVIVAL TIP #23

DON'T SWEAT THE SMALL STUFF – LIKE COCONUTS

I was the last to wake up the following morning. I think I could have slept a lot longer too, if it hadn't been for Lina shouting.

I stumbled out of the shelter, into the brightness of the day to find her standing at the bottom of the coconut tree with Lukas clinging on halfway up it. Lina was bellowing at him to, "Get down this instant."

Francesca, Benedict and Étienne were there too, all looking up. Clearly, something was going on.

Étienne said, "It's no big deal, honestly, Lina," but Lina was not having any of it.

"That's *your* coconut, Étienne. You've been practising hard to climb that tree, you should be the one to get it, not someone who has just this second shown up!"

"I really don't mind who gets the coconut," Étienne said.

"It is the **PRINCIPLE OF THE THING**, Étienne!" Lina blared.

Francesca rolled her eyes. "I don't see why you're getting so worked up about a coconut. What's your problem?"

"It's not just *a* coconut! It's Étienne's coconut and *that's* my problem," Lina said, giving Francesca a dark stare.

"It really isn't my coconut," Étienne said, but no one was paying him much attention.

Benedict said, "Lukas, maybe you should come down if it is going to cause so much fuss. It's not like there aren't other coconuts."

"He's almost there now," Francesca said. "It would be stupid not to get it!"

"Lina's right," I shouted. "Leave the coconut alone. It's Étienne's!"

"Why is nobody listening to me? I don't care about the coconut," Étienne said.

"Yes, you do," Lina and I snapped.

Étienne did a big sigh and sat down on the ground next to Giuseppe, who was lazily chomping on some grass.

Lukas was still hanging onto the tree, looking very

unclear about what to do. "Am I getting this coconut or not?"

"NO!"

"YES!"

"I'm the leader," Lina said, very forcefully. "You do what *I* say."

Francesca laughed at that, which obviously didn't go down well. "You're not our leader."

"While you're on *my* island I am."

Benedict offered Étienne his hand. "I'm so not here for this. How about you and I go for a swim and leave these guys to it?"

"Sounds better than hanging around here." Étienne took hold of Benedict's hand, and he helped him up.

"Hey! Don't go!" Lukas said, but Étienne and Benedict ignored him and trotted off towards the water, leaving the rest of us in a fight over a coconut.

Eventually, Lukas clambered down and said, "I've had enough of this," and wandered down to the lagoon.

Lina looked mightily pleased with herself. "Thank you, Lukas," she said. "I think that was the right thing to do."

He threw a "Whatever," over his shoulder.

Francesca didn't look happy and as she walked past us she said, "I can't believe you two made such a fuss about a coconut."

Lina shouted after her, "We can't believe you did either!"

"Well done," I said. "You successfully defended Étienne's coconut."

She nodded, then cupped her hands round her mouth and hollered, "Étienne, come back up here and collect your coconut."

Étienne stopped splashing Benedict for a moment, then carried on swimming about, pretending he hadn't heard.

"I'm sure he'll get it later," I said.

"It wasn't just about the coconut, Sebastian," Lina said, staring at the others. "That lot need to know who is in charge here."

"I totally agree," I said and leaned against the coconut tree, which somehow caused Étienne's coconut to fall from its place. It landed in the sand with a **whoomph** at my feet.

Lina's mouth dropped open in what I thought was surprised concern.

"Woah! That was close," I said. "I was almost one of those unfortunate people killed by a falling coconut. More common than death by shark apparently. I suppose if sharks lived in trees that might not be the case."

It turned out that Lina was not at all concerned about my brush with death or interested in my fascinating shark fact. She said, "Sebastian! What did you do that for? I spent all that time fighting for Étienne to get the coconut and first chance you get you knock it down!"

"What?" I spluttered. "That was obviously an accident!"

"Everything is an *accident* with you!"

"Exactly! Besides, you said it wasn't really about the coconut!"

"I said it wasn't *all* about the coconut! It was quite a lot about the coconut! Now, get up there and put it back!"

"I can't put a coconut back in a tree!" I said, very reasonably. How would I even do that?"

Lina stomped her foot in the sand and said, very unreasonably, "I suggest you come up with a way, because I'm not having the others think we made a fuss about Étienne having to get the coconut for you to knock it down." Then she flounced off to go and check on the fire.

"I think you may have got a bit carried away with the whole coconut thing!" I yelled after her.

She just held up one hand and said, "Not listening!"

I stood, coconut in hand, genuinely trying to come up with ways to reattach it to a tree I had no hope of climbing to the top of, for much longer than I would like to admit.

Eventually, I gave up, dropped the coconut off at the shelter and went down to the lagoon to join Étienne for a swim.

"Are you coming in?" Benedict said as I stood eyeing

the turquoise waters for Julian.

"I haven't seen Julian, if that's what you're worried about," Étienne shouted.

"I am not," I lied and dived in. I surfaced in front of Étienne and squirted water in his face.

"Sebastian!" he protested, rubbing his eyes and blinking furiously. "Must you always do that?!"

Next thing I knew there were two large hands on my shoulders and I was being shoved under. I burst back to the surface to see Benedict grinning at me. "You give it, you have to learn to take it," he said, which shut me up before I could protest. Still, I was not happy.

I think to diffuse the situation, Étienne said, "You should see how far Benedict can swim underwater! He's like a fish! Show him, Benedict."

"I'm not that good," Benedict said, though he clearly thought he was.

"Go on! Show Sebastian!" Étienne chirped again.

"Oh, okay, if you insist." He disappeared into the blue, the bright soles of his feet flashing a goodbye.

I watched the surface of the water, trying to figure out where he might pop out.

"He's so good! Just watch!"

"I am watching!" I said, unable to keep the annoyance out of my voice.

"He can stay under for ages!" Étienne squealed.

"Of course, he can," I said, a little stroppily.

"Honestly, Sebastian, he's amazing!"

He's a show-off of the most monumental kind, is what I thought. I folded my arms and waited for him to resurface.

"It's been ages!" Étienne clapped his hands excitedly.

It had been rather a long time. How could he still be under? Maybe he *was* a **mutant**. A **merman-mutant**. I wouldn't put it past him. I decided I should check him for gills when he did come up for air.

Eventually we heard an, "Oi oi!"

Benedict was standing on the coral reef grinning. He must have been forty metres out, more maybe. Then, as if he hadn't shown off enough, Benedict did a backwards somersault into the lagoon. When he surfaced, he said, "You guys should swim out here, come see this coral, it is so beautiful! And there are so many lovely fish! We should bring the net out here!"

Étienne didn't want to. It was probably too far for him and, even though it wasn't too far for me, I didn't want to either. There might be all sorts of nasties out by the reef. But because of my stupid ego, I blocked my fears of humongous sharks and shoals of Julians and swam out there.

To see the beautiful coral and all the lovely fish.

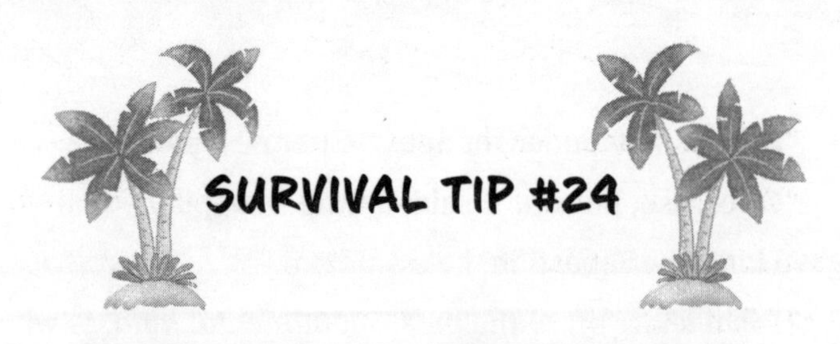

NEVER DROP YOUR GUARD, ESPECIALLY AROUND A JELLYFISH WITH A VENDETTA

I stuck my face in the water and powered over to Benedict, wanting to demonstrate that I was a good swimmer too. I was quite out of breath when I reached him.

"Nice form," he said and smiled, and I wasn't certain if he meant it or not.

I said, "Thanks," anyway.

"Get a load of all the fish!" He ducked back under, then popped up again. "They probably like it round the reef. We'll catch loads if we bring the net out here."

"A good fish supper will set you up for your journey back," I said. "When was it you said you were leaving again?"

"Two or three days – that should give us enough time to prepare. Why, do you want rid of us already?"

"No, just wondering," I said casually.

"You could come too," he said. "I saw that look you gave Lina last night."

"What look?"

"When I mentioned leaving. I got the impression you and Lina might consider it."

I looked over at Étienne, who was waving at us – a huge smile splitting his face.

Guilt rushed over me. "Not without Étienne and I don't know if I could convince him to go out on the ocean again. There's no way I'd leave him behind. He needs me. I know Lina acts like the leader, but really, it's me who makes sure everyone is okay out here. I'm the one who is always keeping my eye out for dang—"

I was going to say danger.

Instead, what I did was scream. Very loudly.

Because **Julian Jehoshaphat** had realized I'd let my guard down and seized his chance.

He only got me with one of his wafty tentacle bits, but my goodness, that was enough. The pain shot up my backside – the point of impact – then up my spine and across my skull. My eyes flew so far open in distress, it's a wonder my eyeballs didn't pop out.

Benedict said, "Are you alright?"

Which seemed an unnecessary question when I clearly was far from alright. Benedict clocked Julian undulating about in the water near me and shouted, "Jellyfish!" Also unnecessary because I was *very* aware of Julian.

I didn't know what to do with myself. I wailed. Then I forgot how to swim, and I thrashed about, in a way Benedict later described as resembling, "a mackerel stuck in an electric fence". But I was panicking and in pain. So so soooooo much pain. I didn't know what to do, other than flap about like a mackerel in an electric fence.

Luckily, I guess, Benedict was there.

He grabbed hold of me with his muscly hand and towed me back to shore, like a proper lifesaving hero, while I howled at the sky, "**MY POOR BUM! A CURSE ON YOU, JULIAN AND ALL YOUR JELLYNESS!**"

The others, including Giuseppe, had gathered on the beach and watched with concerned faces as Benedict laid me face down on the sand. I became aware of lots of pairs of legs, including four furry goat ones, gathering round me.

"What happened?" Lina asked, kneeling down.

I lifted my head and groaned, "Julian," because I didn't need to explain any further. Even though Lina and Étienne had said otherwise and pretended that Julian's obsession with me was all in my head, we'd all known that this day would come.

Étienne said, "Julian is our jellyfish."

And Francesca and Lukas both went, "Ohh," in acknowledgment of my terrible situation.

"The good news is that if you were going to die it would have happened already." This was indeed good to hear, but the matter-of-fact tone of Lina's delivery somewhat dismissed the dreadfulness of my situation.

"Where did he sting you exactly?" Étienne asked.

I couldn't really speak, so I raised a trembling hand and pointed to my rear.

"Oh, Sebastian!" Lina said, like it was my fault.

I wiggled my shorts down a little and was going to ask how it looked, but when I heard a chorus of gasps, I knew there was a serious situation back there.

"It looks like you've been whipped with a skipping rope," Étienne said.

"More like burned by a lightsaber," Lukas said.

"It hurts...so...so...bad."

"You know what we have to do to relieve the pain," Francesca said gravely.

"Ugh. I do," Lina said.

I lifted my head from the sand again. "I don't! What do you need to do?"

If *you* know what they needed to do, good for you – because I did not. That little nugget of information had somehow passed me by.

"Sebastian, I'm afraid we need to pee on you. There's something in urine that helps ease the sting," Francesca said. "There's a chance it's a myth, but I think it's better we do something than nothing."

"Oh. You. Are. Kidding. Me! You *think* you *may* have to wee on me?" I flopped my face back into the sand. "Worst. Day. Ever."

"Er, sorry, did you say this is the *worst day ever*?" Lina spluttered. "You do remember the day you got us all marooned on a desert island?"

"Just get it over with," I wailed. "But can it be you or Étienne?" I know being peed on by *anybody* is awful, it just felt more humiliating to be peed on by one of the others.

"If that's what you want," Lina said. "But we're not going to pee directly on you."

"Why not? Peeing next to me isn't going to help! I'll just be slowly dying next to a puddle of piddle. If you're going to do it, do it properly!"

"No, I meant we'll wee in a coconut shell then chuck – I mean pour – it onto you," Lina explained.

"Ooh yes! Do that!" To this day I feel sad that I was so excited about that prospect.

They both headed off to the toilet cubicle – Étienne telling Giuseppe and the others to keep an eye on me.

When they returned, I noticed they were not holding any coconut shells in their hands.

"Where is the wee? I need the wee!"

"Thing is..." Étienne began, "we're both a bit

dehydrated. I managed to get a tiny drop, but I don't think that will help."

"It hurts so much!" Then I huffed. "Fine, one of the **mutants** can do it."

"One of the *who*?" Francesca asked.

"Nothing." Then, because my bum was literally on fire, I swallowed my pride and said, "Would one of you please pee on me?"

I waited while they all trotted off to pee into a coconut, only for them to return empty handed too.

"Seriously! No one can squeeze anything out! Not even a dribble?"

They shook their heads and looked very sorry.

"We could drink loads of water and try again in half an hour?" Benedict suggested.

"I cannot wait that long!" The pain was becoming quite unbearable. "Please...help me..." I stuttered. "There has to be something you can do, *anything*."

Étienne whispered something to Lina. Her eyes widened. She whispered something back and then they both shrugged.

"What? What is it? If there's something you can do to help, do it!"

"We may have an idea," Lina said slowly, and then she and Étienne looked at **Giuseppe Garibaldi**.

"Why are you looking at Giuseppe?"

"I'm sure goat urine will work the same way," Étienne said, although he didn't sound sure.

Francesca clasped her hand over her mouth, either to hide her horror or to stifle her giggles.

That was not happening. I dragged myself to my knees, then staggered to my feet. Étienne quickly appeared at my side and helped me to straighten up.

"Give me a coconut shell," I demanded. "I will pee on myself before I let a goat wee on me. I have some dignity."

Then I hobbled to the toilet with my shorts round my ankles, which on reflection was not that dignified, but I couldn't bear to have anything touching the sting.

Lina and Étienne followed me, offering words of encouragement and I staggered into the loo and did what I had to do.

I emerged many minutes later. Everyone was waiting. The pain was still there, but not as skull-scorchingly dreadful.

"Are you okay?" Lina asked.

I nodded though I was mildly traumatized. "I'm going for a lie-down and if we ever get rescued and if we ever meet anyone else again, what happened here today on **Sunrise Island**, stays on **Sunrise Island**. Do I make myself clear?"

"Of course," Étienne said, and everyone nodded solemnly but I swear I saw a few faint smiles.

"You had better not be finding this funny. I told you Julian had it in for me!" I said, then shambled off to the shelter – my shorts still slung low.

I stayed inside the shelter for the rest of the afternoon waiting for my backside to stop throbbing and, apart from the few times I went to pee on myself again, I had no intention of showing my face until my dinner had been cooked for me because, considering the circumstances, it was the least I deserved.

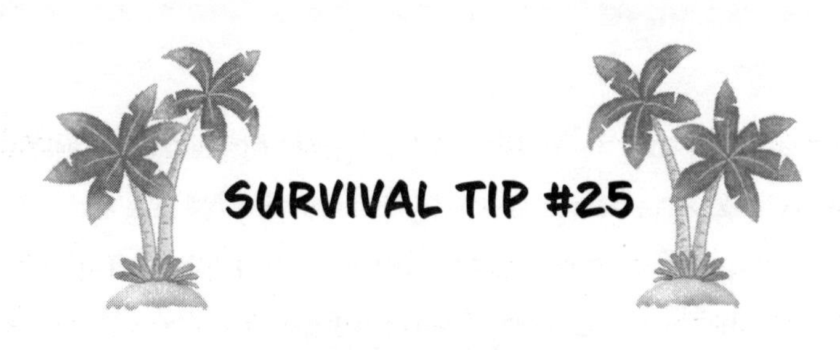

CHECK YOUR SURROUNDINGS BEFORE HAVING A MOAN ABOUT SOMEONE

The following day I was still in a bit of a mood about the whole bum debacle and was the last to get up. I stood, stretched, then spent a little while inspecting the sting, which was still an angry red. Then I spent a little more time commiserating with myself. I found myself blaming Benedict for my whole sorry situation. If he hadn't made me go out to the reef, then I would never have had my run-in with Julian.

I finally emerged from the **Ritz** to find Benedict, Lukas and Francesca returning from the jungle laden with coconuts. They stacked them up next to our pile of date rocks. There were sixty-three now. *Fifty turns into a hundred*, I thought.

Benedict dropped his coconuts when he saw me, then

spread his arms wide, like he was greeting his best buddy. “Morning! And how is our jellyfish warrior feeling today?”

I caught Francesca and Lukas smirking but chose to ignore them. “I am continuing to bravely battle through the pain.”

“I’m really sorry it happened,” Benedict said. “It can’t be much fun.”

“It isn’t,” I said and glared at him because I felt his apology was neither proper nor sufficient. I gestured at the coconuts. “These for your journey?”

“Yup,” Lukas said. “We’re thinking about heading off tomorrow.”

“If the weather is right,” Benedict quickly chimed in. He nodded at the sky. “I don’t like the look of those clouds.”

There were a few white wisps in the sky – nothing particularly ominous-looking – and that’s coming from me, who has understandably become very suspicious of clouds. Lukas and Francesca were clearly wondering what he was on about because they both said, “Hey?”

“I have a feeling,” Benedict said. “You know, like when you sense that you’re going to have a bad game. Can’t explain it, but I think we should maybe leave it a few more days.”

“Huh,” I said, not really buying it. However, the bad game thing seemed to strike a chord with the others.

Lukas shrugged. "Fair enough. Always trust your instincts."

"We can wait until the time feels right," Francesca said.

Benedict slung his arm over my shoulder. I looked at it – draped there – as he said, "You never know, by then these guys might have decided to come with us."

"Really?" Lukas said. "I kind of got the impression that wasn't an option."

"I don't know," I said defensively. "Maybe it is."

Lina and Étienne emerged from the jungle dripping with sweat and laden with sticks. Giuseppe was trundling along behind them with Lina's Converse in his mouth.

"We have more wood for the fire!" Lina announced.

"She sure loves a fire," Lukas muttered.

"I do and you, while you remain here, will love it too," Lina said.

"We were just talking about when we might leave," Francesca said. "Sebastian was saying that you guys might want to come with us."

Étienne dropped his pile of sticks at his feet and looked at me accusingly. "Sebastian?"

"I didn't say that we would," I said. "Just that we might consider it. Maybe. But only if you both agreed."

I looked to Lina for support, but Étienne said, "I don't agree. I'll never agree!" then he stomped off towards the sea. Giuseppe followed him, giving me quite a snotty look as he went by.

Benedict said, "I'll go after him."

I wasn't having that. "No, I'll go."

"*We'll* go," Lina corrected, and she lumped her sticks into Lukas's arms and instructed him to go and tend to the fire.

We found Étienne sitting by Tarquin's eggs, with Giuseppe's head in his lap. Lina sat down on one side of him, and I gingerly lowered myself onto the sand on the other side, letting out the tiniest of yelps when my bum touched the ground.

"If you two have decided to leave me on **Sunrise Island** you had better just tell me," he said.

"We haven't decided anything," I said.

"We would never decide anything without talking to you first," Lina said.

Étienne pushed his glasses up his nose and looked at us. "But you've thought about leaving?"

Lina nodded. Then I nodded.

"I've thought about it too," Étienne said quietly. "And it makes me feel terrible because I miss home so much. I miss my parents so much, but I can't. I can't go out on the open ocean again. I still have nightmares."

Lina spoke gently. "You may feel differently the longer we're here."

Étienne shook his head. "I'm not brave enough."

"But you are brave!" I said. "We thought that, perhaps, after **Tarquin Tarantino** had her babies, we might—"

"Please," Étienne said, tears welling in his eyes. "Can we not talk about this?" He stood up. "I think I want to be on my own for a bit."

Lina and I watched as he and Giuseppe walked off further down the beach.

"He's not going to change his mind, is he?" Lina said.

I shook my head. "I don't know. He might."

"We won't go without him, though, will we?" she asked.

"No," I said. "We won't."

I looked at our boat.

Fifty days could turn into a hundred, a hundred become a year, a year becomes ten, I thought. Étienne would change his mind, he'd find it in himself – we couldn't stay for ever.

Life on **Sunrise Island** felt different with the others there. A little less harmonious. Even though Étienne was his usual cheery self, I would sometimes catch him anxiously muttering to himself or Giuseppe in French. He still seemed worried that we might decide to leave with the others. Lina clearly had a problem with the possible threat to her rule that our new guests presented. Even after she'd read them some of **Lord of the Flies** and they'd said they were fine with her being leader, she was still suspicious that they might try to overthrow her. And I definitely held a grudge against Benedict for the Julian incident and for just being Benedict.

He was irritating. They all were. Even on a desert island, dressed in clothes made from undergrowth, they still looked annoyingly sparkly and shiny and could literally do *everything* better than me. They started fires in next to no time using only dry sticks. They carried more, they climbed higher, they swam faster, and they built an extension to the **Ritz**, which even I have to admit rivalled my luxury toilet.

They didn't do anything wrong. In fact, they did everything right, but their presence on our island began to annoy me. In the two weeks since they'd arrived, we'd heard all sorts of excuses as to why it wasn't the right day for them to row off. Either there was an ominous-looking cloud, or the waves looked too choppy past the reef, or they just didn't have the right *feeling*. I began to worry that they might not leave at all.

Fifty days could turn into a hundred, a hundred become a year, a year becomes ten.

On the morning of the sixteenth day of their stay on **Sunrise Island** and on the seventy-eighth day of ours, I decided to do something about their reluctance to leave. Benedict and Étienne had gone for a swim with Giuseppe – they'd invited me along, but I was too annoyed by their blossoming friendship to go. I was lazing around camp with the others – it was a particularly hot day, and no one fancied doing much. I watched Benedict and Étienne messing about in the water until I was too irritated to look at them. I nodded to Lina, raised my eyebrows and said, "Shall we go and get some firewood?"

Lina, always up for replenishing the firewood, held out her arms for me to pull her to her feet. "Yes, Sebastian, and I applaud you for thinking of the fire!"

When we were out of earshot and Lina was busy hacking away at the trees, I said, "I actually want to talk to you about the others and how long we allow them to stay here."

Lina stopped the hatchet mid-swing. "I want to talk about that too! They don't seem to be showing any signs of leaving anytime soon!"

"Benedict says he senses bad weather coming." I rolled my eyes so she knew what I thought of that.

"Hmmm. Maybe they've lost their nerve."

I shrugged. "It's possible. I think they've realized how great **Sunrise Island** is."

"We need them to sail off so they can send a rescue party back for us!" Lina said. "We've been here long enough! *They've* been here long enough."

"It feels like they've been here *for ever*!" I agreed.

Lina nodded. "Lukas's booming laugh is getting on my nerves. You could probably hear him on the other side of the island. And they are always sprawled *everywhere* with all their long limbs taking up space."

"I hate the way Benedict is always hanging around with Étienne – he treats him like some kind of pet. His little lapdog." I was beginning to enjoy the chance to have a good moan.

"He does!" Lina said. "Of course, Étienne doesn't see it."

"I think we should tell them they need to leave," I said. "It was better when it was just the three of us."

"There's no need." We both turned round to see a dripping wet and hurt-looking Benedict.

"Benedict, er...hi!" I said, cringing and blushing and throwing Lina a guilty look.

"We'll go tomorrow. After Étienne's birthday," he said, and then he walked away.

I looked at Lina. "How much of that do you reckon he heard?"

She pulled a face. "Ooh, I'd say the whole lot."

"Right, well, bit awkward that."

"Just a bit," Lina said.

"I guess we sorted the whole getting them to leave situation though."

She nodded. "We did."

I frowned. "Hang on. Did he say it was *Étienne's* birthday?"

DON'T VOLUNTEER FOR IMPOSSIBLE TASKS

Lina and I took the firewood we'd collected over to the camp and discussed the fact that Benedict had known it was Étienne's birthday and we hadn't. I was not happy about it.

Étienne was shaking water out of his ears and Giuseppe was stretched out, drying himself in the sun. Benedict didn't look up when I said, "How's it going?"

Lukas ruffled Étienne's hair. "Did you know it's this little guy's birthday today?"

"Benedict told us," I said and looked at Étienne. "Why didn't you tell anyone?"

"He did. He told me," Benedict said.

Étienne looked a bit apologetic. "I *think* it might be

today. I'm not sure. I tried to keep track; I might have got it wrong."

"That doesn't matter!" Benedict said. "Today *shall* be your birthday and tonight we will have a party! A party to celebrate you, Étienne! And a party to mark the end of our stay here."

Francesca, who had been lying down with a leaf over her face to shield her from the sun, sat up. "You're ready? You think we should leave?"

"I do. Tomorrow," Benedict said, then looked at me. "I sense it's time."

Francesca nodded and Lukas let out a deep breath and said, "Okay then."

For a moment nobody said anything, and a vague feeling of guilt swirled in me. It had been what I wanted, but I felt bad about how it had come about.

Étienne looked out to sea, his chin wobbling. Benedict saw and gave him a little nudge. "Hey, it will be okay. We've survived before, we can do it again. We'll make it back and we'll get you rescued – you see if we don't."

"Yeah, we will!" Lukas said and jumped up and punched the air. "But first, my fellow **Climate Avengers**, we party!"

Benedict leaped up next to him and so did Francesca and they all started chanting, "**Party, party, party!**"

Étienne looked a little broken. "I don't think I could celebrate knowing that you're all leaving. That we might never see you again."

Francesca held up a finger. "Nope. None of that. Positive attitudes only, please! We are throwing you a party whether you like it or not. It's our parting gift to you. Besides, we want to go out on a high!"

"It doesn't seem right," Étienne said.

"We want to," Benedict said, "to show you how much you mean to us."

Now, I know I had kind of forced Benedict and the others to take a perilous journey across the Pacific Ocean, but my guilt about that was not enough to stem the competitiveness that suddenly surged through me.

I jumped up. "We want to as well, don't we, Lina? It's your birthday and you're *our* best friend and *we* are going to throw you the best party ever."

"Absolutely, *we'll* throw you the best party ever!" Lina said, and we both looked at Benedict so he understood who should be in charge of the party organization.

I jabbed my finger at Étienne. "Yeah, the best party ever. Got it?" I might have sounded a little more threatening than strictly necessary, but the others needed a reminder of who Étienne's *actual* friends were. "We just need some time to plan it."

But then Francesca and Benedict and Lukas started to throw suggestions around before Lina and I even had a chance to think.

Francesca leaped up from the sand and clapped her hands together. "We can play games and make our own party outfits!"

"Party outfits?" Lina didn't look convinced. "I'm not sure Étienne would want that."

"I'm happy for that, if it's what people want," Étienne said unhelpfully.

"Definitely party outfits!" Benedict said. "We can make them from whatever we can find."

"And have a competition to see whose looks the best!" Francesca said.

"I'll go into the jungle and get us a decent feast," Lukas said. "It should be extra-special food for an extra-special day!"

Étienne's smile was quickly replaced with a worried frown.

Lukas laughed his boomy laugh, which, as Lina had pointed out, could probably have been heard on the other side of the island. "Don't worry, I won't hunt any of your beloved animals. But I'll prepare you a birthday dinner to remember."

Lina and I flashed each other a look. The party planning

was getting out of control. We needed to take charge.

"Presents!" I said. "We'll be in charge of presents."

"Great, thanks, guys." Benedict spoke like we were doing him a favour. Lina and I exchanged more scowly looks.

Étienne clutched his hand to his chest and sat down on the sand.

"Are you okay?" Francesca asked.

He lifted his glasses up and used Giuseppe's tail to dab his eyes, which wasn't at all hygienic and something I made a note to discuss with him later. "Yes, I'm good," he said, "just a little overwhelmed, that's all. Thank you. And while I am really missing home and my parents terribly today, I couldn't wish to be **shipwrecked** on an island with better people." Giuseppe gave him a little nudge. "Or goats. I really am lucky."

I was about to say, "We're the lucky ones," when Benedict beat me to it and then bent down and gave him a hug and then Francesca and Lukas joined in.

Lina and I stood there not hugging Étienne and giving each other angry looks.

"Come on," I hissed, "we're going to get Étienne the present to end all presents!" I stomped off towards the jungle with absolutely no idea what we could get him. It wasn't like there was an Argos round the corner.

We hadn't got too far into the forest when Lina finally put into words what I'd been thinking.

"Sebastian, what on earth can we get Étienne as a present in a jungle? He's not going to want a rock or a creeper, is he?!"

I had no idea and it was stressing me out. Though it was not the only thing that was worrying me. "I know, I know!" I agreed. "But I had to say we'd be in charge of something! I didn't know what else to do. They'd already taken all the other jobs."

"They did, didn't they?! What did I tell you about them coming here and taking over?"

"You told me you were worried they would come here and take over."

"That was a rhetorical question, Sebastian! But they'll be gone soon, which is what we wanted." She let out a sigh. "So why do I feel bad that they're going?"

"Because we know what it's like out there on the ocean. Because we're letting them take that risk in the hope that they'll save us. Because it's us who had a problem with them staying here."

"That was a rhetorical question too, Sebastian! Way to make me feel worse than I already do!"

"They always said they'd leave. We just gave them the nudge to do it."

"I feel rotten."

"Me too, but we can apologize to Benedict when he's boarding their boat. In the meantime we've got a gift to find."

She groaned. "What on earth are we going to get him?"

"We know Étienne better than anyone, I'm sure we'll figure it out."

She raised a disbelieving eyebrow. "You're sure?"

"Yes." I was not sure in the slightest, but I thought it would be best to approach the task with some confidence. "I'm sure we'll know when we see it."

We spent ages trawling through the jungle trying to find things that might be suitable presents for Étienne and, once we had a selection of items, we worked on our outfits for the party.

That evening, we sat round the campfire looking quite **magnificent** in our home-made coconut-shell swimwear and palm-leaf headdresses and vine-creeper armbands. Lukas had made an excellent feast – he'd managed to catch loads of fish as well as a hermit crab who I hoped wasn't **Herbie Herbertson**.

Lina and I went to collect Étienne, who was waiting in the shelter.

"We're ready for you!"

Étienne came out in a towering headdress and grass

skirt that was so long it trailed on the floor behind him. He held a stick with a curved end that he had wrapped in a creeper vine. Giuseppe was also wearing an outfit that was a smaller version of Étienne's.

"Wow! Étienne! You look like a tropical Bo Peep!" I said.

"Thank you?" he said uncertainly.

"I think what Sebastian is trying to say is that you look fantastic," Lina said.

We started the party with the costume competition. Francesca had marked out a runway with stones and rocks and made little fires inside coconut shells to light our way. We went in alphabetical order, with Benedict going first. He'd obviously paid attention to how catwalk models work it because that boy could strut. At the end he pulled a series of poses and we all cheered, Lina and I whooping especially loudly, probably in an attempt to make up for what had happened earlier.

Étienne and Giuseppe were up next, but Giuseppe got stage fright and Étienne practically had to drag him down the catwalk. I think he was overcome with the spectacle of it all because at the end instead of posing he did the most ginormous wee. Giuseppe, not Étienne.

Lukas stomped down in quite an alarming way. Francesca took ages because she kept stopping to pose and flick her hair and flash her teeth. Lina got a bit carried away on her go. I think she was trying to better Francesca. She took even longer posing and hair-flicking, but I don't think she quite achieved the effect she was going for, because her hair-flicking was quite ferocious. Then, when she finished, she had to sit down and take a quiet moment because she felt a bit dizzy.

As I was up last, I knew I would have to pull something **spectacular** out of the bag if I wanted to win, so I did a cartwheel at the end. Unfortunately, my coconut top came loose and hit me in the face, which everyone else seemed to think was hilarious.

We decided that, as everyone looked so brilliant and had tried so hard, we all should get ten out of ten and all be winners, which I suppose was nice, but I think everyone knew that I had done that little bit extra with my cartwheel.

We stuffed ourselves until our bellies swelled and then Benedict announced it was time to give Étienne his gifts.

Lina and I had worked out a big, long spiel to say, in the hope that it would make what really were rather dull jungle items seem more special.

"Happy Birthday," Lina said and handed over the first gift, which we had wrapped in a large banana leaf.

I cleared my throat and began, "Étienne, our bestest friend, on your birthday as a token of how much you mean to us, we would like to present you with this—"

"Rock?" he said, holding it up.

"If you allow me to continue, this is no ordinary rock—"

"It looks like an ordinary rock to me," Lukas rudely interrupted.

"It is not just an ordinary rock—"

"What, does it have special powers?" Francesca asked, sounding very sarcastic.

"No, it does not have special powers," I said.

"So just a rock then?" Benedict said.

"Would you all just close your cakeholes and let me finish!" I shouted. Then I realized I may have overreacted and added a "Please."

"Sorry, do explain about the magical rock," Lukas said.

"Thank you, I will. This rock is no ordinary rock. This rock is special because it is special. Just like Étienne."

Lina looked at me, her eyebrows ramming into each other like they do when she's annoyed. "That's not what we discussed. You said you were going to make it sound really good."

"I haven't finished yet. The rock is special like you because it is not as big as some other rocks, but it is still strong and determined—"

"Rocks can't be determined, can they?" Francesca interrupted.

"This one is. And it is reliable and strong—"

"—you said strong already," Lukas interrupted but Benedict shushed him.

"And it's a little bit shiny if you hold it up to the light and Étienne is shiny too and the rock will always be here, so it is loyal like Étienne—"

Luckily, Étienne put me out of my misery and jumped up and gave me a hug and said, "Thank you, this is the best rock ever. I love it."

Which was a lovely moment but ruined by Lukas saying, "It's not better than Ayers Rock though, is it? Now that's what I call a rock," which earned him a very strong look from Lina.

"What else did you get him?" Francesca asked. "A *special* stick perhaps? To show how you'll always stick by him?"

We did indeed have a stick for Étienne, which we had carved his name into using a sharp flint. Well, most of his name. We'd only managed Étie, but it was very hard work and we had to sort out our costumes. I'd been planning on saying that while it wasn't the biggest of all the sticks it was still a very strong stick just like Étienne, but what Francesca had said sounded better so now I didn't know what to do.

"For your next present, Étienne," I began, "we would like to present you with a—"

"**Boat!**" Lina said.

And I said, "Hey?"

"**BOAT!**" Lina shouted this time.

I turned to Étienne and said, "I'm sorry, we don't have a boat for you, but what we do have is this stick which might not be the biggest—"

Lina walloped me quite ferociously on the shoulder. "No, you wally! **BOAT!** Out there on the horizon!"

We all turned round.

And there it was.

A tiny black dot of hope, way out where the water met the sky.

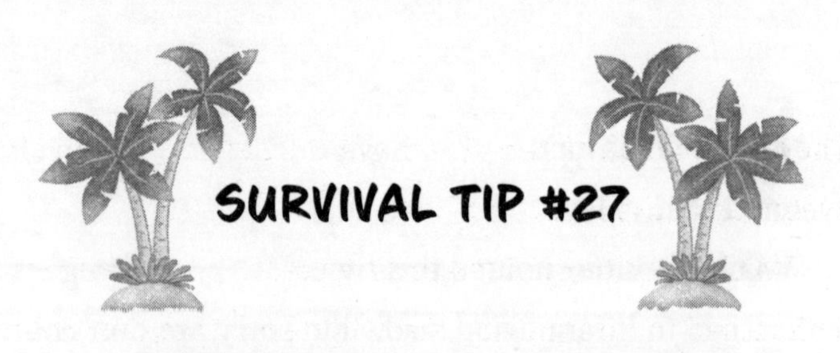

SURVIVAL TIP #27

TRY NOT TO FALL ASLEEP WHEN HELP ARRIVES

For a moment, no one knew what to do. We just stood there, dressed in our jungle finery, gawping at the sea.

A **boat**.

There really was a **boat**.

I wondered, for a moment, if my dad might be on board and felt a wave of desperate emotion roll through me. I thought about him standing at the prow, in his crisp, clean uniform. Of what I'd say to him. Of what he might say to me.

It was only when Giuseppe bleated very loudly that we realized we should probably stop gawping and do something.

Lina quickly started ordering everybody about. "Quick, load more wood onto the fire. We need it to be big! Huge.

They have to see it! They just have to!" she said. Then she eyeballed Giuseppe. "If only we still had a flare!"

Which was a fair point but, as we didn't, we sprang into action, moving frantically, throwing everything we could find onto the flames. When we had run out of wood to burn, we went to the jungle and cut down more and more. We only stopped when the flames and smoke were billowing high into the sky.

"There," Benedict said, standing back and crossing his arms. "They're bound to see that."

"For sure," I said, squinting at the silhouette of the boat, my skin tightening against the heat of the fire. "Although, it looks like they've stopped still."

I felt the worry ripple through us. The thought that whoever was on the ship might not come to our rescue was too dreadful to consider.

"They've probably anchored up. I don't think they'll approach until morning when they can see to navigate around the reef," Lina said and everyone agreed that was probably, hopefully – no, definitely – the reason.

"Should we row out to it?" Étienne asked.

"I don't think we should chance getting through the reef at night either," Benedict said. "They're far out and with that current we might not make it to them, even if we make it past the coral."

We stood a little longer, staring at the boat, worried that if we took our eyes away from it for even a moment, it might disappear.

"I don't believe it's really there. That there's really a boat," Étienne whispered. He was standing with one hand on Giuseppe's back and his birthday rock under his arm. He was quite a sight in his headgear and skirt, illuminated by the light of the raging fire. Possibly looking a little intimidating – warrior-like, even – if it hadn't been for the tears glistening in his eyes.

"It's there alright," Lukas said. Then he did something quite unexpected. He burst into tears too. "Thank God we won't have to row out on the ocean again."

Francesca placed her hand on his back and he sniffed and shook himself and forced the tears away.

Benedict bumped Étienne gently with his shoulder. "What a birthday, hey, little guy!"

Étienne nodded, cried a little, then wiped his eyes, thankfully not on Giuseppe this time, and said, "What a birthday." But his words were stifled by a yawn so big it was as though all the weeks of tiredness and emotion had suddenly been expelled from his body.

I suddenly felt overwhelmingly tired too. "Maybe we should take it in turns to sleep so we can keep a watch out and the fire burning?"

"That is an excellent idea," Benedict said. "Lukas, Francesca and I will take the first shift, if you like?"

"Sounds like a plan," Lina said.

Without bothering to change, we stumbled into our wing of the **Ritz** and crumpled down onto the floor, Giuseppe taking his usual place across the doorway and Étienne using his back as a pillow.

"My heart is beating so fast but my body is so tired, and I don't know whether I'm going to fall straight to sleep or start spinning in circles," he said.

"I know what you mean," Lina said. "I never thought—"

She stopped but I knew what she was going to say. She never thought we'd get off the island. As much as we'd talked about someone showing up to rescue us, I don't think any of us truly believed it would happen.

"What's the first thing you're going to do when you get back?" she said.

"Hug my parents," Étienne said, "and never let go."

"Me too," Lina said.

Even though Dad and I weren't that good at hugging each other, I said, "Me too." Because at that moment I couldn't think of anything else I'd rather do than hug my dad – and my mum. The hope that I might soon be able to do that felt too big and I thought I might cry so I said,

"Then order a pizza and a bucket of Coke," to change the subject before anyone noticed.

"Oh yes! And have a hot shower and wash my hair with actual shampoo," Étienne said with a happy sigh.

"Use a flushing toilet," Lina added.

"Sleep in a real bed," I said as I tried to find a comfortable position on the floor.

"We're going home," Lina whispered. "We're really going home."

"Yes, we are," I said, a rush of happiness filling my heart and sleepiness closing my eyelids.

But we weren't – not then, anyway.

Benedict and the others must have taken a long first watch, because when they shook us awake the first thing I noticed was that the sun was just peeking out from behind the horizon. The second thing I noticed was that the fire was out.

"We have to go," Benedict said, with a tightness in his voice that I didn't like.

I sat upright, my headdress tilting dramatically to one side.

Étienne rubbed his eyes and yawned. "What's going on?"

“We fell asleep…and that boat…the people, look, we just need to go,” Benedict said.

“Francesca and Lukas have gone on ahead.”

“You fell *asleep*?!” Lina said in a truly terrifying manner.

“I’ll explain later but we need to go now. Come, quickly.”

“No! You explain now!” Lina jumped to her feet and stormed outside, tripping over a sleeping Giuseppe.

We all raced after her as she headed towards the shore.

“Lina, stop!” Benedict shouted.

She spun round, her eyes wild. “Where’s the boat, Benedict?”

We all stared at him. I could hear blood pounding in my ears. The world began to spin. The boat can’t have gone.

“Where’s the boat, Benedict?” I said slowly. “Seriously, where’s the boat?”

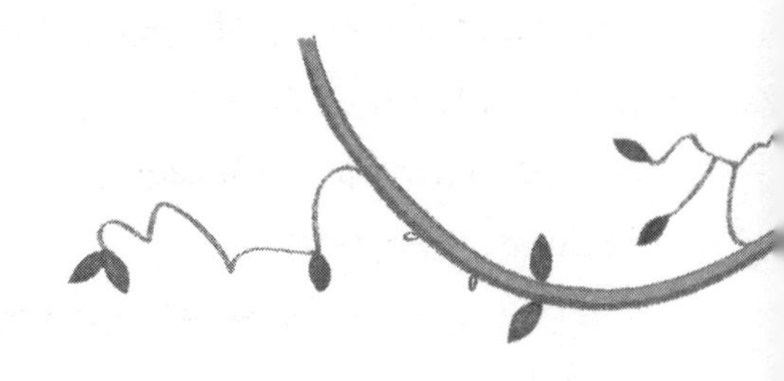

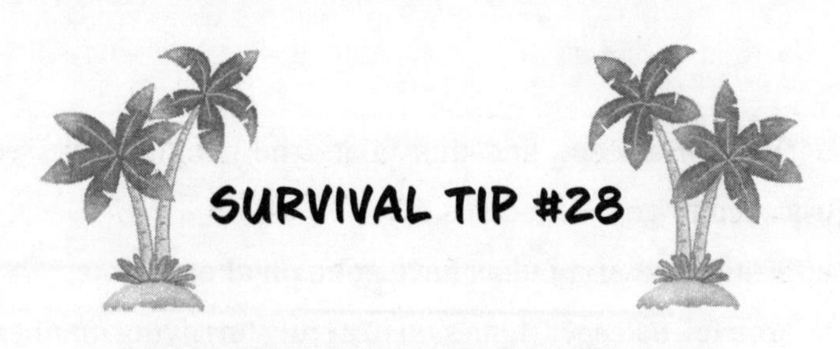

ASSESS THE SITUATION CAREFULLY – HELP ISN'T ALWAYS WHAT IT SEEMS

Benedict shifted from foot to foot and looked at each of us in turn. "Don't panic," he said but as *he* looked fairly panicked it was hard not to think that panicking was a suitable reaction. "Current thinking", he said, "is that the boat is on the other side of the island – to the north-west beyond the cave. We woke up and spotted it as it sailed round the corner. Francesca and Lukas have headed that way already."

My legs felt weak under me. Benedict couldn't have lost an entire boat.

"Current thinking? *Current thinking?*" Lina grabbed hold of Benedict's arms and shook him. "You mean you don't *know*? Tell me you know!"

"Er...well...we suspect—"

"*You suspect?!*" Lina shook Benedict about some more. Then she let go of his arms and promptly began to hyperventilate, although quite angrily and loudly. "This isn't happening, *this isn't happening*—" She bent over and took three deep breaths.

"Unbelievable... *Unbelievable!*" Then she dropped to her knees. "NO...! No!" Three more deep breaths. "Can't... can't...breathe." More big breaths. "You. Are. An. Idiot!" Lots of short fast breaths. "Can't...can't...breathe! You idiot!"

Étienne said, "Calm your breathing, Lina. It's going to be okay."

"This is not okay! I can't breathe!" she howled and flopped forward onto her face.

"You're making an awful lot of noise for someone who can't breathe," I said, but very quietly, so she couldn't hear and direct all her rage at me.

Benedict put his hands under Lina's armpits and lifted her up and popped her back on her feet.

"We were going to eat shampoo on a flushing loo while Étienne washed his hair with pizza in a hot shower!" she wailed.

Benedict tilted his head to the side. "You were going to do what?"

"We weren't going to do any of that!" I said, slightly horrified at the image Lina had conjured up. Then I whispered, "I think Lina is having a difficult moment right now, which is understandable seeing as you lot may have ruined our chance of ever getting home."

Lina started stomping about in circles and yelling out random words like, "**Pizza! Duvet! Showers! Toothpaste!** I miss them all!"

"Are you okay?" Benedict asked, which I think was brave of him in the circumstances.

"Am I okay? *Am I okay?*" Lina said and then began laughing maniacally.

It was clear to everyone that the answer was no, she really wasn't okay. But to make sure, she started throwing rocks into the sea and shouting, "**I HATE THIS PLACE! I HATE THE SAND! I HATE THE SUN! I HATE THE SEA! I HATE THE JUNGLE! I HATE THE INSECTS! I HATE THE TOILET!**" Which was taking things too far if you ask me. "**AND I REALLY, REALLY HATE BREADFRUIT AND I JUST WANT TO GO HOME!**"

I was a little surprised, to be honest. Not by the fact that she wanted to go home – but that she hated **Sunrise Island** so much. I'd thought we all liked it here.

Then she shouted at Giuseppe, "**AND WHAT ARE YOU LOOKING AT, YOU STUPID FLARE-DESTROYING ANIMAL?**"

This was too much for Étienne. You don't insult a boy's goat. "Lina Lim, you stop this right now and apologize!" He stepped forward and waggled his finger at her. "This is no way for a leader to act. That is, if you are still our leader. Now is not the time for tantrums, young lady. Now is the time for action. I think Benedict is right. We need to go over to the other side of the island and see if we can find this boat."

"That was very brave," I whispered to him out of the side of my mouth.

Lina glared at him with a slightly unnerving look on her face.

Étienne gulped, then continued – although with a little less confidence than he had started, "So...are you coming? Or are you going to stay here shouting at the sea and stamping your feet?"

Lina stared at him for the longest time. Then she pushed her knotted hair behind her ears, adjusted her coconut bikini top and nodded. "Yes, Étienne. I am going with you. I apologize for my outburst."

"Thank you, but it's not me you need to apologize to." He nodded towards Giuseppe.

Lina did a big, exasperated scream. "Fine! Giuseppe, I am sorry for calling you a stupid flare-destroying animal. Even if it is true."

Then she marched off up the beach, her leafy skirt flapping furiously behind her. And even though our situation wasn't brilliant, witnessing Lina apologizing to a goat was definitely one of the best things I have ever seen.

We made our way to the cave, then climbed up it and through the jungle beyond. We passed the stream and the place where we'd collected bananas and blongberries and rambutans, and continued until we reached the rocks that looked out over the north-west side of the island. They weren't as high as the ones we had climbed on the east side, but they were steep and difficult to navigate.

We found Lukas and Francesca just below a ridge. They were sitting cross-legged, sharing sips from a coconut. I threw myself down, grateful for a chance to rest. The climb had been hard going – only Giuseppe had made relatively easy work of it, pretty much skipping up the rocky face. We, however, had needed to concentrate on where we put our feet the whole way, in case we stepped on a loose stone and tumbled to our deaths, as Lina kept telling us would happen if we weren't careful. What with the threat of imminent doom and her being in quite a snappy mood, it had been rather a stressful journey.

"We found the boat," Lukas announced as we clambered

up and joined them in their resting place.

"You found the boat?" Lina closed her eyes and exhaled. "What a relief!"

Francesca nodded and passed round another coconut half. "It's down the other side of this hill. There's another little beach and they are moored up out there but—" She paused. I could sense something was wrong.

"But what?" I asked.

"I think we need to approach carefully," Lukas said.

"Why?" I asked.

"If we approach," Francesca said, "and that's a big *if*."

"Why wouldn't we approach?" I said. "That boat is our ticket home!" By the looks on Lina and Étienne's faces, they were as confused as me.

"The people – they don't look that friendly. I don't think they're here for good reasons. Have a look for yourself," Lukas said, nodding towards the top of the hill.

"But don't all of you go – there's not much cover up there," Francesca warned. "You don't want to be seen."

I thought being seen was exactly what we were aiming for. I wanted to shout and leap about to attract attention, but there was something about the fearful look in Francesca's eyes that stopped me. I needed to see what the problem was. "I'll go and report back."

"I'll go with you," Benedict said and set off up the cliff.

I followed him as he climbed the short distance up over the ridge to where we could see the boat anchored in the shimmering waters of the cove. I was expecting to feel excited, but my heart sank a little when I saw it. This wasn't the type of boat my dad would sail. It was a medium-sized vessel with a motor and battered and rusty around the helm. There was a torn black flag flapping about in the breeze. I counted three people on board. Although there may have been another crew member in the cabin at the front where the steering wheel was. At the back there were stacks of crates and in the crates were... I wasn't quite sure what they were. I leaned over the ridge a little further.

"Benedict, what are those?" I said. "In the crates...are they moving?"

Benedict nodded. "Those, Sebastian, are turtles."

"Turtles?"

Benedict ran his hand through his hair and puffed out a long stream of air from his cheeks. "The boat is crewed by turtle traffickers, Sebastian."

"**Pirates**." I sort of breathed the word. "That's not the most brilliant news, is it?"

"Probably not the best, no."

We stayed looking at them for a while as they busied themselves about the boat. They were the first other people I'd seen in ages. They almost looked like other-worldly beings. We could hear an occasional shout but weren't close enough to make out what they were saying. Two of the crew seemed to get into a bit of a fight and there was some pushing and shoving, but the biggest guy pulled them apart and they settled down. Even from where we were, they didn't seem like the friendliest people. The hope I had for rescue twisted into a fear that it might not happen. That these people might not be the ones to save us. Then the fear twisted again into an anger at the injustice of it all.

"Oi! You two, what are you doing? Sightseeing?" Lina hissed up at us.

We climbed back down to break the news that our rescuers were in fact a band of probably dangerous turtle-trafficking pirates.

"Turtle traffickers!" Étienne gasped. "They're not after Tarquin's babies, are they?"

Francesca swallowed. "Maybe. Probably. But what might be slightly more important is that I doubt these guys are going to risk rescuing a group of missing kids, considering the business they're in."

"And why's that?" Lina asked.

Francesca sighed and kicked a stone off the ledge. "What they're doing is illegal. They could go to prison for years if they're caught."

"Good!" Étienne said.

"What's not good is that they won't be happy about there being witnesses to their crime. I don't think we should approach them – we don't know how they might react," Francesca continued.

I thought she had a point. I'd been thinking the same.

But Lukas had a point too. "I think we should still try. This could be our only chance to get back home."

"But what about the turtles?" Étienne said.

"What about *us*?" said Lukas.

I was with Lukas on that. It was typically lovely of Étienne to be more worried about Tarquin's offspring than our ticket home. Typically lovely, but also a bit daft.

"What if Francesca's right and they don't want people around who could tell on them?" Lina said.

Lukas said, "They might just drop us off somewhere if we promise to keep our mouths shut."

"They might," Benedict said, "but they might not. Are you willing to risk that?"

DO YOUR RESEARCH SO YOU KNOW WHAT YOU'RE UP AGAINST

As no one was saying anything, I quickly weighed up the arguments for both sides and said, "I say we go for it. What's the worst that could happen?"

To which Francesca then explained, in quite gruesome detail, what she thought the worst could be – what such people might be capable of.

I gulped. "Oh, that is quite bad, isn't it? Maybe we should give these guys a miss and wait for someone else to show up and rescue us."

Étienne had gone completely white and was clinging onto Giuseppe like he was a furry comfort blanket.

"Don't worry, Étienne," I said, "we won't let any of those things that Francesca described happen. Your eyeballs will remain exactly where they are."

"But what if no one else shows up? This really could be our only chance," Lukas said, which sent us all back into quiet thought again.

Until Lina inconsiderately clapped her hands loudly and shouted, "I know!" and made everyone jump. "I say we spy on them, figure out if they are dangerous. Or...this is better! We could also sneak onto their boat and steal their radio and call for help!" She was becoming more and more animated as she was speaking. "Yeah, that's what we'll do. We'll wait until they come ashore and, when they're busy, we'll creep onto their boat and use their radio!"

"If we're on their boat, why don't we just steal the boat?" Lukas said, which seemed like a reasonable suggestion.

"Steal the boat?" Étienne said in a very small voice.

"I like it!" Lina said, nodding furiously.

Benedict rubbed his chin. "It could work."

"Stealing a boat from dangerous pirates?" Étienne said in a now very small and very shaky voice.

"It seems quite risky," Francesca said. "What if it goes wrong?"

Étienne brought his hands to his glasses and said, "I like my eyeballs."

"They are very lovely," I said because I felt he needed to hear something nice at that point. He was not dealing with the whole dangerous turtle-pirate thing well at all.

He said, "You've got lovely eyeballs too. I like that one is blue and one is green."

"It won't go wrong," Lina said. "Neither of you are going to lose your lovely eyeballs."

Lina was proven to be fifty per cent correct about that statement. Luckily for us, it was the latter part that she got right. Étienne is still in possession of two rather lovely, if slightly myopic, eyeballs. And I still have one eyeball that reminds me of Mum and one that reminds me of Dad. Our attempt to sail off in the turtle-trafficking-pirates' boat, however, did go wrong.

Spectacularly wrong.

It was decided that, as we weren't totally committed to stealing the boat, we'd just spy on the pirates a bit and see if: 1. They actually were friendly and might offer us a ride home and 2. An opportunity would arise for a spot of non-perilous ship-hijacking.

"You never know," I said. "They might head off for a bit of sightseeing and leave the boat completely unattended."

Obviously, that didn't happen.

We made a plan to watch from the top of the ridge, but the pirates didn't come to shore until nightfall, and we spent many hot, uncomfortable hours sitting on the rock, eating bananas and drinking from coconuts while our bums grew numb. We'd almost given up when they finally brought the boat into the shallows. It was dark, but the men had head torches on, so we could just about see what they were up to. The boat anchored and three men climbed down the ladder and into the water. They waded through to the beach, carrying something on their heads.

"Are those crates?" Étienne said, squinting behind his glasses.

One of their light beams paused on something in the sand.

"Do you see that?" I could just about make out that sand was being flicked about by some unseen thing.

"What *is* that?" Francesca asked.

Étienne pulled himself up a little higher. "Turtles." He took a deep breath. "Those are baby turtles hatching. Another turtle must have laid its eggs on this side of the island!"

Étienne was right as, from under the sand, the first tiny turtle body burst its way into the world, its little flippers flapping about energetically. It pulled itself forward towards the sea, making a little trail behind it. But before it got very far, the spotlight on it grew smaller and the pirate approached.

"No!" Étienne cried. "We have to do something."

"What can we do?" Francesca asked.

It was terrible to watch. The little fella was plucked from the sand and tossed into one of the crates.

The torch beam tracked back across the sand, pausing when it fell on more movement.

Another turtle had dug itself out.

I felt my stomach clench. *Hide, little turtle dude. Hide!*

But the turtle couldn't see the threat that we could, and it began wiggling across the sand, searching for water, only to find itself chucked into a box.

More and more turtles started to emerge. So many baby turtles.

"We can't just sit here and watch this happen," Étienne said. It was dark but I could tell by the catch in his voice that he was crying. "We should go down there and stop them!"

"How are we going to do that?" Lina asked. "I don't think appealing to their better nature will work. And I don't see a way we can steal their boat with them so close."

"I can't watch this." Étienne dropped down from his viewing position and hugged his head in his knees. Giuseppe, who'd been sleeping, stirred and nestled his head against him. The rest of us carried on watching the beach until the very last turtle had been plucked from the sand. The men then loaded the crates back onto the boat and climbed aboard. After a while, they turned off their lights and we decided that they must have gone to sleep.

We would have to work out what we were going to do in the morning – try and hijack their boat and rescue the turtles, or ask them to take us home, or do nothing and let them and our chance of rescue go.

With it being so late and everyone being so tired and our hearts so heavy, we thought that we should sleep too. Nobody fancied climbing down the mountain and walking back through the jungle in the dark, so we all slept together on the ledge, using each other for body heat.

That night, Lina said she didn't want to go round and say what made us proud and nobody objected. I guess none of us felt particularly proud. We'd just sat by and watched all those baby turtles being taken and done nothing about it.

"Let's wait until tomorrow," Benedict said. "We might have something we're proud of then."

I hoped he was right.

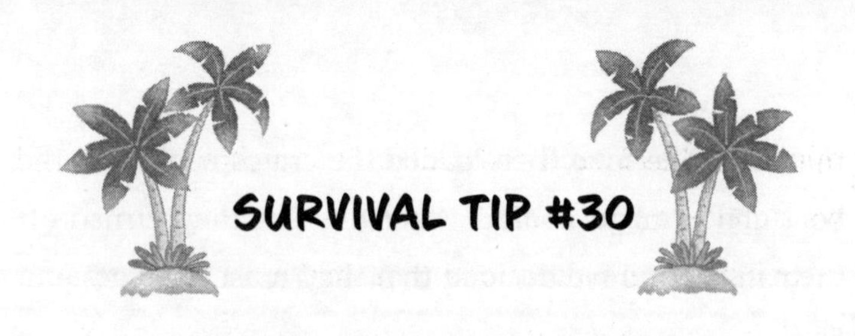

HAVING A GOAT ON YOUR TEAM CAN PROVE TO BE VERY USEFUL

I woke up hot and sweaty. Sleeping with your head between a goat's legs and under Lukas's giant arm will do that to you.

We all peeled ourselves free of each other and sat up under the blazing island sun. Benedict was first on his feet and quickly scrambled to go and see what the pirates were up to.

"Guys!" he shouted, furiously scratching a patch of mosquito bites on his arm. "They're not there!"

"What do you mean they're not there?" Lina said as she climbed to the viewing point.

"I don't know how to say it any more simply – the boat – it's gone."

"What **AGAIN**?!" Lina threw her hands in the air and

tipped her head back and wailed. “I don’t believe it! Could we stop losing the boat!”

Soon we were all squeezed up on the ledge, staring out at the place where the boat had been. I didn’t know whether to feel sad or relieved.

Lukas did know how to feel though. He let out an almighty **roar**, picked up a rock and chucked it as far as he could. “I KNEW WE SHOULD HAVE GONE AND SEEN THEM! What were we thinking? Any chance of getting back home is better than no chance.” Then he turned on Francesca and said, “This is your fault. With your stories of them chopping us up and feeding our eyeballs to the fishes!”

“I can understand why you are upset,” I said, “but in all fairness, I think that the possibility of being turned into fish food was right to have given us pause for thought.”

Lukas swung round and glared down at me. “I’ll turn somebody into fish food if they keep talking.”

I held my hands up and leaned away from him. “I can see emotions are running high right now. Maybe we should just head back to camp and calm down.”

“You calm down,” Lukas fired back.

“Okay...” I said. “I am actually quite calm.”

“Stop being such a jerk, Lukas,” Francesca said. “This isn’t anybody’s fault.”

"*Me* a jerk?" Lukas fired back.

"Would everybody **STOP!**" Étienne shouted and we were so surprised by how loud and cross he sounded and how terribly upset he looked, that we did stop. "Haven't any of you realized? They might be after Tarquin's babies. *Our* babies! We have to do something!"

Étienne turned and started to scramble down the cliff, Giuseppe bolting down after him. Both of them ignored our pleas to stop.

"I have to protect them!" Étienne said, in full-on **Climate Avenger** mode.

I chased after him and managed to catch up faster than I expected, since I slipped and slid down a couple of metres on my bum. "Étienne," I said as I crashed face first into Giuseppe. "Please stop a moment! We can't just go charging into a group of turtle traffickers. We need to have a plan!"

Étienne came to a stop, chest heaving and breath ragged.

"Étienne, please." I took hold of his hands. "We need to think before we do something rash."

His shoulders dropped and his eyes became less wild. "You're right."

"We'll head back to camp together and figure out what to do," I said, although I had no clue what that would be.

Lina and the others had reached us now. "We'll think of something," she said, but when I looked at my friends, I could see from their expressions that they had no idea either.

Nobody spoke much on the journey back to camp. I guess we were all trying to make sense of everything that had happened. Thoughts rolled in my mind like waves. I thought about turtles, the ones stuck on crates on that boat and of our turtles that might end up joining them. How, like us, they'd be trapped. I thought about the happiness I'd felt the night before when we'd seen the boat, and how completely that happiness had been dashed. I thought of home, and how it seemed to be getting further and further away. And I tried to think of a plan to make everything right, but it seemed impossible.

When we came to the edge of the jungle near our camp, Benedict, who was leading, suddenly gave the signal to be quiet and get down.

"They're here!" he whispered.

Even though we were hidden in the undergrowth, we could just about see the boat anchored up in our lagoon. Two of the pirates were sitting around *our* campfire. They were cooking something in a pot while they munched through *our* stores of food. If that wasn't bad enough, the third one came out of my luxury toilet! We were far enough away not to be seen or heard but we had a decent view of what was going on.

Étienne crept forward and peered round a tree. "The ring of stones round the nest site hasn't been disturbed – Tarquin's eggs are okay!"

"Right, enough is enough, I'm going to speak to them," Lukas said. "They're going to know somebody's here anyway. They've seen all our stuff."

"No, Lukas!" Francesca tried to grab his arm to stop him, but he brushed her away and started to walk purposefully towards them.

"Lukas!" Lina stood up and blocked his way. "Wait a minute!"

Lukas didn't wait, he just ploughed straight through her, so Benedict rugby-tackled his legs and he dropped to the ground like a falling tree.

"Get off me!" Lukas spat.

Lina shushed him and I thought the pirates must have heard all the fuss, but they didn't seem to have noticed – they were too busy helping themselves to our supplies.

Lukas tried to get up, but Benedict pinned him down and then they started wrestling around in the dirt.

Francesca hissed, “Stop it, both of you!” But they didn’t listen.

“That is it!” Lina threw her hands up in the air in resignation. “I knew this would happen. Didn’t I say this would happen? It’s just like in **Lord of the Flies**. It all descends into **chaos** and **misery** from here.”

“She’s right.” Étienne pushed me towards them. “Sebastian, do something!”

“Like what?”

I don’t know why he thought I would be able to stop two **mutants** mid-wrestle, but I tried to persuade them anyway. I suggested that they should discuss things maturely, but I don’t think they were keen on that idea because they just rolled about even more. Things came to a head when they bowled into Étienne and knocked him over. **Giuseppe Garibaldi** was not happy about this and launched himself at them. Two strapping basketball players sporting grass skirts wrestling a goat is not something you see every day and the rest of us just stood there, watching.

Surprisingly, Giuseppe emerged as the victor, pinning them both down with his hooves.

Lukas thrashed about but Giuseppe held strong. “Étienne, tell your goat to stand down!”

Then Étienne, sounding very leader-like, said, “No,

Lukas. Not until you promise to listen to what I have to say."

Lukas started to say that he would do as he liked and would not be listening, but Étienne said, "I should warn you – Giuseppe can pee on demand."

I have no idea whether that was true or not, but I wouldn't have taken my chances, and neither did Lukas.

He held up his hands. "Fine, you have two minutes."

Étienne said, "Giuseppe, you can release them." And Giuseppe did as he was told, which really is quite incredible if you think about it. "What we are going to do now is what we planned to do before," Étienne continued. "We are going to spy on those pirates and see what they are up to, and I'll tell you this for nothing, if they go after Tarquin's turtles, we are not going to stand by like we did last night. We are going to stop them. As soon as the opportunity arises – maybe at night when they're asleep – we get on that boat and sail off, so they have no chance of trafficking **Eggbert** or **Ethel** or **Ernest** or **Edward** or—"

"You don't need to name them all, we get the picture," I said.

Étienne snapped a look at me and I shrank back.

"Does everybody understand?"

Our response was a bit muted, so Étienne said, "Are we

or are we not **Climate Avengers**?"

The others looked at him like he was off his coconut, but not wanting to leave a friend out on a limb I said, a little uncertainly, "We are?"

"That's right, Sebastian, we are. Now follow me. I know a place we can hide to listen in on them."

With that, Étienne strode back into the jungle and we followed him, Lukas and Benedict still scowling at each other, and all of us a little confused as to what had just happened.

"What is going on with Étienne?" Lina whispered to me.

"I'm not quite sure, but would you look at him! He's quite **spectacular**, isn't he?"

We both looked at the small figure of Étienne leading the way, his grass skirt trailing behind him and his faithful goat at his side, and Lina said, "He really is."

SURVIVAL TIP #31

BOOKS REALLY CAN GIVE YOU THE ANSWER

Étienne found us a great spot near our camp, behind a thicket of tightly woven creeper vines. From there, we had an excellent view and were able to hear everything the pirates were saying, while remaining safely hidden. It quickly became clear that the pirates *were* intending to stay until Tarquin's turtles hatched. Although obviously they didn't refer to her by name. Apparently, they'd been tracking turtles in the area for quite some time.

"May come tonight, may come in a couple of nights, but they'll hatch soon enough," the biggest of the men said as he stirred the cooking pot. He was wearing a pair of dirty grey tracksuit shorts and a very dirty white vest. He stretched back in the sand, rubbed his stubble and grinned. "We'll wait and we'll make good money. Easy times."

"Not if we've got anything to do with it," Étienne hissed.

Lina whispered to me, "Who even is he right now?"

"Boss, do you still think some other gang made this camp?" I couldn't really make out what the guy who said that looked like because he had his back to us, but he was wearing a black T-shirt and shorts and flip-flops. I'd never considered flip-flops to be top choice of footwear for a pirate, but there you go.

"I've never seen anyone in these parts who wasn't after making money from turtles."

"The two fishing boats – do you think that means they're still here?"

"No one could get all the way out here on those two tired-looking boats. My thinking is that they came on a bigger vessel, rowed ashore and staked the place out then scarpered when they saw us arrive."

"Without the rowing boats?"

"You know our reputation is enough to send a man fleeing."

The third pirate, the much older of the three and the one we hadn't heard speak yet, said in a low voice, "Or maybe something happened to them. Something bad."

The boss shook his head slowly. "Are you starting up again with your superstitions? You place too much belief in old stories."

"They might be hiding in the jungle," the flip-flop guy said. "The fire was still warm when we arrived."

I managed to stop myself from giving Lina an accusing look.

"Then maybe you should go and check," the boss said.

The guy looked towards the jungle, and we all shrank back.

"Get ready to run," Benedict whispered.

Flip-flops pulled a face like he didn't much fancy it. "I'm not checking the jungle." He probably realized he wasn't sporting the correct footwear for forest exploration. "You're right – they've likely taken off."

The boss nodded, then pulled what must have been a cocktail stick out from behind his ear and started working on his teeth. "They'd better not show up in our waters now, if they know what's good for them. These are our turtles, am I right?"

Étienne jutted out his chin and I swear I heard him do a little **growl**, like a very angry but ever so cute-looking tarsier monkey. Benedict put a hand on his shoulder, and because I was Étienne's actual best friend, I put my hand on his other shoulder.

The boss guy jabbed his teeny-tiny stick at the air. "Remember what happened to the last lot who tried to take from us?"

"They took a holiday at the bottom of the ocean," the flip-flop guy said.

"You want to go speak to them now, Lukas?" Francesca whispered.

Lukas didn't say anything, but I imagined his answer was no.

"No mistakes. We collect the turtles and we go, you hear?" the boss guy said. "We've a lot of money riding on this. A lot of money."

The older guy suddenly rose to his feet and stared directly towards our hiding place.

"I feel eyes on us," he said.

We all froze. Well, all of us except Giuseppe, who seemed to be busy trying to catch a butterfly in his mouth. Étienne held onto him, but Giuseppe *really* wanted that butterfly.

"Strange things," the old guy continued. "There are stories of beasts in these islands. Beasts that could snap the head clean off a man. Places like this seem like paradise, but you have one eye in heaven and the other in hell."

"Hush yourself!" the boss guy said, then pelted him with what looked like the last of the rambutans from Étienne's birthday party. "Sit down and enough with your myths. You are wrong in the head, old man."

The old pirate pointed his finger towards us. "I tell you there are bad things in these parts. I sense it. We should sleep on the boat tonight."

We were all trying to stay completely still and quiet, but Giuseppe was becoming increasingly animated in his pursuit of the butterfly. Francesca and Lina grabbed hold of him to stop him from making too much noise and giving us away, which Giuseppe wasn't thrilled about.

"Enough!" the boss guy said. "We'll build up the fire and sleep by it. That way we can keep an eye out for the turtles." He snarled. "There are no beasts, you fool."

Our own little beast, Giuseppe, continued to get more and more excited by the butterfly and Lina and Francesca desperately tried to restrain him, while the older guy kept his eyes fixed on the jungle. "I tell you, there's something in there. Something bad. I feel it in my bones. You can stay here, but I will sleep on the boat."

All the pirates turned and stared in our direction. I could see that, for all the boss guy's bravado, there was a small flicker of fear in his eyes. The jungle does that to you.

"Sleep in the boat with your fear for company," the boss guy said. "There's no such thing as beasts."

At that moment, the butterfly landed on Giuseppe's nose. Giuseppe went cross-eyed, trying to focus on it, but then the butterfly flew off and Giuseppe went a teensy bit **berserk**. He kicked himself free from Lina and Francesca and charged after the butterfly who, unfortunately, was heading straight towards camp. We watched in horror as he crashed through the thicket, his bandy legs bounding out onto the beach and a look of pure joy on his face.

Oh, Giuseppe.

The pirates shouted in alarm and leaped to their feet. The boss guy grabbed a filleting knife from his belt and held it up. Étienne lunged forward to go after Giuseppe, but Benedict and I grabbed hold of him.

The boss's face, which had been fixed in horror, relaxed and he started laughing. "You see, you old fool? Your beast is nothing but a goat. No goat I've heard of can snap the head off a man!"

The flip-flopped pirate joined in with the laughter, but the old guy kept his eyes on the jungle. "There are beasts out there, I tell you. I can feel them."

"You want to eat goat tonight?" the boss asked, nodding at Giuseppe, who was turning in circles, trying to catch the butterfly, which had settled on his bum.

I don't know if goats can gasp but on hearing the pirate's words, it sounded like Giuseppe did. He stopped spinning and eyeballed the men as though he was noticing them for the first time. His little face looked from the boss to Mr Flip-flop to the old guy and the sudden realization that he was not in the best company seemed to dawn in his bright goaty eyes.

Étienne tried to wiggle out of our grasp but, let's face it, that was never going to happen, not with Benedict's and my combined strength. Luckily, Giuseppe activated his own escape plan.

I've never seen a goat move so fast. He darted about the camp, kicking up sand everywhere. He knocked over a stack of breadfruit, then the cooking pot and dodged round the flip-flop guy as he made to tackle him.

Once he'd completed three full circuits of the firepit, he bolted back into the jungle, straight to our hiding place and into Étienne's open arms.

Giuseppe lapped his flicky pink tongue all over Étienne's face and Étienne kissed him back on his nose. The rest of us – while pleased about his return – shushed them both because we didn't want the joyous yet totally revolting reunion to blow our cover.

When their enthusiastic show of affection had finally finished, we stayed where we were, waiting to see if the pirates said anything else important. When they started discussing some TV soap called *Rainbow Days*, Lina whispered, "I think we've heard enough. Let's go."

Quietly, we moved deeper into the jungle, heading

back towards the stream where we had decided to make a new base. Lina and Benedict led the way with Giuseppe and Étienne taking up the rear. We spoke only to warn of a sharp rock or thorny branch to avoid. I felt an urge to sing something uplifting and triumphant to brighten the mood, but I'd only managed "**Hakuna Mata**", when Lina said, "No, absolutely not."

So I spent the walk in quiet contemplation and the most surprisingly **spectacular** thing happened.

I came up with the most surprisingly **spectacular** idea.

I know. I was shocked.

"I don't believe it!" I said, coming to a sudden halt which resulted in Giuseppe's face becoming way too familiar with my backside.

"You don't believe what?" Lina said. We'd just arrived at the stream, so she sat herself down on a large flat rock and Benedict positioned himself beside her.

"Okay, so...I think I have a plan that might be the answer to all our problems."

"I can't wait to hear this," Lukas said in a tone void of any belief.

"Give him a chance," Francesca said. "If it had been up to you we'd have bowled straight up to those traffickers and probably ended up being—"

I'm not going to go into all the details of what Francesca said next because they were truly terrible, but let's just say Étienne turned very white again and said, "But I like my feet almost as much as my eyeballs. I need my feet."

I said, "They are very wonderfully large flappy feet, Étienne, it is no wonder you like them. They're even a bit like flippers. Ooh, Beecham was right, you are like a turtle."

Lina looked at me rather strangely, then said with far more doubt in her voice than was polite, "Are you sure you have a plan?"

"Yes," I said confidently, "I absolutely do, and you can thank your man William Golding for the idea."

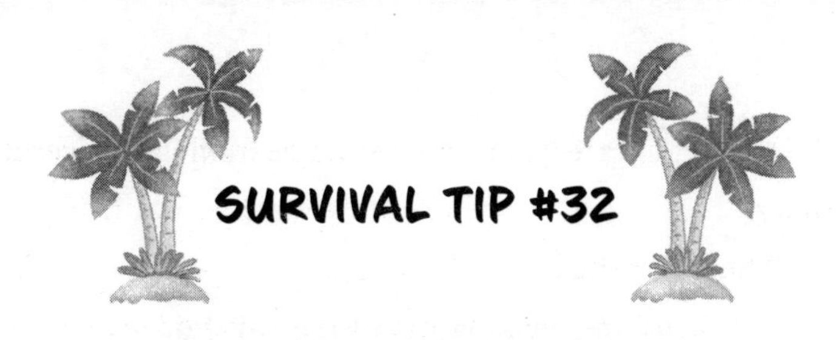

SOMETIMES YOU NEED TO CHANNEL THE BEAST INSIDE

After I finished telling everyone my **spectacular** idea about how we could stop the pirates stealing our turtles *and* then end up sailing off for home in their boat, everyone was disappointingly quiet.

I hadn't expected them to hoist me up onto their shoulders and call me a genius, but I was hoping for some sort of positive reaction. A light smattering of applause, for example.

Finally, Francesca broke the silence. "But do you really think we could be that scary? I mean..." Then she looked over at Étienne, who was cradling Giuseppe in his arms like an oversized and overly hairy baby.

"It's not about what we actually are, it's what we make

them think we are," I said. "The imagination is a powerful thing."

"Yours certainly is," Lukas said.

I knew he was making fun of me, but I decided to be the bigger person. "Thank you, Lukas."

Benedict leaned in – his face serious. "Do you really think it will work, Sebastian?"

I shrugged. "Look at what happened in **Lord of the Flies**. Those kids managed to convince themselves there was a **beast** in the jungle, scared themselves silly and there was nothing there, it was *all* them."

"You were actually listening?" Lina said quietly.

"I was. I mean, you didn't give me much choice but, yes, I was listening. Look, I think that old guy is already scared. All we need to do is frighten them a bit more. Make them think there is really a beast in the jungle."

"He did say he felt eyes," Francesca said. "The idea *is* already in their heads."

"But there is no beast," Lina said.

"But there is," I said, "it just happens that the beast is us."

"You really think we can scare away those nasty old turtle-trafficking-pirates and then take their boat?" Étienne said.

"I don't know, Étienne, but I think we should try," I

said. “We’ve been here seventy-nine days. We’ve not seen another boat in all that time. If we don’t take this chance we’re back to rowing across the ocean and we all know that’s not much fun. The turtles need us to help them find their way home but we need to find our way back, too.” I thought of my dad and of my mum and my chin trembled. “I want to go home.”

“So do I,” Étienne said.

“Me too,” Lina said.

Francesca nodded. “I’m in.”

“Benedict, Lukas, what do you think?” I asked.

“I think we should try,” Benedict said. “Lukas?”

Lukas grabbed a stick and rammed it into the ground. “Me too. You want me to find a pig’s head to put on a stake?”

“Ooh,” I said, “I appreciate your enthusiasm, Lukas, but I don’t think that will be necessary.”

“What exactly are we going to do then?” Lukas said.

“We are going to get in their heads, and then we’re going to get that boat,” I said. “We start as soon as the sun goes down.”

The plan I had come up with was that we would torment the pirates in a beastly way. We would make them think there was something in the jungle and that it was coming for them. It would work best if we had a few nights to build up the scaring. We just had to hope Tarquin's babies stayed safely in their shells long enough to give us time to put the fear of the beast into the pirates.

"Ultimately, we want it to look as though the beast is coming for them from the west side of the island to drive them east along the beach and away from their boat. When they're far enough away, we make a run for it. We'll have to stay alert and be ready but, most importantly, we mustn't get caught."

"It's risky," Benedict said.

"We've sailed the Pacific in a fishing boat," I said. "We can outsmart some pirates."

When the sun went down that first night the pirates stayed in our shelter, we were ready. We repurposed our jungle costumes, tying extra leaves to our arms and legs to look like spikes, and smeared mud on our faces and across our bodies.

"We actually look like savage beasts," Lina said.

"Does everyone know what they need to do?" I asked.

Determined faces nodded back at me.

"Hands in," Francesca said.

Lina put her hand on top of Francesca's, then Lukas put his hand in and then Benedict.

I put my hand on top of his and he nodded at me, and I don't think I've ever felt so good about a nod.

"I've always wanted to do this," Étienne said, placing his hand on top of mine.

"On three," Lina said.

We counted down from three and shouted, "**Climate Avengers!**" and Giuseppe joined in with a tremendous bleat.

On swift, silent feet, we made our way through the jungle, then when we were close, spread out in pairs to our various positions surrounding the west side of the **Ritz**. My body felt like it had been charged with electricity – my heart was racing and my breathing was rapid. Benedict and I were together, Lina was with Francesca and Étienne was with Lukas and Giuseppe.

When we reached our spot, Benedict whispered, "Go on, Sebastian, you go first."

I cupped my hands together and, with even more motivation than when I had sung the **Circle of Life**, I let out my best impression of a beast and growled.

And then we fell silent.

A minute later I heard a growl from further along the jungle. Even though I knew it was Lina or Francesca, the hairs on the back of my neck stood up.

"That sounded great," I whispered to Benedict.

"It really did."

A third growl came a minute later.

"That had to be Lukas," I said.

"Terrifying," Benedict agreed.

I listened for any reaction from inside the shelter, but there was no sound. Yet.

We waited for a little while before it was Benedict's turn. We wanted a slow build – for the pirates to question whether they were really hearing things.

Benedict then let out his growl, which, I admit, was very impressive.

Then the girls growled again, and then Lukas and Étienne.

We waited a while, as planned, before we unleashed a third round. Lina added an ear-piercing scream too, which was very menacing. Then Lukas made his move. It was so dark I could barely see him charge from his position to the shelter. I heard the clacking sound of the stick though as he ran it along the walls of the **Ritz**. He'd made it safely to me and Benedict when we heard the first raised voice from the pirates.

"My turn," Benedict said and he raced off, his feet barely grazing the sand as he ran the stick across the uprights of the shelter. He made it to Étienne just as the rest of us growled.

The voices inside the shelter grew louder. They sounded like they were arguing.

I let out one more growl and the now flip-flopless pirate emerged from the shelter.

Then we retreated back into the jungle.

That was enough for the night.

We were all buzzing when we got back to our temporary camp by the stream. We hugged and high-fived and congratulated each other on our incredibly convincing beastly growling and how well we had executed the plan.

"Now we wait," I said, "and then when we can be sure they're asleep, Benedict and I will go back and implement **Beast Plan - Part Two**."

Benedict rubbed his hands together. "The footprints!"

We'd spent some time earlier that day searching the jungle for the perfect rock. A little further down the stream, Francesca had found exactly what we needed. It was large and flat and jaggedy on one edge - it would leave a perfect impression in the sand of a beast's trail.

Once all the excited chatter had died down, Benedict and I moved a little way away from the group to let them sleep and waited until we decided it would be safe to go back to the pirate camp.

We sat in a small clearing, the moon full and high in

the sky above us. It reminded me of the night the turtles were born.

Benedict picked up a stick and started scratching it about on the ground. "Do you ever think about that night?"

He didn't need to say which night. I knew exactly what he meant.

"The night of the boat race? All the time," I said.

"It's all my fault."

"Your fault?" I nearly fell off the stump I was sitting on. "How do you figure that?"

"I should never have agreed to your bet. It was stupid – pointless. No offence, but you had zero chance of winning."

"Er, offended. Would we say zero? I mean, there is always a chance."

Benedict did a sad little laugh. "I suppose so. There was an exceedingly small, teeny-weeny, minuscule chance you might have beaten us."

"I'll take that," I said.

"I just feel so guilty," he said.

"I was the one who made the bet. It's my fault not yours. However...if you're happy to take the blame in front of the others, I can live with that... But it wouldn't be true. I'm sorry, Benedict, truly I am."

"I should have said no." He stopped poking the ground

with his stick and looked me in the eyes. "I just have this need to make sure everyone knows I'm the best. Even if it isn't true. It's like my dad says," he put on a deep stern voice, "*Winning is a way of life. Win at everything, Benedict, show people the kind of person you are – a winner.* Funny thing is, no matter what I achieve, how many times I win, it never feels enough."

"Sounds exhausting. I think your dad might get on well with my dad."

"I don't know why but I need to prove myself all the time. Like *all* the time."

"I know that feeling. Doesn't result in me appearing in Beaufort's *Rising Stars* newsletter though. Usually results in me doing something disastrous, like getting stung on the bum by a jellyfish." I was quiet for a moment, then I said, "Thinking about it now, I always knew this was going to happen."

"You always knew you were going to end up **shipwrecked** on an island pretending to be a beast to scare off some turtle-trafficking pirates? That's some seriously specific foresight, Sebastian, and you probably should have mentioned it when you challenged me to a boat race."

I gave him a playful nudge. "You know what I mean. My dad tried to tell me that the course I was steering was the wrong one. I just wish I hadn't got all you guys involved in it."

"You know what, Sebastian? I think I was probably on course for something disastrous too."

"Really? But you're so good at literally *everything* you do."

"That might be sort of true, but between you and me, I'm not very good at being happy."

"Is anybody?"

"I think Étienne is. I wish I could be more like him."

If Benedict Phan had said that when I first met him at the **Climate Avengers** Camp, I would have thought he was being mean, but that day, sitting in the moonlight, I knew he meant it. I knew he'd meant all the nice things he'd said. I'd just chosen not to believe in him. But I believed in him now and I was starting to believe in myself too.

"Come on," I said jumping to my feet. "If we want to reset our course for one that gets us home, we have some pirates to scare."

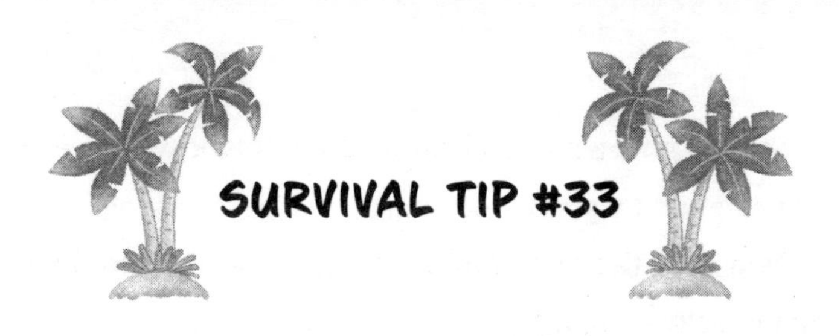

SURVIVAL TIP #33

HAVING A GOAT ON YOUR TEAM CAN PROVE TO BE A COMPLETE DISASTER

The following morning, we left Giuseppe sleeping and all crept down to our hiding place behind the pirates' camp, to see what effect our night of tormenting had had on them.

From our position we could see the footprints Benedict and I had made in the sand. They led from the jungle to behind the **Ritz** and then back again.

"They look great – believably beastly," Étienne whispered.

We drew back a little when the two pirates emerged from our shelter.

"They don't look like they've had the best night's sleep," Lina observed as they staggered about outside, rubbing their eyes and groaning.

The old guy, who was wading up to the beach towards them, shouted a good morning.

"You hear the noises in the night?" the flip-flop pirate called back.

"Was it you trying to mess with our heads?" the boss one said.

The older man stopped, his yellowing eyes moving from one pirate to the other. It was clear that he had no idea what they were talking about.

"There was growling coming from the jungle," the flip-flop one explained. "It sounded like an animal. A big animal."

"It was nothing! Probably just the wind," the boss guy said angrily.

The older pirate didn't seem to hear him. He held up a trembling finger and walked towards the edge of the forest. Quietly, we retreated a little so as not to be seen.

"I have a bad feeling about this place," he said. "Beasts roam in these islands. We shouldn't have come here."

"There are no beasts!" the boss guy said.

But then the flip-flop guy said, "Er, boss…if there aren't any beasts, what are these?" He was round the back of the hut, looking at the markings. Benedict and I exchanged glances – it was working!

The other two joined him and, when they saw the

footprints, the older guy started shaking and mumbling quietly to himself until the boss guy shouted at him to shut up and frantically kicked up the sand until the footprints were gone.

"There is nothing here but two men with wild imaginations. It was probably a boar or something."

"We should leave," the old man said. "Now."

"Not until we have the turtles. But you will stay here with us on the beach tonight. We'll take it in turns to keep guard," the boss guy said and then he stormed off towards the shelter.

Mr Flip-flop shouted after him, "Maybe we should go. Plenty more turtles on other islands."

The boss swung round. "Enough! Your heads are full of nonsense when they should be thinking of money!"

Benedict cupped his hands round his mouth and let out an ear-piercing caw, which sent a flurry of colourful birds flapping and squawking into the sky.

Startled, the boss guy leaped backwards. He looked down at the place where the footprints had been, then back at the forest. He muttered something then quickly disappeared inside the shelter.

"That was good, Benedict," Lina whispered. "He's spooked for sure."

The plan was working. The beast was in their heads

and a sense of determination was building in mine.

We headed back to our new base by the stream, to prepare to ramp things up that evening. Buoyed by the success of our first night of scaring, I set everyone to work. Lina and Francesca went off into the jungle scavenging for scare-supplies and Étienne and Lukas kept watch over the turtle eggs from afar, praying that they didn't hatch too soon.

By the time the sun was weak in the sky, we had dressed ourselves in our beastly finery and we were ready. From our vantage point in the jungle behind the **Ritz**, we could see the flip-flop guy sitting by the fire keeping watch. Luckily, he seemed to be more interested in digging dirt out of his toenails with a stick than doing any actual watching.

I nodded at Francesca and Lina and, with their arms full, they tiptoed down towards the shelter. Lukas, who was further along from us, let out a growl and then another. The flip-flop guy's stick flip-flopped right out of his hand, and he stood up. With him distracted, Lina and Francesca scattered the items I had asked them to collect – bones and corpses of birds and rodents – around the **Ritz**. My heart was racing in my chest as I tried to make out their movements in the darkness, and it continued to beat double time even after they got back safely.

"You covered your footprints?" I asked.

"Of course," Lina said.

Lukas began to shake some trees and howl, which was the signal for Benedict and me to get ready to run down to the base and set about making more footprints with the flat rock. We watched the pirate walk uncertainly in the direction of the moving trees and then we raced down and made the mark of our **beast**.

We worked quickly and were safely concealed in the undergrowth by the time he was back digging out his toenails and muttering to himself that it was only the wind.

We did another round of growling. Louder this time and increasing in volume. Mr Flip-flop leaped up, grabbed a flaming stick from the fire and roared, "What's there? Show yourself!"

The other two pirates came bursting out of the shelter, shouting and flashing their head torches around until they scanned the freshly laid beast tracks and animal corpses.

The older pirate cried, "I told you evil waits in this place! Now will you listen?!"

The boss's face was distorted in the torchlight, but the fear in his eyes was clear. He wiped his hand across his face. "One more night. If the turtles don't hatch then, we go."

The old guy grabbed hold of his T-shirt. "No! We go now!"

The boss guy shoved him back and the old guy stepped on the bones of some long-dead jungle rodent. He shrieked when it cracked under his foot, which made the other two scream. Then they started shouting at each other and there was more pushing and shoving.

We could still hear them going at it by the time we got back to our camp, panting and laughing and fizzing with adrenaline.

I whipped off the leaves that were tied onto me. "That was good, but did you hear what they said? One more night and they'll leave. Tomorrow is our last chance to scare them far enough away from the boat so we can commandeer it."

Everyone's faces grew serious.

"We ramp everything up to **maximum beast level** tomorrow," I continued. "We're going to come at them hard from the west side of the **Ritz**. We pelt the camp with everything we can lay our hands on. We throw coconuts and animal bones and rocks – Lukas, Benedict, can you be in charge of missile collection?"

They nodded.

"Lina, Francesca, Étienne, I want you to collect anything that can burn easily – dry grass, sticks, coconut husks – that sort of thing. We'll hide it all close to the camp today. Then tonight, you're going to start a fire."

"Fire is my speciality," Lina said.

"I know. You need to make sure it forces them eastwards and then, when they run, we do too. Straight out to the boat."

"I'm guessing we're talking a conservation garden-sized fire," Lina said.

I grinned. "Bigger."

"What are *you* going to do?" Lina asked me.

"I'm going **blongberry** picking."

As everyone set off to gather what we needed, a feeling of resolve set deep in my bones. I was really beginning to think that the plan, *my* plan, would work.

But on the third night, things didn't quite go as I had hoped.

We were a little later getting down to the camp than we would have liked and the moon was high and the sky black. Giuseppe had wandered off into the jungle and hadn't returned. Étienne had wanted to go and find him, and we'd traipsed about in our beast costumes looking for him until I'd said, "This is ridiculous! Why are we looking for a goat?!"

Étienne had said something about Giuseppe being *more than a goat* and, as I was feeling tense and anxious about what we were about to do, I'd lost my temper and snapped at him about misplaced priorities. Then Lina had snapped at me and then we'd all got a bit overemotional and there had been some crying then some apologizing. I think we were all on edge. If our plan worked, we'd be on a boat sailing for home that very evening. And if it didn't, well, no one wanted to think about that.

When we finally set off through the jungle, my whole body shook with nerves as I replayed over and over what we had to do. But when we arrived in the undergrowth behind the **Ritz**, where we had stacked our improvised jungle missiles and flammable material, the pirates weren't at the camp.

They were on the beach, with their crates ready and their head torches pointed at the sand. My stomach dropped to somewhere near my knees. Immediately we knew what was going on. The turtles were hatching.

"No," Étienne said quietly. "Please, no."

I could see by the number of tracks that a least a dozen baby turtles had already tunnelled their way out into the world. They'd probably been plucked from the sand and loaded into a crate already.

I couldn't move. Couldn't speak.

"We can't scare them from here," Benedict said. "They're too far from the jungle – too close to the water, they won't hear. We're too late."

"They're going to take the turtles and go!" Étienne said.

"Sebastian?" Lina said. "What do we do? The plan's not going to work."

I knew she was right, but I couldn't think for panicking. I looked over to the boat bobbing gently in the moonlight. Then back to the pirates, their attention solely focused on the turtles. The boss man was rubbing his hands together, looking at the baby turtles and whooping excitedly.

"Sebastian?" Lina pressed.

Everyone turned to me. I didn't know what to do, but then I looked back to the sea and I heard my dad's voice.

Time and tide wait for no man, Sebastian.

"We abandon the plan and we go. Now," I said, my heart quickening in my chest. "Forget scaring them, we make a run for the boat while they're distracted. I think we can make it. We can release the turtles they have on board later."

"What about our babies?" Étienne asked. "We swore an oath to protect them. We're **Climate Avengers**, remember?"

"If we get the pirates' boat, they aren't going to be trafficking those turtles anywhere, they'll have to let them go."

Étienne didn't look convinced.

"They'll be stuck here. We can report them once we're home."

Everyone nodded. Except Étienne.

"Étienne," I said, a little more forcefully, "are you ready?"

He shook his head. "What about Giuseppe? I can't go without him."

"We can't bring a goat back with us!" Lukas spluttered. "Besides, his home is here."

"His home is with me," Étienne said. "I'm not going without him."

"Étienne," I said, as gently as I could manage considering I really wanted to shake the silly out of him. "We need to go. Think of your family..."

"Giuseppe is my family."

Oh, Étienne.

"Étienne, this is our chance to get home! *Home*, Étienne. Think about that!" Lina said.

Étienne looked behind him into the jungle and, when there was no sign of **Giuseppe Garibaldi**, his eyes filled. "Okay," he said, "let's go."

“It’s for the best,” I said, but Étienne didn’t answer.

We snuck along the forest until we were at the best point to make a dash for the boat – a hundred metres or so from the pirates.

“We’ll go two at a time, swim slowly and smoothly,” I said.

Francesca and Lina went first. They flew across the sand to the shore, then quietly submerged themselves. They moved through the black inky waters, barely making a sound. We charted their progress to the boat by the ripples. Once they were hidden on board, it was time for Lukas and Étienne to make a run for it. But just as they were about to go, we heard a bleat from the jungle.

“Giuseppe!” Étienne said, turning back from the beach. “I have to get him.” And off he ran through the creepers.

“No!” Benedict and I whisper-shouted after him.

“Seriously, you are kidding me! He’s going after a goat?” Lukas hissed. “We should have eaten the thing when we had the chance.”

“You two go, I’ll get Étienne – he’ll listen to me,” I told them, hoping it was true.

Lukas nodded and took off across the sand, but Benedict hesitated. “I should come too.”

“No, the others may need you.” Before he could stop me, I charged off into the jungle, chasing after the kindest

but possibly daftest boy in the world, who was chasing after the daftest but possibly most inconsiderate goat in the world.

SURVIVAL TIP #34

UNDERSTAND YOUR ENEMIES' FEARS

I raced through the jungle, desperately searching for any sign of Étienne or Giuseppe. Creeper vines blocked my way, and I stumbled in the dark, tripping over the mess of roots and rocks that covered the jungle floor. I kept running and running but I couldn't find them anywhere.

I stopped a moment to listen. It was hard to hear anything over the sound of the pounding of blood in my ears and my own ragged breathing. I tried to hold my breath. When I did, all I could think about was that I was holding my breath in the middle of a desert island looking for a goat called Giuseppe to escape some turtle-pirates and I realized how far one stupid, reckless bet had taken me. But I wasn't prepared to lose Étienne because of it. Although, arguably, his decision to chase after Giuseppe was more ill-advised than my boat race, but hey, who's counting?

I couldn't hear anything and could barely see anything in the darkness anyway, so I closed my eyes to see if that increased my listening powers. I'm sure I read somewhere once that it worked. I'm not convinced, though, because it was only when Étienne and Giuseppe bashed into me that I heard them.

"Sebastian, what are you doing standing there with your eyes closed?" Étienne said, like *I* was the mad one, when it was him giving **Giuseppe Garibaldi** a piggyback.

"I was looking for you!"

"With your eyes shut? Seems strange."

"You're wearing a goat like a backpack! Now come on! We need to get to that boat before those awful turtle traffickers notice what we are up to."

"Giuseppe's coming with us," he said. "I'm not leaving him here with those pirates. They might eat him!"

"Fine," I said, and we hurried back through the undergrowth taking it in turns to carry Giuseppe, who would not walk no matter how much we encouraged him.

As we drew closer to the edge of the trees, I prepared myself for the fact that I would have to try and tow a goat across the lagoon, but when we got to the beach we stopped in our tracks and quickly scuttled back into the undergrowth.

Sitting round our fire, their hands tied behind their backs with rope, were our friends. Their faces were pale and full of fear. Three very angry-looking turtle-pirates stood over them.

Étienne started hyperventilating immediately. "Sebastian...Sebastian...Sebastian," he repeated.

"Try and stay calm," I said, though I wasn't feeling particularly calm myself.

The boss guy shouted at the others. "Look what you've done!" He was pointing his torch towards the lagoon.

Étienne and I rose up from our hiding place a little to get a better look.

The dark waters of the lagoon were filled with even darker shapes. Hundreds of them – of all different sizes – making their way out to sea.

It was quite **spectacular** to watch, even in the circumstances.

"It's the turtles from the boat," Étienne whispered. "They freed them."

"But got caught in the process," I said.

"What are we going to do?" he said, taking my hand and gripping it tightly. "This is all my fault."

"I told you not to – that there'd be trouble if you let the turtles go!" the boss went on. "And now we have ourselves an issue." He was clearly very, very agitated.

"All we have left are the ones in these crates!" the flip-flop guy said, gesturing to Tarquin's turtles, who were stacked up at the edge of the water.

The boss guy picked up a stick from the fire and pointed the fiery end at Benedict, who was looking at him defiantly despite his obvious fear. "You kids cost us. You've cost us big, and now we have the added problem that your whole presence here brings." He kicked the sand and let out a frustrated shout.

"They're just kids," the old guy said. Then he handed him a bowl and ladled in some of the soup that had been bubbling away on the fire.

"They don't look like kids." The boss guy took a big slurp of the soup and wiped his chin with the back of his hand. "They look like savage beasts to me."

"You're the only beasts round here!" Lina yelled, which was brave, if a little foolish.

The boss drew his stick through the air so the flames flickered dangerously close to her face. "It seems you are forgetting your situation, young lady."

The old guy took a step towards him, his hands held up. "We should go. Let's leave them here. What harm can they do stuck on this island?"

"What if someone finds them and they run off their mouths about us?" the flip-flop guy said.

"We never leave witnesses," the boss guy said.

I didn't like the sound of that. "Come on," I said, pulling Étienne to his feet. "I have an idea."

With Giuseppe bouncing about on my back, we hurried through the jungle until we were positioned in our hiding place right behind the camp. "We have to scare them, Étienne."

Étienne blinked behind his glasses. "Sebastian, there's

three of them and only two of us and those men are dangerous. How are *we* going to scare them?"

"We need to bring back the **beast**."

Étienne shook his head. "It won't work."

"It will." I spoke with surprising conviction, despite my own serious misgivings. "It has to. Our friends are counting on us. Look, we know we got into their heads. We might not be particularly terrifying to behold –" I paused for a moment, realizing just how far from terrifying Étienne actually looked – "but the scariest things are the ones that people make up in their own minds."

"I don't know, the whole being-stranded-in-the-middle-of-the-ocean thing was pretty frightening."

"Étienne, I'm trying to make a point here. I believe we can do this – I need you to believe it too. For Lina and Benedict and Lukas and Francesca."

He looked towards the camp, his face looking tortured.

"They need you, and so does **Eggbert** and **Ethel** and **Ernest** and—"

"You're right!" Étienne said. "We'll do it for them!"

"That's the spirit!" I said, trying not to dwell on the fact that it was the turtles that had finally swung it for him. "Now, growl, growl like you've never growled before."

Étienne and I tipped our heads back and let out a tremendous roar. The pirates immediately stopped talking and looked towards the jungle. I saw Benedict look in our direction. He couldn't have seen us from where he was sitting, but he knew we were there. I picked up one of the dead animal skeletons from the pile and launched it into the camp. It landed with a *thwump* at Benedict's feet.

The old pirate wailed, dropping his bowl of soup and the other two jumped back.

"It's the beast!" Benedict cried, and I smiled – he'd realized what we were doing.

"There is no beast!" the boss guy shot back.

"There is, we've seen it!" Benedict said.

Étienne and I growled again. Then we grabbed hold of some tree branches and shook them with all our might.

"Untie us!" Francesca shrieked. "It's coming!"

"There is no beast!" the boss guy shouted again.

"There is. It's been tracking us for weeks," Lina cried. "Please untie us, please! It will kill us. It will kill us all!"

While the pirates started arguing about what to do, Étienne and I moved further along the bushes, pulling Giuseppe with us and then, from our new position, we growled again and I threw over another animal carcass.

"It's closing in!" Lukas hollered and started to wrestle with his bindings.

The men were becoming more and more agitated.

"Go and check," the boss guy said pointing towards the jungle. "If there's a beast, prove it!"

The old guy and the flip-flop guy did not look like they wanted to prove it.

"I told you evil lurks in that jungle," the old guy said, "and now it has come for us. I will not go and meet it."

"You are a stupid old man," the boss said, forcing his torch into the man's hands. Then he drew his knife from his shorts. "We will go and see this beast."

SURVIVAL TIP #35

THE BEST WAY TO LEARN TO CLIMB A TREE QUICKLY IS TO BE CHASED BY KNIFE-WIELDING PIRATES

The boss guy stomped across the beach towards our hiding place, his knife blade glinting in the moonlight, the other two pirates trailing behind.

"Follow me," I said to Étienne. We needed to move before they found us.

Étienne grabbed hold of Giuseppe, but the goat squirmed free and bolted off ahead. We tore through the undergrowth after him. My heart was thumping so violently I thought it might burst out of my chest.

"Do you hear that?" the old guy said. "The beast is out there!"

They were in the jungle now. Giuseppe sensed the danger and had charged off so fast we had no hope of keeping up with him.

I raced on further then stopped and growled again, expecting Étienne to join in. I looked behind me, to tell him to growl, but he wasn't there. I twisted round, panicking, trying to catch sight of him.

I heard footsteps. Moving branches. A thud.

Then a shout of "What is this I have here?"

It was the boss guy and I knew what it was without looking.

Who it was. The realization was like a punch in the gut.

"Leave me alone!" Étienne cried.

"Another kid! You're coming with me!" the boss guy snarled.

I waited helplessly, listening to the sounds of Étienne being dragged off through the jungle.

I chased after them, as quiet as I could, but hung back in the trees as they emerged out of the undergrowth and onto the beach. The boss guy pushed Étienne to the ground.

"Étienne!" Lina cried and Francesca said, "You leave him alone!"

The boss guy, bent over him. "How many of you are there?"

I'll give it to Étienne, he thought quickly. "The b-b-beast," he stammered, looking as traumatized as he had back when we were on the boat. "It's c-c-coming!" He pointed a trembling finger towards the jungle waiting for me to growl, but I just stood there, frozen. I don't know if it was from fear or from the sudden hopelessness I felt knowing all my friends were in danger.

"It's coming!" Étienne cried again. Then he grabbed hold of the boss guy and stared up at him, his eyes wild. "I've seen it!"

"You lie!" the boss guy roared then struck Étienne hard across the face with the back of his hand, sending his glasses flying. Lina screamed, Francesca yelled and Lukas and Benedict both fought against their bindings.

And something in me snapped.

A growl came out of me so vicious and guttural and raw that even I was shocked.

A sudden silence fell over the camp which was immediately broken by Étienne shrieking, "Beast! Beast! Beast!"

"Enough!" the old guy hollered, visibly quaking. "I'm not staying here to look hell in the eyes."

The boss gave Étienne a good shake. "You lie!"

"He isn't lying!" Francesca cried.

"I don't like this, boss," the flip-flop guy said, his eyes darting about madly. "What if there is a beast? These kids seem petrified."

I growled again – as loudly as I could and shook the trees.

Étienne scrambled to put his glasses back on, then screamed, "God help us!" It sounded so desperate and real that he almost convinced *me* he was scared of a beast.

The pirates flashed their head torches along the tree line, and I ducked back as the lights drew close to me. There was a sudden rustle in the undergrowth, then out from the jungle burst **Giuseppe Garibaldi** going at a lightning pace, as though sent by Étienne's God himself.

Giuseppe, head dipped and hooves a blur, rammed straight into the boss. The sound on impact was startling and the pirate toppled backwards and fell. I flinched – I knew first-hand how much a goat in the stomach hurts.

Étienne didn't miss a beat. He was up and running. The boss guy staggered to his feet and, clutching his belly in one hand and the knife in the other, chased after him. Étienne's little legs flew over the sand and then, when he reached his coconut tree, he scrambled up it quicker than any tarsier monkey.

"Come down!" the boss guy snarled, then swayed a little.

But all Étienne would do was shriek, "Beast! Beast! Beast!"

I rustled the leaves again, growling, and I picked up the skull of what once might have been a pig ready to launch it. I wondered if I could hit the boss from this distance – take him out – but when I drew my arm back, I saw something that caused me to stiffen with fear.

The old guy.

He was standing in front of the bush I was hiding behind, staring through the branches. He'd seen me.

We locked eyes. He brought his torch to my face. I glared into the beam – certain I was done for. That the game was up.

But then he staggered backwards, tripping as he went, and letting out a guttural scream.

"What's wrong with you?" the flip-flop guy said.

"Beast!" The old guy got to his feet and grabbed hold of the boss by the T-shirt. "I saw it! The beast. I saw the beast!"

I retreated backwards and growled again.

"I saw it! I saw it!" the old guy cried. "Listen to me! I saw it! I saw the beast! It has one eye in heaven and the other in hell! One green, one blue!" and then he raced off up the beach and thrashed his way through the water towards the boat.

The flip-flop guy glanced at the jungle then looked up at Étienne, who was clinging onto the tree doing an excellent job of looking utterly terrified. Flip-flop then gulped and fled towards the lagoon too.

The boss guy shouted at him to come back and, while

he was busy shouting, Étienne shot down the tree. They stared at one another for a second, then Étienne made a break for it into the trees. I ran to meet him and when we found each other, he screamed right in my face.

I must have looked a bit shocked, because he thumped me and hissed, "Growl then!"

I growled again.

Étienne screamed, "NO!" and shook the trees and screamed some more, then made some agonizing-sounding cries of "**HELP ME!**"

The others all started screaming, "It's got him! The beast has got him! Untie us before it gets us too!"

Lina wailed and cried, and the boss guy stood motionless and horrified as he listened to Étienne splutter and cry out then finally pretend to die what sounded like a **spectacularly** gruesome death.

When Étienne had fallen silent, I made some snorting, chomping noises and then threw the pig's head as hard as I could. It landed by Lina's feet. She screamed, I think in earnest because she wasn't expecting it and because she already had issues with pigs' heads courtesy of old William Golding and his **Lord of the Flies** book.

Now, if the boss guy had been of more sound mind, and if he had taken the time to go over and inspect the skull that had landed on the sand, he might have realized that it wasn't the head of the boy he had just seen run into the jungle. But the imagination is a powerful thing, and the beast had taken hold of his.

And so too, perhaps, had the litre of green **blongberry** juice that I had poured into their cooking pot earlier that day.

The knife dropped from the pirate's hand and his mouth fell open. I thought he might scream too, but no sound came out. Instead, he cast one look at the jungle, then sprinted down the beach, stumbling and crying, until he reached the water and dived in.

Étienne and I watched from the jungle as he thrashed his way to the boat.

"Do you think they're actually going?" Étienne said, through laboured breaths.

As if to answer him, a moment later, the motor started up.

"I think they are," I said. "They really thought I was a beast."

"I think it was your eyes. A lot of cultures are superstitious about different coloured eyes."

"I think it was my general all-powerful beastliness."

"Oh yes, that also." Étienne laughed, then threw his arms around me. "But we did it, Sebastian! They've actually gone." Then he burst into tears.

I rested my chin on his head and felt the weight of something warm and goat-like lean against our legs. "They've gone," I said. But so too had the boat and our chance to get home.

SURVIVAL TIP #36

SOMETIMES IT IS NECESSARY TO SET A COURSE THROUGH FEAR IF YOU WANT TO SURVIVE

I could have stood with my chin on Étienne's head for ever. I didn't want it to stop, because stopping would mean that we would have to face reality again.

It was Lina bellowing, "Étienne, Sebastian? Do you think you could come and reassure us that you weren't actually eaten by a jungle beast! We're still tied up over here if you haven't forgotten!" that finally made us move.

Giuseppe, Étienne and I came out from our hiding place. I felt all shaky and a little bit sick and a lot overwhelmed. I think I was trying to process everything that had just happened – I think everyone was, because when we arrived at the camp nobody said anything, we just looked at each other.

"So that was an eventful evening," I finally managed to say.

Benedict nodded. "Yup."

"Didn't quite go as planned," I said.

"Nope," Lukas said.

"We lost the boat," I pointed out.

"Yup," Francesca said.

Giuseppe looked around at us all, shook his head, then reared up on his back legs and bleated long and loud into the night. It was a victory cry, to remind us of what we had just done, and it sent a wave of emotion through us.

"That's right, Giuseppe, we survived!" Étienne said, then he dropped to his knees and punched both fists in the air and shouted at the top of his lungs, "**WE SURVIVED! WE SURVIVED!**"

Giuseppe bleated some more and soon we were all whooping and cheering, "**WE SURVIVED! WE SURVIVED!**"

Then Lina shouted, "PRAISE BE TO WILLIAM GOLDING!"

I stopped and stared at her. "Excuse me? Praise be to *who*?"

I used the knife to cut the bindings and set everyone free, and while I know we were all thinking about the chance we'd lost to get home, we had something else to focus on first.

Lina and Benedict took two sticks from the fire for torches and, together, we walked over to the crates that the pirates had left on the beach.

"Would you look at those," Lukas said, his eyes glistening. "I don't think I've ever seen anything more wonderful."

"We saved them!" Étienne said. "We saved **Tarquin Tarantino**'s babies."

"I reckon we must be the best **Climate Avengers** that have ever enlisted," Lina said and we all agreed that we probably were.

We carried the crates down to the water's edge, Giuseppe following behind, and one by one we set the turtles free. Doing it that way was Étienne's idea. Lukas had suggested that we just chuck them in like they had done to the ones on the boat, but Étienne was very insistent that, as there was no direct threat from the pirates, we should give them a proper send-off.

I gave the lagoon a quick scan to check Julian wasn't about to ruin things for everybody and when I was happy the coast was clear, we began.

We started with **Eggbert**. "God speed, little **Eggbert**, may your journeys all be happy ones," Étienne said, releasing him into the water. I admit, we all got a little emotional as we watched the little fella flippering his way out into the big, wide ocean.

"**Ethel**, stay safe, precious turtle," Étienne said when he released the second.

Lina picked up the turtle we decided was **Ernest**. "If there is someone up there, I hope they're looking out for you, but if there isn't you can always call on us **Climate Avengers**."

I found the one that most looked like an **Ermentrude** and sent her on her way. "Good luck," I said, "and if you have a moment, could you possibly send someone back here to rescue us?"

Francesca, **Lukas** and **Benedict** then placed their turtle namesakes into the water and held hands as they watched them swim off.

It took quite a while releasing the turtles that way. But I'm glad we did it.

It felt like an important moment.

As we walked back up to camp, the sun was just promising to rise. "I know that, essentially, we lost our ticket off this island, and we are essentially still very much **shipwrecked**, but I think we should still chalk that up as a success," I said.

"I agree," Lina said. "I refuse to feel anything but positive about what happened today, but would someone please put some more wood on the fire before it goes out. I'm still hopeful we may attract another boat, hopefully one that isn't full of pirates this time."

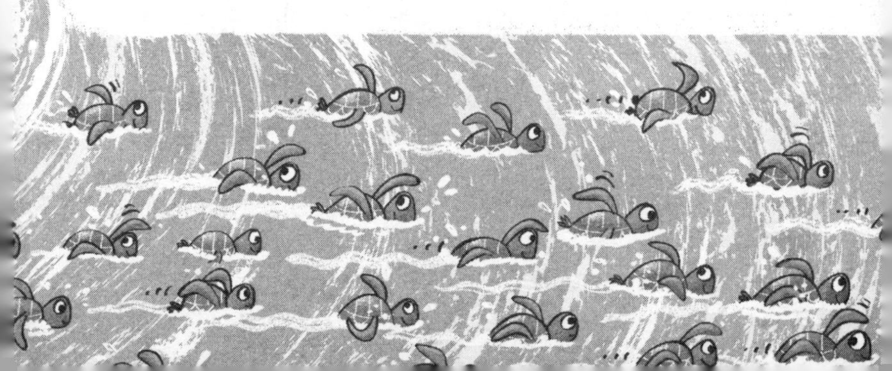

Neither she nor Étienne caught the looks that passed between Benedict, Lukas and Francesca when she said that. But I saw how they gazed out to sea with quiet determination in their eyes. I knew what they were thinking, and I knew that night would be one of our last times together as a six.

We sat round the fire eating more burned breadfruit and talked about what made us proud. We spoke about how proud we were that we had scared off the turtle traffickers and saved Tarquin's babies and that we had done it as a team, and that we were still surviving on the island and looking out for each other.

Étienne said, "I'm also very proud of Giuseppe for ramming into that boss pirate with no thought to his own personal safety."

We all agreed and gave Giuseppe an enthusiastic round of applause, extra breadfruit, and decided he was the Lord of all Goats.

Then Étienne looked a little bit bashful and said, "I'm a little bit proud of climbing that tree too."

And we whooped and cheered and told him he should be *very* proud of climbing that tree.

But then Lina said, "It is a shame Sebastian knocked that coconut down or you could have got that too."

I opened my mouth to tell her just what I thought of

that, and she said, "Sebastian, that was a joke," so I shut it again and smiled.

Then, when everyone had fallen quiet and we watched the sun rise up from the horizon, I told everybody what I was most proud about. "You know, guys," I said, "my dad told me he thought I was lost before, and I guess he was right. But now, here with you, I've never felt more found. I'm proud that I know you all. And I'm proud of who we all are."

It was hard when Benedict, Lukas and Francesca left.

A couple of days after the pirates left, Lina, Étienne and I awoke to find them standing by their boat. It was full of supplies and, immediately, I knew what was happening.

"It's time," Benedict said as he loaded up the last of the food. "We've put it off long enough."

"It was watching those turtles, you see," Francesca said, hugging Lina. "A sign maybe? Seeing our namesakes head out into the ocean made us think it was time for us to go too."

"But was it a sign?" Étienne said. "I think maybe you are looking into things a little too deeply."

"Our plan was always to row for help. We meant to go sooner, but it turned out that **Sunrise Island** and its inhabitants were harder to leave than we expected." Lukas hugged us all in turn tightly, and I mean tightly. I thought about how Lukas had burst into tears when he'd thought he wouldn't have to sail the ocean after he saw the turtle-trafficker's boat, and of how brave he was being now.

"You could all come too?" he said.

Étienne looked out at the horizon, the pain in his face so clear. I knew he wanted to go but I also knew how terrified he was.

"We'll stay," I said. Even though every part of me was burning to go, to set my course for home, I couldn't do it to Étienne.

Benedict clapped a hand on my shoulder. "We'll make it, I promise, and we'll send help."

On the morning of our eighty-third day on **Sunrise Island**, Lina, Étienne and I stood at the edge of the lagoon and watched three of the most **spectacular** people I have ever met row off into the ocean to try and make it home. I don't know if they were scared, I can't see how they couldn't have been, but they didn't show it.

Étienne prayed for them that day down on the sand. He prayed that the oceans would be kind to them and that they would navigate the waters safely home, and even though Lina and I don't have faith like Étienne does, we joined in, because we wanted that for them too.

But now, two weeks later, there has still been no sign of rescue. Étienne didn't speak much after our friends went. He's spent every day with Giuseppe at the shore, looking out to sea, waiting, hoping, praying. Yesterday, I woke early and realized he wasn't in the shelter. I found him there, down by the lagoon and, as we watched the sunrise, he turned to me and said, "**Sunrise Island** doesn't feel as sunny any more. Not without the others."

"It doesn't."

"It's day ninety-seven," he said.

"I know."

"I don't want that to turn into a hundred, to turn into a year, to turn into ten. I'm ready to leave. If our friends are lost somewhere out at sea, we have to try to save them. It's what they'd do for us."

"It is." I put my hand into his and squeezed it. "I know you're scared. I am too."

"I realized something," he said. "Everything I want – for us to get home, for the others to be safe – it's all on the other side of fear." He smiled. "That and a humongous ocean."

"That's very true," I said. "So how about we set a course to cross them both?"

"I say that sounds **spectacular**."

We woke up early this morning, our ninety-eighth morning on **Sunrise Island**. I had one final trip to the luxury toilet. I think we shall all miss it when we have to pee in a bucket on board **HMS Saviour**, but I do look forward to triple-ply toilet paper. We spent yesterday loading the boat with enough coconuts and breadfruit and water to last us for weeks, hopefully.

"Are you ready?" Lina asks.

I turn and take one last look at the **Ritz**. "I'm ready."

Étienne turns to Giuseppe. "Are you ready? Then climb aboard, fella!"

We had much debate about whether taking a goat out into the Pacific Ocean was a wise idea but when Étienne point-blank refused to go without him, Lina and I had no choice but to give in.

But Giuseppe doesn't move when Étienne tells him to.

"Come on, Giuseppe. You'll love it where we're going, I promise. I have a whole cupboard full of trainers you can chew." Étienne tries to lift him up and load him on, but he's having none of it.

"Giuseppe, please, come on. We're not leaving you here. *I'm* not leaving you here." The desperation in

Étienne's voice is painful to hear, but Giuseppe just hangs his head and sits down on the sand.

"Étienne," I say and put my hand on his shoulder. "Étienne, this is Giuseppe's home."

"No, but I need him, he's my best friend!"

I try to ignore the fact that Lina and I have somehow been usurped by a goat and put Étienne's comment down to his state of high emotion.

"Étienne, he's not coming. We can't force him to."

Étienne tries one last time, "Giuseppe?"

But Giuseppe looks up at him sadly and shakes his head.

Étienne drops to his knees, tears running down his cheeks, and throws his arms around his friend. "I can't leave you."

Giuseppe begins to nudge Étienne with his snout. He's pushing him towards the boat, pushing him home. "Giuseppe," Étienne protests, but the goat butts him again then looks up at him with his wet, bright goaty eyes for what will be the last time and nods. It's only a nod but, even to me, it feels like so much more – a thank you, a promise it will be okay, an understanding of the friendship they had. And we watch as he turns and races back towards the jungle.

"Oh, Giuseppe," Étienne cries after him. "I shall miss you. I shall miss you so much."

I look over at Lina and see she is crying, and I realize I'm crying too. And for some reason, we understand that we have all fallen in love with a bandy-legged goat called **Giuseppe Garibaldi** and an island somewhere in the Pacific Ocean that, for a little while, felt like home.

But **Sunrise Island** isn't our home.

Our home is with our families, so we pick up the oars and with a rousing call of "Onwards through fear!" from me, we begin to row and sing at the tops of our lungs a very emotional rendition of the **Circle of Life**.

IF YOU PUT GOOD OUT INTO THE WORLD, IT MIGHT COME BACK TO YOU IN UNEXPECTED WAYS

Sunrise Island becomes smaller and smaller until it's just a tiny dot on the horizon, and then our home for the last ninety-eight days disappears altogether.

"That's it," I say, "just us and the sky and the sea and our boatload of breadfruit and hope."

We row for a couple of hours and when our arms start to cramp, we decide it's a good time to take a break. We pull the oars in and sit back. We eat a little, then listen to the waves lapping against the side of the boat.

"It's incomprehensibly beautiful out here," Étienne says, his voice filled with awe.

I close my eyes for a moment and feel the sun on my face and, despite my worries about what lies ahead, an unexpected sense of calm washes over me. Whatever happens, I know we've tried our best. We've been our best. We can feel proud of that. We let the boat drift, and the current takes us further and further out to sea. We talk a little. My eyes become heavy, Lina and Étienne's voices become muffled and I feel myself drift off.

I'm woken by Lina shaking me. I sit up a bit fuzzy-headed and Étienne sits up too, also blinking away sleep. Lina's pointing at the water, a smile on her face. "So, guys," she says, "**Tarquin Tarantino** popped by."

We peer over the side. There, swimming alongside the boat is a sea turtle.

"**Tarquin Tarantino!**" Étienne cries.

"It can't be him!" I say.

"Her," Lina corrects.

"I think it is!" Étienne says determinedly.

"I think so too," I say, because I want to believe it is.

"Undoubtedly," Lina agrees. "I'd recognize her shell anywhere."

I give her a questioning look and she winks back, so I know she's just saying it for Étienne's sake.

I point to the sky and spot a gull flying over and trying to get into the spirit of things, I say, "Look! It's **Gloria Goldberg!**"

Étienne scowls at me. "Don't be ridiculous. That wasn't Gloria," which makes Lina giggle.

Tarquin comes closer to the surface and Étienne hollers, "Ma'am, your babies are all okay!"

I don't know if she hears, but she dips down lower, and we watch her as she moves through the water – her strokes smooth and unhurried. It's almost hypnotic. Maybe, I think, it actually is her.

We're so busy watching Tarquin that when we hear a long, loud blast of a horn it's so unexpected we jump with a start and then scream.

Lina pushes herself to her feet, her voice trembling. "Oh, your God, Étienne!"

It feels like all the air is rushing out of me, because heading towards us is the most **spectacular** sight.

There's a **boat**.

And on board it is my dad.

I spot him straight away and I think that my heart might burst. He's standing right up on the prow next to Beecham, and on the other side of him is my mum and Benedict, Lukas and Francesca. They are shouting and cheering and jumping up and down and hugging each other. I guess the people behind them waving are their parents. I spot Lina and Étienne's parents too.

There's a moment – a pause – where time seems to slow down and Lina, Étienne and I just stand there, not quite trusting our eyes, not knowing how to react.

I suppose when your hopes are so huge, when they come true, they can almost feel impossible to believe.

Lina says, “Tell me you two are seeing what I’m seeing?”

Étienne smiles. “I’m seeing what’s on the other side of fear.”

I swallow and say, “Me too.”

That is possibly a little ambiguous for Lina, and she grabs me and shakes me. “The boat? Tell me you see the boat!”

“Yes! I see the boat!” I say and her face breaks into the most wondrous smile and we all start shouting and cheering and hugging each other. Then the emotions become too much and too many, and we start to sob uncontrollably.

My feet are barely on the deck before my mum has rushed over to me. She cups my face in her hands and pebble-dashes me with kisses. Then she looks deep into my eyes. "Sebastian, I...I am..." Her voice gets caught in a sob and I wrap my arms round her and say, "It's okay, Mum. I know. I'm sorry too."

She pulls me into her and says, "I'm here, Sebastian. I'm here."

I can see Dad hanging back, watching us. Waiting. I unwrap myself from Mum's arms, giving her hands a final squeeze, and walk over to him. I stop a pace from him, trying to find the words to apologize for what I've put him through. Trying to find a way to bridge the gap between us, but I don't have to. He steps forward, picks me up and hugs me so tightly that I wonder whether he might cause me some permanent skeletal damage.

When he puts me down, he runs his thumb across my cheek and says in the most tender of voices, "Sebastian, my Sebastian."

All I can do is hold onto him and say, "I'm sorry, I'm so sorry," again and again.

I can feel the sobs coming out of his chest as he says, "Everything is okay now, son, everything is okay."

For the first time in a long time, I feel safe, and I let myself cry in his arms.

When I finally pull myself away, I apologize for making a snotty mess of his top. I laugh when I see what it says. "Is that a **Climate Avengers** T-shirt? That's a change from your usual attire."

"There's a few things about me that have changed, Sebastian."

"I've changed too," I tell him. "Granted, I may not currently look it, but I'm much less wild. I know who I am now. I know the course I want to take."

Dad pulls me into another hug and kisses the top of my head and says, "Oh my son, I am so very proud of you. Wherever life steers you, I will be right there with you."

"That", I say, "is a very excellent naval quote."

Later, when we are sitting in the canteen on the boat, eating food we haven't tasted in months with people we have missed more than is possibly imaginable, I try to find the words to thank the others for saving us.

Benedict smiles and says, "It wasn't us, Sebastian. It was **Tarquin**."

Lina, Étienne and I all say, "What?"

Beecham fills us in. "Some pals of mine have been tracking a turtle we tagged for years now. It was time for her to lay and once we picked up on her signal, they headed out here. That's when they came across a boat of traffickers we've been trying to arrest for months. Scared half out of their wits, talking of beasts and kids on an island."

"Those are our pirates!" I say.

"They're not pirates any more. They're prisoners. Anyway, my friends phoned me, figuring they might be talking about my missing **Climate Avengers**, and I called your dad immediately. He'd flown out here and chartered a boat the day you went missing. He's been scouring the waters ever since. Once we had an idea of where you might be, I brought your mum and the other parents out to his boat. That was four days ago."

"They found us on their way out to **Sunrise Island**," Lukas says, taking another huge bite of his pizza. He rolls his eyes like it is the most delicious thing he has ever eaten.

"I couldn't believe what I was seeing," Dad says, "a boat of full of kids, rowing across the Pacific! It was incredible." He smiles at me. "You are all incredible."

"You know what else is incredible?" Étienne says, thoughtfully. "We saved Tarquin's babies, and she saved us."

"In a way, yes," Beecham says. "I told you our reptilian relations are truly magnificent."

"I am very glad we didn't eat her now," I say.

Beecham looks aghast, Étienne smacks me on the back of the hand with his ice-cream spoon and Lina shakes her head and sighs, "Oh, Sebastian."

This evening, Dad came to tuck me into my bunk. He hasn't done that for years, but today I'm so glad when he does. Honestly, I want to hold onto him and never let go.

"So, you and Mum?" I say when he goes to turn out the light.

He shakes his head and sits back down next to me. "No, Sebastian we're not getting back together. But we are two people who love you. Very much."

"I know you do," I say.

"She wants to move to Singapore. Get an apartment so she can be close to you. I think losing you like we did made her realize what really matters." He closes his eyes for a second and lets out a breath. "No, that's not fair. Your mother has always known how important you are, but sometimes people act in ways that they themselves don't understand."

"I think I was like her," I say quietly. "But I want to be like you now, Dad."

"Your mother is fun and loving and free-spirited – I see

those parts of her in you and they're wonderful – you shouldn't lose them. And I don't want you to be like me, I want to be you, Sebastian. **Spectacular** you." He takes hold of my hand and kisses my palm. "Now, don't you ever disappear on me again, you hear that?"

He has tears in his eyes. I've never seen him cry. When I point that out, he says, "You should have seen me lately. I've been an absolute blubbering mess."

I know it's awful but that sort of makes me feel happy. Not that he was upset, but that he cared so much. "Have you really?" I say.

"Have I? Barely stopped. I've been dreadful. A complete state! You are part of me, Sebastian and it so transpires that I simply cannot be without you. I need you – you know?"

And finally, I do.

I need him too. Because my dad is my home. I guess he was right, sometimes it takes navigating your own waters to find out what's truly important. Sometimes you need to be taken so far away from somewhere to know just how much it means to you.

So, as helpful as that **Lord of the Flies** book turned out to be, I would like to politely disagree with the late, great, Mr William Golding. I don't think dreadful situations bring out the evil that is lurking inside humankind. I think tough times can bring out the best in us. Benedict and Lukas and Francesca, and my best friends, Lina and Étienne and even **Giuseppe Garibaldi**, have shown me that. I believe people (and some exceptional goats) are **spectacularly** good and will find a way to bring joy to others, even in the darkest of times.

As my dad might say, life's toughest storms prove the strength of our anchors and reveal the true depths of our hearts.

And as *I* say, that is a pretty **spectacular** way to survive.

THE END

READ EVERY JENNY PEARSON ADVENTURE!

"As funny and tender as it could ever be."
FRANK COTTRELL-BOYCE

"Funny and touching storytelling."
DAVID BADDIEL

"A big-hearted comic journey."
DAVID SOLOMONS

"Hilarious and heartwarming."
A.F. STEADMAN

"A gorgeous, heartwarming story full of hope, humour and love."
HANNAH GOLD

JENNY PEARSON has been awarded **six** mugs, one fridge magnet, one wall plaque and numerous cards for her role as **Best Teacher in the World**. When she is not busy being inspirational in the classroom, she would like nothing more than to relax with her two young boys, but she can't as they view her as a human climbing frame.

Jenny's debut novel, ***The Super Miraculous Journey of Freddie Yates***, was shortlisted for the **Costa Children's Book Award** and the **Waterstones Children's Book Prize**, and was the winner of the **Laugh Out Loud Book Award**.

SHORTLISTED

Costa Book Award
Waterstones Children's Book Prize
Branford Boase Award.

WINNER

Laugh Out Loud Book Award

PRAISE FOR JENNY PEARSON:

"Funny and touching storytelling." David Baddiel

"Hilarious and heartwarming." A.F. Steadman

"A gorgeous, heartwarming story full of hope, humour and love." Hannah Gold

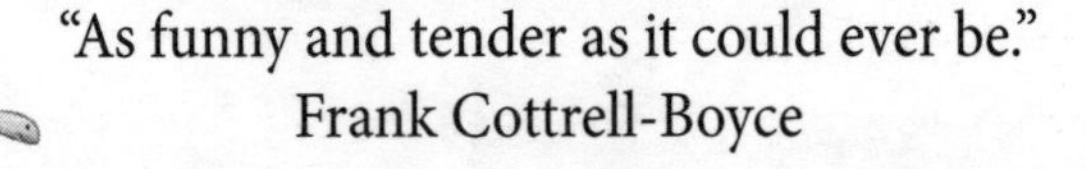

"As funny and tender as it could ever be." Frank Cottrell-Boyce

"Jenny is one of the finest storytellers we have." Phil Earle

"No one writes humour and heart quite like Jenny Pearson." Katya Balen

"A big-hearted comic journey." David Solomons

"Heartwarming and genuinely funny." *The Times*

"Full of laugh-out-loud escapades." *The Sunday Times*

"One of the funniest books you'll read this year, with bundles of heart to boot." *The Bookseller*

"[A] heartbreaking and hilarious book." *Sunday Express*

"An action-packed and funny adventure story, written with lots of heart." *The Irish Independent*

"Pearson deals with tricky subjects with her customary blend of poignancy and humour." *The Mail on Sunday*